A VERY CHRISTIAN CHRISTMAS

JOSIE RIVIERA

INTRODUCTION

To keep up on newly released ebooks, paperbacks, Large Print Paperbacks, audiobooks, as well as exclusive sales, sign up for Josie's Newsletter today.

As a thank you, I'll send you a Free PDF ... The Beauty Of ...

Josie's Newsletter

Did you know that according to a Yale University study, people who read books live longer?

5 STAR READER REVIEWS

"Josie Riviera has written this book with the sensitivity of the soul of a genuine musician who also has a deep understanding of God's love and His power of restoration in every area of life. She carefully crafts the personalities of her characters so that each one is unique, and the reader can easily identify with one or all of them. Her attention to detail is remarkable as she allows you to see people and places and to become a citizen of Cherish. You will want to stay there! Thanks Josie Riviera for enriching the Christmas season with this inspiring story." - Amazon Reviewer (*A Christmas To Cherish*)

"A nice combination of characters....Max, Sarah and also the message of Christmas. Loving nature, the environment was perfect with the birds and the others of the forest. Toss in a harmonica and a puppy....(who doesn't love a little puppy?) and the scene is set.

Truly a wonderful positive story for this upcoming season. Most highly recommended…" - Amazon Reviewer (*A Christmas Puppy To Cherish*)

"A holiday inspired series with a unique believable premise, delightful small town Colorado setting, diverse relatable characters, often gut wrenching dilemmas, twist and turn plot and satisfying resolution. Each holiday novella is a stand alone. Josie Riviera is a talented writer addressing contemporary issue of homelessness and homeless shelters, especially in small communities." - Amazon Reviewer (*Holly's Gift*)

This book is dedicated to all my wonderful readers who have supported me every inch of the way.
THANK YOU!

CONTENTS

HOLLY'S GIFT

PRAISE AND AWARDS

USA TODAY bestselling author

DEAR FRIENDS

A heartwarming story is the hallmark of a romantic read. Savor the magic of this collection with three clean and wholesome inspirational romances, brimming with Christian values.

Find out why readers are falling in love with *A Very Christian Christmas* & staying up all night reading! Let's keep the Christ in Christmas. These stories will warm your heart.

This collection contains 3 books. Available in ebook, paperback, and Large Print paperback.

Each book and audiobook also sold separately.

A Christmas To Cherish

There's nothing a Christmas kiss won't cure. Except perhaps a shattered heart…

When Emmanuelle Sumter steps off the train in Cherish, South Carolina—a town simply glowing with the promise of Christmas—she finds herself praying God will help her find the broken pieces of her life. Shattered, like her beloved harp. Her dreams. And her trust in men.

Her friend Dorothy told her Cherish is a safe haven. But

she never expected Dorothy's brother, Deputy Nicholas Thompson, would relight the one thing she thought she'd lost forever. A spark of hope.

Not long ago, while Nicholas' sister was in rehab, Emmanuelle's voice and smile on his Skype screen held him together. After that, she seemed to disappear, an absence he felt keenly when his ex-fiancée left his faith in God dented but not broken.

Now she's in Cherish, even more stunning in person. Yet she's holding tight to a private pain she refuses to reveal. Nicholas resolves to be patient, vowing that he'll never let anyone hurt her again. Even when her past rears its ugly head to destroy what's left of her heart.

Note: Contains references to verbal and physical abuse.

A Christmas Puppy To Cherish

You don't need ears to hear God's plan. All you need is an open heart…

Music of both birds and harmonicas fills Max's life, but it's the near-silent forest guide he meets in Cherish, SC, who captures his attention. Small and slim, pretty Sarah's smiles and graceful hands speak louder than her voice. In fact, she's so quiet, he's not sure he's made much of an impression. But with her, he can imagine making this temporary stopover into something permanent.

Sarah has found a comfortable niche in Cherish, working miracles with plants, arranging flowers for church, and taking in stray animals. In fact, her house is so full, she's not sure she can say yes to the Sheriff's plea to take in one more puppy for Christmas.

Max has definitely captured her interest, and he shares her love of nature. But maybe she should take in that puppy after all, because a ball of fur that needs her will fill the empty space in her heart when Max's research sends him off looking for bluer skies.

Holly's Gift

Miracles don't always come easy. Sometimes it takes a secret wish to light an angel's way.

Holly steps into a homeless shelter looking for an MIA piano student, she notices a distinct lack of Christmas cheer —because a handsome building inspector is forcing the shelter to temporarily close down.

Holly knows bad guys—she was married to one. Yet when the man asks her out, she finds *absolutely not* warring with *absolutely yes.*

Tim Stewart doesn't hold his breath waiting for God to answer prayers. He went from homeless desperation to television stardom to relative obscurity while God stayed silent. But when Holly barrels into his life, her steady faith sparks hope for a dream of his own. Even if it means praying for a Christmas miracle—one last time.

GOD IS AT THE CENTER

JOSIE RIVIERA

a Christmas to Cherish

A SWEET AND WHOLESOME
HOLIDAY NOVELLA

PRAISE AND AWARDS

USA TODAY bestselling author
#1 Bestseller Women's Religious Fiction
#1 Bestseller Contemporary Religious Fiction
#1 Bestseller Inspirational Religious Fiction
#2 Bestseller Inspirational Prayer

CHAPTER 1

*E*mmanuelle Sumter surveyed the picturesque town of Cherish, South Carolina, brightly lit in crimson and green holiday decor. The town looked as if it had emerged from a Christmas card. Glittering frost framed bare tree branches, and local artists were setting up their canvases for an art walk. The coldness in the air was soundless and serene, comforting in its own way.

She exited the Cherish Central train station, zippered her cobalt-blue puffer coat to her chin, and stepped onto the curb.

Who believed an actual, breathing town could resemble a holiday snow globe?

Evidently, her friend Dorothy did, considering her enthusiasm whenever she described her idyllic South Carolina town.

Emmanuelle stood on the curb and shoved her hands in her pockets. A cold December gust slapped her cheeks, sharp streams of frigid air. She swept a wisp of hair from her cheek and searched for Nicholas, Dorothy's older brother. He was supposed to pick her up. People were shouting greetings, kissing, cooing over babies. A teeming mass of humanity.

But no Nicholas.

A taxi's horn spiked. Emmanuelle jumped, an involuntary nervous reaction.

Take a deep breath. Relax. Dorothy had assured her Cherish was a safe haven, a harbor in a storm.

Repeating her mantra, Emmanuelle hailed the black-bearded taxi driver parked at the curb. She still didn't see any sign of Nicholas, so she'd take the cab.

She handed the driver her suitcase, then slid into the backseat and gave the address of Dorothy's music store, Musically Yours.

They passed charming shops decorated in glittering lights, and a sign advertising a historic home tour. A few minutes later, the driver pointed at the Musically Yours lighted outdoor sign and idled at the corner of Myrtle and Magnolia Streets.

"The store's two hoots and a holler away, ma'am." He hoisted her suitcase from the trunk and set it on the sidewalk. "We've reached your destination."

Destination. Was this where her journey ended after a year filled with pain and abuse? Did hope and encouragement wait for her in this little town?

A new life. With perseverance, she could start fresh.

"Thanks." She climbed from the taxi, paid the driver and grabbed her suitcase.

Daylight faded as dusk crept in, and she tipped her head to take in Evergreen Street. Family-owned businesses had switched on their storefront lights, transforming the town into a fairy-tale sparkle of miniature white lights. The tantalizing scent of honey roasted almonds wafted through the air. Boughs of fragrant holly tied with red velvet bows hung cheerily from tall solitary lampposts. Bright-faced children skipped by, lifting their faces skyward to catch a sprinkling of snow. Their conscientious parents followed close behind.

"Emmanuelle! You arrived right on time!" Dorothy flung open the door of the music store and pressed a welcoming kiss to Emmanuelle's cheek. Dorothy's brown hair was swept up in a French braid, her creamy complexion glowing with an enthusiasm Emmanuelle didn't recall from their days working as struggling musicians in New York.

Dorothy had lived there before moving back to Cherish, her hometown, and marrying her high school crush, Ryan Edwards. He had been an opera star in the making and had given up his touring career to settle in Cherish. They were newlyweds. They were in love.

Love. The beginning was always so alluring. It was the end Emmanuelle feared.

Dorothy regarded the departing taxi. "Apparently Nicholas didn't pick you up?"

"I didn't see him so I took a cab."

Emmanuelle turned from Dorothy and admired Musically Yours' frosty window display, bedecked in an infinite array of treble clef signs. A pine wreath, embellished in antique ornaments—tiny pianos, violins, and harps—adorned the front door.

"It's wonderful," she said. "You've worked so hard to set this up."

"Thanks. Ryan and I are still learning the business, and we're inspired by anything musical."

Emmanuelle smiled, but then shivered. "It's colder here than I expected. At least the blizzard that threatened to shut down New York never came."

"The storm hit after you left," Dorothy replied. "You escaped the worst of it."

Did she? She couldn't answer at first, finally whispering, "Hopefully."

Dorothy raised a delicate eyebrow, but Emmanuelle didn't elaborate. Sure, she'd escaped the snowstorm. An escape from George, her ex, was yet to be determined.

Please God, be with me now in my dark season, when I'm so out of place. The world around me is glowing with the promise of Christmas and I feel dark and empty inside.

She leaned forward to admire two animated polar bears sitting amidst the treble clef signs in the shop's window. Beneath a starry sky, the bears tapped drums to the tune of "Jingle Bells."

"Very clever." She couldn't help a grin. "Thanks for the invite to Cherish."

"We're thrilled you agreed to join us for Christmas." Dorothy grabbed her hands for a reassuring squeeze. She was so pleasant and gracious, Emmanuelle thought. So jovial.

On the other hand, Emmanuelle felt the opposite. All she had become in twenty-five years—a dependable, straightforward woman as well as an esteemed harpist—she'd lost in six months to George.

She'd once been like Dorothy, resilient, independent and a woman of God.

Her ex had taken it all away.

Deep in her coat pocket, her fingers worried an angel ornament she'd purchased at the New York airport. For her, the ornament symbolized the sacred Christmas season, its optimism, dreams, and promise.

She hadn't taken it out of her pocket yet.

"You've been difficult to reach these past few months." Dorothy studiously appraised Emmanuelle. "You hardly ever answered your phone."

"I've been busy with concert engagements." Emmanuelle forced her features to remain blank. "You know, musician stuff." It was a lie, and with the lie came heaviness, a wide band of disapproval. Where had her sense of decency gone?

She tightened her paisley scarf around her neck. Although the violent purple and yellow bruises had faded, she still felt self-conscious.

Dorothy guided her into the music store. "My brother will blame his forgetfulness on his new job, or that gigantic puppy he adopted at the animal shelter. You'd think he'd know better at thirty years old."

"He's a good guy," Emmanuelle said. "Nicholas and I Skyped every night for months when you were in rehab."

"Thanks to you both, I'm better." Dorothy smiled. "And most important, thanks to God."

Once, Emmanuelle would have readily agreed. God was her salvation, her refuge. Now she didn't know how to answer because her faith had wavered.

Truly I tell you, if you have faith as small as a mustard seed, you can say to this mountain, "Move from here to there," and it will move. The verse from Matthew 17:20 came to her mind, a reminder of her strength. All she had to do was reach for it, if she was brave enough.

Inside the store, Dorothy ran a finger along one of the shelves, grinning when she was assured it was dust free. "Ryan and I purchased a cottage-style bungalow four blocks from here and there's an extra bedroom."

"This is your first Christmas as a married couple." Emmanuelle set her suitcase out of the way of a passing customer. "Please celebrate the holiday without me in the middle."

"I insist you stay with us."

"For an entire month?" Emmanuelle shook her head. "Insist all you want. I booked a room at the Cherish Hills Inn. You raved about the inn's accommodations being top-quality when you returned to Cherish for your brother's wedding last year."

"The wedding that didn't happen." Ruefully, Dorothy

sighed. "Nicholas is still healing from the embarrassment and heartbreak."

The ending stages of love. Dreams shattered.

Without warning, the front door burst open. Instinctively, Emmanuelle held up a hand, shielding herself from view.

A heavy-set woman, her hair helmeted in a tight gray bun, ambled inside. She called out a jovial hello to Dorothy.

"Be with you in a minute, Mrs. McManus." Dorothy gave a flap of her hands, and then turned back to Emmanuelle. "Sorry. What were we discussing?"

Emmanuelle blew out a breath. This uneasiness, this fear of being followed, had to stop.

Still shaken, she kept her focus on a Mozart statue topped with a red plush Santa hat sitting on the counter.

"We were discussing the wedding that didn't happen," she replied. "Whenever Nicholas and I talked when you were in rehab, he always reminded me we should place our trust in God."

"Sadly, people change, beliefs change." Worry replaced Dorothy's earlier smile. "Hard knocks can shake the faith of the most devout. I pray he'll go to church again because he's faltered since the breakup."

Suggesting Emmanuelle put her suitcase behind the front counter, Dorothy led her past a display table. As Dorothy paused to rearrange two pairs of oboe earrings so they lined up side by side, she said, "God had other plans for him and for me. I believe things work out for the best."

Emmanuelle frowned and nodded, aborting both actions.

For Dorothy, perhaps. For Ryan. For anyone in this idyllic snow globe town. But not for me. And apparently not for Nicholas.

Her cell phone buzzed. She retrieved it from her tote bag and scanned the screen. *Unknown caller.* Her heart stopped. A telemarketer? A wrong number?

"Who is it?"

Looking up, she saw Dorothy was studying her with keen interest.

"No one." Fumbling, Emmanuelle tucked the phone back into her faux leather tote. "You're right. People change for many reasons." And she'd changed most of all. She'd been a competent, successful woman. Now a chill crept up her spine when a door opened into a harmless music store.

"Are you okay?" Dorothy asked.

"I'm fine, just tired from traveling." Emmanuelle's eyes welled with tears, and she averted her gaze. She'd applied makeup, the first time in months, attempting to conceal her sleep deprivation. The endless worrying and crying had taken a toll.

"We're organizing a concert in the town square the weekend before Christmas," Dorothy was saying. "I meant to ask you to bring your harp—"

"My harp weighs nearly eighty pounds." She picked up a pair of piano earrings and fingered the tiny keyboard. "It's in New York."

Broken. She wouldn't reveal how George had destroyed her harp in one of his lightning-fast rages. The memory caused a block of ice to form in her stomach, a block that she knew would be slow to thaw. She hated the thought of her beloved instrument, splintered into pieces, lying on a New York curb under a pile of snow.

Better the harp than you splintered into pieces.

But his shouted insults and rough slaps had been her fault. She'd provoked him.

No, no, no. Her inner voice took on a sharp edge. That was the old Emmanuelle talking. The new Emmanuelle knew she wasn't a dishtowel to be thrown around on a whim. In hindsight, she should have known George was abusive. The warning signs were there.

She blew out a breath. She'd resolved to find peace and comfort in this holiday … in this town … somewhere … and find her footing again.

"Enough about me." She set down the earrings and dismissed herself with a flutter of her fingers. "Where's Ryan?"

"He's rehearsing in nearby Stanley Valley today and will arrive this evening. He'll be singing 'O Holy Night' for a Christmas Cantata service. He gives so freely of his talent." Dorothy's smile was as radiant as a Merry Christmas bouquet. "He's featured throughout the Carolinas in many guest appearances. Plus, the Atlanta opera house asked him to perform the role of Zoroastro in Handel's opera, *Orlando*. I'm incredibly proud of him."

"You should be." Dorothy's smile was contagious, and Emmanuelle managed a warm grin. "He's famous and extremely talented."

"And you? Any upcoming concerts?"

"None." She answered in a firm tone that she expected would discourage her friend from probing. Judging by the way Dorothy's eyebrows drew together, she'd succeeded.

Fortunately, an acoustic guitar arrangement of "Lo, How a Rose Is Blooming" piped in the background, the ideal holiday music to smooth a lull in the conversation.

"I'm sure you're keen to check in." Dorothy broke the silence. "I'll deal with these last few customers, close the store, and give you a lift. Unless you'd rather walk the three blocks to the inn?"

"No, no. I'll wait for you."

She'd never walk alone again. Not in New York, not in Cherish. Not anywhere, because she'd never feel safe again.

Dorothy gestured toward the front of the store. "If you care to browse, the Christmas music section is on your left. There's a lovely harp arrangement of *The Nutcracker*."

"Thanks. Your store is a music-lover's dream."

Intrigued, Emmanuelle stepped past a buyer laden with music bookmarks and made her way to the sheet music. She thumbed through endless arrangements of Christmas solos, wondering what madness had brought her to this town. She didn't belong here among all this gaiety. Her sadness was a burden refusing to go away.

Disheartened, she stared, trancelike, at the display window. A whimsical model train circled the polar bears, and the sight was enchanting.

Beyond, past the cheery town, past the exuberant children and the enormous Christmas tree illuminating the town square, a darkened sky had followed dusk.

CHAPTER 2

*A*s he entered his apartment, Nicholas Thompson pulled off his deputy badge and set it on a table in the foyer. Except for one traffic violation, a minor fender bender and endless meetings, the day had been relatively calm for a newbie deputy.

He looked forward to relaxing in front of the TV with a good cup of coffee and a chocolate-glazed doughnut. Ever since he'd become a deputy, he'd acquired a taste for both.

All fifty pounds of his six-month-old golden retriever greeted him with an energetic stretch. He'd purchased the dog from an animal shelter in Stanley, two weeks to the day after his fiancée, Alice, had broken up with him. The dog surveyed Nicholas with expectant black eyes and a fiercely wagging tail.

"No, Molly Belle, I'm not taking you for a—"

The dog ran in circles around him and barked.

Nicholas groaned. He'd no sooner walked in and he was forced to turn around and walk out again. "All right, take a tater and wait a sec." He weaved around a mountain of laundry and strode to his bedroom. His bed was unmade, an old sweatshirt tossed over a side chair. He removed the gun from his holster and locked it in his bedroom closet's safe. Then he loosened his tie and changed out of uniform—white shirt and khaki pants—dragging on jeans, a long-sleeved T-shirt, and work boots. Pausing, he ran a critical survey of his apartment, particularly the coffee table piled with remote controls and junk mail and old catalogues. The large sofa begged for a skilled reupholster, and his sister, Dorothy, had admonished him countless times to hang curtains on his bare windows.

He darted a glance at the motorcycle calendar propped on a shelf. Today was December first, and Christmas was less than a month away. At the very least, the season merited a Christmas tree in the corner and a wreath on his apartment door.

Nope. Not this year.

Despite Molly Belle lightening his days, Nicholas didn't have the heart for celebrations and feasts. What other man in the state of South Carolina had experienced the humiliation of his fiancée leaving him on their wedding day? And by text, no less. Not even in person.

The dog's impertinent barking prompted him to grab the leash, button his navy pea coat and open the front door. With an eager yelp, Molly Belle ran ahead, down his short flight of stairs and onto the sidewalk.

"Slower, girl." The dog, as usual, didn't obey and tugged harder on the leash. Nicholas made a mental note to sign her up for obedience classes.

His cell phone buzzed. He hoped it wasn't a call to drive back to the police station. Relieved to see Dorothy's caller ID, he clicked on.

"Nicholas, are you through with work?" she asked.

"Yes, I just got in." He restrained the dog from sniffing

every blade of glass in a neighbor's garden. "I'm taking Molly Belle for a walk."

"Emmanuelle arrived an hour ago. Did you forget?"

He sighed and slapped a hand to his forehead. He forgot a lot of things lately. "I got sidetracked by last-minute meetings at the police station. Please tell her I'm sorry."

"You can tell her yourself. We're at the Cherish Hills Inn and she's unpacking. Meet us here, then join us at Frank's Pizzeria for a slice. It's your favorite restaurant."

His first response was *no* before he thought better of it. He should extend a polite apology, considering he'd forgotten to pick up the woman. He'd swing by and make his amends and then leave.

As he and Molly Belle neared the inn, it was all he could do not to reverse direction and head back to his apartment.

He could work. He could take care of his spirited dog. But he didn't relish small talk with a woman, especially a woman he'd grown close to during their many phone conversations. What would he say to her after all these months?

"Oh, by the way, Emmanuelle, do you remember me talking nonstop about Alice, my fiancée? She left me the day of our wedding."

Molly Belle ignored his command to walk slower, nearly choking on the leash as she lunged forward.

CHAPTER 3

$\mathcal{B}$attling for control of the leash, Nicholas strode into the Cherish Hills Inn's lobby. Briefly, he admired the boxwood wreath hanging on the wooden door, the lighted village scene on a round cherry tabletop in the foyer. He greeted the white-haired innkeeper, Tom Canning, with an apologetic shrug and lifted the dog's leash.

Tom scowled. Crevices grooved the sides of his mouth. "No animals."

"Just this once—for someone you've known your entire life?" Nicholas asked. "For a man who upholds the law in our town?"

Tom sighed, unbending a bit, and peered at Nicholas above the cheaters perched on the bridge of his nose. "Go ahead, deputy." He rewarded Nicholas with a brief nod, but raised his index finger to issue a one-minute warning.

"Thanks." Nicholas strode across the wide plank floors to the parlor where a fire blazed in the stacked rock fireplace, so large an ox could stand upright inside it. On the center of the mantel sat a handsomely carved Nativity set in burnished wood. Artistically arranged seasonal fruit—oranges and apples and pears—were loaded high in a wide pewter bowl on a side table.

He directed his gaze toward Dorothy, who stood near the fireplace, and that was the last thing he remembered.

The undeniably beautiful woman who stood beside Dorothy, clad in a white lace sweater dress, resembled a dainty, sweet confection. Her complexion was pink, her dark lashes slightly lowered, her lips plush and generous. A puffy blue jacket was slung over her shoulders, and she held a tote bag close to her side.

His mind reeled with memories.

Emmanuelle Sumter. They'd Skyped many times, so he'd known she was attractive, but in person she was positively breathtaking. Silky blonde hair rioted around her face in impossibly tight curls, and her huge blue eyes acknowledged a tentative welcome.

"I assume you remember me." He fumbled with Molly Belle's leash as the dog sniffed the rug incessantly. "You look … different in person." *Better*, he amended to himself. *She looked better. More than better.* He extended his free hand. "Please accept my apologies for forgetting you."

"Apology accepted." She placed her small hand in his large one. "How could I forget our nightly conversations? You guided Dorothy through a challenging season in her life."

Emmanuelle's features were so petite, her fingers so fragile. "And you were the friend she counted on." He tightened his grip and vigorously shook her hand.

"You were the person who prayed with her every day." She pulled away, politely, decisively. "You encouraged her."

"Hold on you two, I'm right here!" Dorothy laughingly stepped between them. "Are you competing in a compliment contest I'm not aware of?"

Emmanuelle's dimples winked in a slight smile. "Your brother's the winner."

"Please don't boost his ego, or he'll expect you to treat for pizza." Dorothy chuckled. "Frank's Pizza is within walking distance. They advertise the best pizza in town."

"Because they're the only pizzeria in town." Nicholas helped Emmanuelle on with her coat, then swung Molly Belle's leash up and down. "Unfortunately they don't allow animals and I won't be able to go."

Molly Belle responded with a defiant stare and Emmanuelle leaned down to pet her. "Aww, your dog is so friendly." Soon, the dog was lying on the rug legs up, outstretched in doggy ecstasy while Emmanuelle crouched to rub her stomach.

"You said you'd just gotten home from work," Dorothy said as she encouraged Emmanuelle and the dog to stand, then steered the threesome to the doorway. "Have you eaten dinner, Nicholas?"

"I'll whip up something." He couldn't imagine what although there was a slight possibility a frozen pizza sat in his freezer behind a carton of peanut butter ice cream.

Molly Belle had different ideas, having decided Emmanuelle was her new best friend. With a wiggle of glee, she changed direction and hurled straight into her.

Emmanuelle fell back and Nicholas let go of the leash to stop her fall. Freed from her leash, the dog shot in another direction and knocked over a crystal vase filled with red roses. The vase shattered on the floor.

Tom, eye-glass cheaters in hand, tore into the parlor. His face colored to a beet-red as he tapped his watch. "Your one-minute dog visit was up five minutes ago, Nicholas."

"Sorry. We were just leaving." Nicholas righted Emmanuelle as Dorothy picked up the roses, then he dashed forward to retrieve the leash.

"Shoo, all of you!" Tom said. "I'll clean up the mess."

The women followed Nicholas. They exited to a whip of

icy wind that blew Emmanuelle's curls around her face. Nicholas lifted his hand, an automatic response to protect her from another gust. She flinched, tightened the pink paisley scarf around her neck, and moved a step away.

He tossed an inquiring glance toward her. She ignored him.

As if by mutual agreement to cover up Emmanuelle's skittish behavior, Dorothy began talking about every holiday event scheduled in three counties between Christmas and New Year's.

"Frank's boasts an outdoor enclosed eating area," Dorothy continued, talking in a loud voice to drown out the quiet. She stopped briefly to commend the florist shop's front window decorated in scarlet-red poinsettias and twine wreaths. "I'm sure Frank's will allow Molly Belle inside, Nicholas. She's leashed and we'll take an out-of-the-way table."

Before Nicholas could comment, Dorothy's cell phone pinged. She grabbed it from her tote bag, read the text, then extended an unapologetic grin. "Ryan returned early from Stanley. A few weeks ago, he bought a cookbook called *Southern Charms* at a fundraiser for encouraging women empowerment, and he's been learning to cook gourmet. He's preparing a romantic dinner of rosemary chicken and pasta salad and he wants me to come home now. He has a surprise for me."

"I applaud your husband for buying a cookbook and supporting a beneficial cause." Despite his words, Nicholas sent his sister an exasperated glance. "So, you invited me to join you for dinner and now you're leaving?"

If she was trying to fix him up with Emmanuelle, he refused to go along with it. From what Dorothy had revealed, Emmanuelle had accepted his sister's offer to visit Cherish for the holidays primarily to get away from New York. The result of breaking up with a man. It was always because of a man, he thought, reflecting on his cheating fiancée and her new boyfriend.

He wanted to extend a sympathetic ear, for surely Emmanuelle wanted to talk at length about the break-up, although he wasn't in the proper frame of mind to attend to anyone's problems other than his own.

Yes, he'd gotten along well with her. They had talked nightly for months because of their shared interest in Dorothy's welfare, plus their unshakeable faith in God. But his life was different now. His faith teetered. If he had to define it, he'd say his faith was lukewarm.

He tuned back in when he heard Emmanuelle say, "Don't disappoint Ryan." She put her hand on Dorothy's arm, then flashed a look at Nicholas. "I'll double back and finish unpacking if you don't mind walking me."

This was his out. A polite response and he'd be sitting in his recliner watching television within fifteen minutes flat. Instead, he found himself saying, "We're almost at the restaurant so we might as well enjoy dinner."

Besides pizza, the restaurant had good coffee.

"Perfect! You two go on without me. I'm sure there's a lot to catch up on since you haven't talked in a year." Dorothy tucked her brown hair under the black wool cap she produced from her handbag. With a satisfied wave, she swung in the opposite direction.

"This way." Nicholas touched Emmanuelle's arm. She sidestepped him and ran a hand over the zipper of her jacket. Although she appeared to be an elegant and poised woman, she was as edgy as a newborn fawn.

Perhaps there was nothing left to discuss? Dorothy, their commonality, no longer required their help, and he obviously wasn't interesting enough for pretty and popular Emmanuelle. The thought left him maintaining a chilly and reserved silence as they walked toward the restaurant.

His gaze landed on two tow-headed toddlers running ahead of them. They pointed to the fairyland of Christmas lights in the town square and the sight made Nicholas smile. He loved children, although now he'd never have any. He'd never subject his heart to another battering. He'd successfully barricaded himself behind a solid, protective shell.

Lonely? Sometimes.

Safe? Definitely.

He headed Emmanuelle and Molly Belle toward the next block.

Molly Belle had a mind of her own, though, wanting nothing more than to loll on the sidewalk and hug the ground. He encouraged the dog with an assurance of a treat, and Emmanuelle added a "C'mon girl."

When they resumed walking, he asked, "Are you still the principal harpist for ... I forgot the name of the symphony. It was in a town somewhere outside New York."

"No, I'm not playing the harp anymore. It's gone." Stillness reigned for several beats after her self-deprecating laugh. He recognized the defeat in her shining blue eyes, and sympathy flickered in his hardened heart.

"What about you?" The audible stress in her tone made him hesitate. "I remember you were studying for an important exam."

"The police academy. I passed and I'm a deputy."

Her eyes widened. "A—a deputy ..." She blanched and missed a step.

"And here I thought congratulations were in order," he half joked.

"Yes, of course." She clutched her tote bag and kept her head down. "Umm, congratulations, Deputy Thompson."

Something had happened to her in New York. Something bad, although he couldn't offer any support because he was empty. The woman whom he'd thought had loved him had

24

left him flat. He'd been a blind fool while she'd deceived him for months, but he'd learned a painful lesson and he'd learned it well. Relationships with women were well off his radar, especially when a woman clearly had a hang-up about men.

Bachelorhood was serene. Naught to fear, because nothing—no hearts, no feeling, no plans—would be broken. Besides, a dog was excellent company.

Despite himself, his gaze lingered on Emmanuelle's profile, her slim figure she kept well-hidden beneath her winter jacket and high boots.

Molly Belle barked a little too enthusiastically, prompting Emmanuelle to jump when a black lab trotted past.

"She's high-spirited," Nicholas offered as an explanation.

"Who's in control here?" she asked him. "I used to work around dogs. They were a big part of my life." She patted Molly Belle's head, then smiled when the dog put a wet nose in her hand.

"I'm considering dog obedience classes. Do you think it's a good idea?"

Emmanuelle opened her mouth, closed it again, grinned. "Yes, it's an excellent idea. In the meantime, begin with simple commands like *sit* and *wait*. Can you do that?"

"Certainly. I'm the master."

An irreverent chuckle burst from her lips and he fought the insane impulse to kiss her.

He knew her through those lengthy phone conversations, and every night he'd looked forward to their discussions about God, and their everyday lives, and their pasts. Their comfortable hour-long chats had become easy and familiar. If he hadn't been engaged to his fiancée at the time, he might have admitted the attraction he'd felt for Emmanuelle.

This stiffness between them was foreign. She had frequently sought his advice, the comfort of his faith coinciding with her hard-won beliefs. She'd been orphaned when she was in her teens, but she had persevered, studied hard, and become a virtuoso harpist.

They walked the last block to the restaurant at a quick pace. Her knee-length dress glided along her legs and her suede boots fit high above her knee. Nicholas kept stealing glances at her. The self-sufficient woman he'd known had evaporated. She'd become breakable, her voice soft, her movements hesitant.

They walked up the steps to the pizzeria's entrance, and he reached around to open the door.

"I'm ordering Frank's deluxe-meat lovers special," he said. "Are you the salad type?"

"Salad? Salad is for vegetarians." She walked past him into the restaurant, her expression amused. "I'm the barbecue and corn fritters type."

The next day was Saturday, and Nicholas worked a half day. The morning had started with an arrest for drunk driving and ended in the police station with multiple copies of blank forms to fill out. He loved his job, but he could do without the written procedures and minute details.

When he returned home at noon, he changed out of his uniform and into jeans and a shirt, a white pullover hoodie, and running shoes. He dashed off a reminder note to price affordable curtains over the weekend, then leashed Molly Belle for a quick jog.

Ryan's surprise for Dorothy the previous night had been tickets to a tuba Christmas concert in Stanley, and Dorothy had given Nicholas the not-so-subtle hint that Emmanuelle would be spending the day alone. Despite telling himself a firm *no*, he found himself veering toward the Cherish Hills Inn.

Their dinner at the pizzeria had ended abruptly when Emmanuelle had pleaded tiredness soon after he began telling her about his job as deputy sheriff. He'd started off by regaling her with amusing tales of some of the absurd arrests he'd made. One had been for drunk and disorderly conduct when a spectator ran onto the field of a high school football game declaring he was the sixth offensive lineman. On another occasion, he'd walked an eighteen-year-old home to face his parents after a keg party had gotten out of control, only to have the boy get sick on their front lawn.

As he talked, Emmanuelle's shoulders had tightened and her hand quivered as she'd pushed the barbecue around her plate. Her fear was tangible, stretching across the red-checkered tablecloth, and the pizza set neatly in the center of the table.

He got the hint and stopped talking about his profession altogether, carrying on instead a reasonably normal conversation, albeit one-sided, observing the average winter temperature in South Carolina and New York.

The inn neared, and he closed the distance to the porch steps in five long strides.

He leaned forward to catch his breath and wipe his brow on the sleeve of his hoodie. Wide-slatted rocking chairs were assembled on the expansive front porch and evergreen garland and holly berries were strung across each window.

Although he normally would simply walk into the inn, after the mishap the day before, he thought it best if he knocked first.

Pushing his cheaters down his nose, Tom Canning peered through the entry's side glass, glowered, and flung open the door. "No dogs allowed inside, Deputy Thompson." He tried to sound polite, but there was no mistaking that he was issuing an order. "No exceptions."

"I'm sorry about yesterday, Mr. Canning, and I'll be happy to pay for any damages."

"Good. I'll write up a bill for you."

"No hurry. I mean, please do." Nicholas kept a sneakered

foot in the door as the innkeeper attempted to shut him out. "Will you let Emmanuelle know I'm here?"

Tom took off his cheaters and polished them. "Is she expecting you?"

"Probably not."

"Hi Nicholas." Emmanuelle appeared at the bottom of the curved staircase, looking bewitchingly beautiful. Her blonde hair was piled high at the crown, her ever-present pink scarf around her neck, her puffy blue jacket all zippered.

"I guess she was expecting you." With a conspiratorial half grin toward Nicholas, the owner ushered them outside, then slammed the door, leaving Emmanuelle and Nicholas standing on the porch with Molly Belle.

Annoyed, Nicholas fixed his gaze on the door. "I thought everyone loved animals. Apparently, Tom doesn't like dogs."

"His reasons are excellent." She didn't withhold her chuckle. "That vase of roses spilled water across his rug and cost him thirty minutes of clean-up, not to mention the cost of the vase and flowers."

"I offered to pay for the damages." Nicholas inspected her trim, shapely form. Today, black jeans and high boots accentuated her long legs. A green sweater peeked from beneath her winter jacket. "Were you … expecting me?"

The color on her cheekbones rose to a flattering blush against her creamy complexion. The afternoon sun gilded her blonde hair to streaks of platinum, and he favored her with an unabashed smile. She was stunning.

She stretched on a pair of pink knit gloves that matched her scarf. "Dorothy mentioned you might stop by."

"Several local booths in the town square are selling Christmas items. Are you up for some last-minute shopping?" He was prepared for her to refuse. However, he didn't expect the wariness on her face, the absolutely motionless air between them.

"I have no reason to shop. I'm not buying any Christmas gifts this year." She focused a pained stare on the mixed greenery placed around the white rocking chairs.

An unexpected fury flowed through his veins at whoever had hurt her. When? Where?

"Surely there's something you'd like." He grinned, an attempt to disarm her. "The locals sell handmade jewelry and artwork and leather goods. And I have it on excellent authority that one of my friends, who owns a restaurant called The Grill Room, set up early this morning and is smoking South Carolina barbecue as we speak."

She considered her watch. "It's a little late for lunch."

"It's just shy of two o'clock. We'll call it an early dinner." He hooked his thumbs in the back pockets of his jeans and felt the leash go slack. In an instant, his dog had raced off the porch in a mad chase after a squirrel.

"Molly Belle!"

What happened next occurred in slow motion.

The dog ran into the road. Brakes squealed. A sickening thud.

"No!" Unmindful of traffic, Nicholas dashed for his dog, seeing only Molly Belle's limp body lying helpless in the middle of the road. Blood seeped from her stomach, matting her glossy golden fur. He sank down, right there with his dog, and did something he hadn't done since he was a child.

He cried.

CHAPTER 5

*E*mmanuelle sat in the passenger seat of the innkeeper's lime-green Volkswagen and held the dog in her lap while Nicholas drove. She controlled her voice as she rubbed Molly Belle gently behind her ears. She'd secured a makeshift muzzle using the dog's leash, assuring Nicholas even Molly Belle, a sweet dog, could lash out when she was in pain.

"Looks like a surface wound," she said. Carefully, she lifted the dog's lip, murmuring about capillary refill time. When Nicholas didn't seem to hear her, she added, "Fortunately, the driver stopped in time."

Everything had happened in a blur. Visibly distraught, the driver had burst from his car in a frenzy and groped for the words to apologize. Tom Canning rushed out and offered Nicholas his car, and then dashed to the inn. He was back almost instantly with sterile gauze and a yellow crocheted blanket an instant later. A bystander stopped traffic, which allowed Nicholas and Tom to use the blanket as a sling and carry the dog to the car. Emmanuelle placed gauze over the dog's stomach and applied pressure, murmuring relief when the blood didn't soak through.

Nicholas drove quickly and silently to Cherish Animal Hospital. She took in his granite profile, his short blond hair shoved back from his forehead. He hunched behind the wheel stuffed into a car not made to fit his six-foot frame.

"She doesn't appear to be in shock." She kept her voice quiet and upbeat.

His dog might not be in shock, but Nicholas was. He had taken immediate action, though, and had phoned the animal hospital to tell them they were on their way.

"You don't know that," he finally responded.

"Yes, I do. I've been around plenty of sick dogs."

When they arrived at the hospital, Nicholas parked near the entrance. Once more using the blanket as a sling, they carried the dog past a red-haired receptionist who announced that her name was Scarlett Evans.

Dr. Judson Troutman, the veterinarian, waited for them in the examining room. Nicholas had mentioned to Emmanuelle that Dr. Troutman had been widowed two years earlier.

Slim, serious, and sandy-haired, the vet was casually dressed in khaki pants, a button-down shirt, and a white lab coat. After brief introductions, he checked Molly Belle's lungs with his stethoscope and confirmed Emmanuelle's evaluation. The dog wasn't in shock.

"My father was a veterinarian," Emmanuelle said. Reverently, she ran a hand along the stethoscope after the vet had laid it to one side.

"You learned well, Emmanuelle." His deep-brown eyes were kind, his demeanor innately gentle. He angled toward Nicholas. "I'm going to give Molly Belle all the time she needs, Deputy Thompson. After her fluids are stabilized and the diagnostics run, I'll give you an update. For now, there's nothing else to do except sit and wait."

Scarlett ushered them into the reception area. A nervous-looking woman in her fifties cradling a quivering black dachshund bobbed a brief hello.

Emmanuelle slid onto a thinly padded chair and nudged aside a half-finished cup of coffee set on a corner table. She rubbed her arms and then dropped her head into her open hands. Now that her adrenaline had settled, she felt chilled and kept her jacket and scarf over her shoulders.

Nicholas paced the hallway for several minutes before coming to sit beside her. "I don't know why I wasn't paying attention and didn't hold onto her leash tighter. If only I had …" He stared down at his hands.

She scanned his clenched fists, the skin bunching at his eyes. "Molly Belle is blessed with the ability to love life. You're the most important part and not to blame. She's always on a leash and you do all you can to keep her safe."

Her quiet reassurances seemed to help, for he sat straighter.

"Still, I was lax. Will she ever forgive me?"

"Of course."

She didn't know where to put her hands, so she rested them on her lap.

Scarlett ushered the nervous woman cradling the dachshund down the long hallway. A door banged shut.

"The accident should never have taken place." Nicholas scrubbed his fingers over his face. "I can't make sense of it. Lately, I can't make sense of anything that's happened to me."

"Everything in our lives is a result of God's favor."

"Favor? What favor? My cycle of believing has been broken."

"So was mine. Whenever I think about the person I became these past few months, it makes me sad."

"What happened, Emmanuelle?" He studied her expression. "When we last spoke on the phone you were so upbeat."

She chewed her bottom lip. "A lot happens in a year. Don't ask me about the in-between because I'm not ready to talk about it." Mentally reliving George's abuse, a heavy despair settled in her gut. Whenever he'd banged her body into a wall, he screamed that they belonged together, and he was trying to teach her who was the master. No one had ever hit her before. She'd come from a kind and loving home.

"You were only meant for me, Emmanuelle."

The psychological, and then physical, abuse was always worse after George drank. The sharp smell of whiskey on his breath predicted the flashes of unpredictable anger sure to follow. A familiar sweat of panic slid down her neck. On a jerk, she swung her gaze from Nicholas and locked the terrifying remembrances in a safe compartment in her mind.

"Emmanuelle?"

She faltered, found her axis and drew a fortifying breath. "Dorothy stopped by the inn this morning."

"Why?"

"To talk. And she reminded me I shouldn't rebuke myself for past circumstances. She encouraged me to keep my attention on God and not dwell on myself."

"How can a memory upset you if it already happened?"

"Now there's a question I ask myself. Memories can only upset you if they have your attention. The key is to focus on what really matters." Despite her brave declaration, she couldn't meet his probing stare. Instead, she eyed the white-lighted snowman, accented with sheer purple ribbon, hanging on a far wall.

After breakfasting with Dorothy in the inn's sunny conservatory, Emmanuelle had confessed the beatings she'd suffered while tears had streamed down her cheeks. With every frightening scene she confided, heavy chains had been lifted from her heart.

Dorothy was kindhearted and understanding, a true friend, her intentions always in the right place.

Emmanuelle's rapport with Nicholas was different. He had commended her on her talent and independence, complimenting her on countless occasions. What would his opinion be if he learned she had been foolish enough to allow a man to control her?

She released a sigh and hid her face in her hands. She carried a shame she couldn't describe, not even to herself.

"Care to discuss what happened to you, Emmanuelle?" Nicholas repeated. "You can trust me."

He stared at her. She stared at the snowman.

She could hear a cell phone ringing in the hallway. She could smell the cold, stale coffee on the corner table.

Yes, she trusted Nicholas, even as she feared his admiration would change to disapproval once he understood her situation.

Why hadn't she left George sooner? She'd asked herself the same question more times than she could count.

"Because, Emmanuelle, you were meant only for me."

She shuddered, recalling his bloodshot gray eyes, as he was liquored up more often than not. When had he changed? He'd been so charming at the outset of their relationship, wooing her with lavish dinners and dark chocolate truffles and evenings at the theater.

"Emmanuelle?"

Despite her resolve to start a new life, she pressed her lips tight and didn't acknowledge him.

"You know," Nicholas went on, "I once was a person of great faith." He inclined his head and spoke softly. "This dejection I've felt ever since Alice—"

Emmanuelle's words came quick with no apology. "Your sister said, "'If you despair, you will live in despair.'"

"Dorothy is admirable and Ryan has taken her lead. Together their faith is anchored in God. I want to trust in the Lord again, I really do." He lifted his hand and cupped her chin, raising her face to his, forcing her to meet his gaze.

She didn't flinch, knowing that he needed a fresh start, needed her full attention.

"Begin by reaching out in prayer." She took his hand, holding it as he bowed his head and whispered praises to God. Silently, she joined him.

Scarlett strolled over, stacking used coffee cups and folding morning newspapers. "Do you two want anything? There's coffee in the vending machine."

Nicholas looked up at her. "Is it any good?"

"No. It's instant, and cold, and shuts off sometimes. Often, actually." She grinned. "Anyway, I brought in extra junk food from home. You know, candy and cupcakes, bottles of soda. Want anything?"

Emmanuelle smiled. "We're fine, thanks."

"My motto is to embrace life and indulge yourself."

Scarlett's full-figured form, Emmanuelle noticed, was pleasing and curvaceous. She was empathetic and sunny, a person who saw the bright side, even on a bleak afternoon. Upbeat, she finished cleaning up the waiting room and retreated to her desk.

As afternoon slipped into evening, Dr. Troutman emerged from the hallway. He drew up a chair to sit across from them. "Delightful news, Deputy Thompson. Surgery isn't necessary. There's no internal bleeding, organ damage, or broken limbs."

"She's going to be all right?" The guarded hope in Nicholas's voice prompted Emmanuelle to place her hand on his arm.

"Molly Belle will be fine." The vet came to his feet. "You can take her home tonight. Find a comfortable spot and get her settled with some heating pads. Given time, she'll heal with no scars."

"Thank you, doctor."

"Clean the wound and apply an antibiotic cream. I gave her an injection for her discomfort." Dr. Troutman rooted in his lab coat for a pad and pen. "I'm prescribing an anti-inflammatory and I recommend not leaving her alone for extended periods of time."

Nicholas's face paled. "For how long? A week?"

"Recovery time varies. She's a young bouncy dog, and I predict she'll be fit in a few weeks or less. Incidentally, she might be a mixed breed. Although she's mostly a golden, I'm thinking there's a bit of yellow lab mixed in." He scribbled the prescription and handed it to Nicholas. "I'll ask Scarlett to schedule Molly Belle for a check-up next Saturday."

"Are you sure I can properly care for her at home in the meantime?" Nicholas hesitated before starting for Scarlett's desk. "If it's safer, please keep her overnight for observation."

"Nothing to observe. You and your girlfriend are quite capable," Dr. Troutman said. "She knows her animals."

"I'm not Nicholas's girlfriend," Emmanuelle clarified, quick to get to her feet. "I learned a tremendous amount when I helped my father. We lived in Remsen, a little town outside of New York. For years, I visited his office every day after school."

From the corner of her eye, she saw Nicholas's thick eyebrows raise as he busied himself with paying the bill.

"How far outside of New York is your father's office?" the vet inquired.

The memories flickered, faded, a million miles away. Once, she'd felt safe and happy, living like other people. How easy it had been when she was a child.

"He died ten years ago when I was sixteen." She spoke carefully, not letting her sense of loss, her free and easy childhood, creep into her voice. "He was a highly regarded veterinarian in our little town. Cherish reminds me of Remsen. Without Remsen's snow."

"I've never been to Remsen," Scarlett chirped. "I bet it's pretty there."

Dr. Troutman gave Scarlett an indulgent smile, then turned back to Emmanuelle. "A small town's down-to-earth values and its focus on what matters most in life ... Well, there's not much that can beat that."

"You're absolutely right." Emmanuelle extended her hand. "Thank you."

Over at the reception desk, Nicholas handed Scarlett his credit card, then peered over his shoulder at Emmanuelle. "All those hours we spent on the phone and you never mentioned your animal expertise."

She shrugged. "There were more serious topics to discuss."

Saying he would get Molly Belle, the vet walked down the hallway. He and Nicholas transported a muzzled Molly Belle to the rear seat of the Volkswagen using a large dog crate.

On the drive to Nicholas's apartment, Emmanuelle pondered what to do. Torn between the belief that helping for a week wouldn't matter because she had no other plans, and the fact she'd be immersed in his personal surroundings, she considered how to word her offer before she spoke.

He needed help, especially when he reported to work on Monday. Yet, he hadn't asked for any. A proud, stubborn man, Dorothy had once described her brother when she'd become frustrated at his inability to talk about his hurt after his marriage plans fell apart.

"Once Molly Belle is situated tonight," Emmanuelle began, "I'll stay with her while you fill her prescription."

"I appreciate that."

Guarded, yet so polite.

"Once Monday rolls in, I'll watch her while you're on duty, deputy."

"Wouldn't you rather kill time checking out the Christmas markets and visiting Dorothy and Ryan?"

"I'd rather kill time being of some use."

"All day nursing a sick dog isn't a vacation." His expression indicated his willingness to accept her offer, although he kept his tone carefully noncommittal.

"Who said my visit is about a vacation? Christmas is the season for giving."

What else could she say that was a reasonable justification for offering to help? She simply *wanted* to because Nicholas and Molly Belle had become important to her, but she certainly couldn't say that. "I have experience tending to sick animals."

"I'll pay you." He offered a quick, grateful smile.

"Do you cook?"

"Do frozen pizzas count?"

"You're describing the extent of my cooking skills as well." She grinned. "Fortunately, Ryan is learning gourmet cooking so I'll throw out some hints. Or better yet, I'll borrow his *Southern Charms* cookbook."

With Molly Belle settled on a blanket near the recliner in the living room, Nicholas went off to get her prescription. Emmanuelle applied a heating pad to the dog's belly, where it seemed she had the most pain. When she was assured the dog rested comfortably, she removed the heating pad and waited for Nicholas to come back with the prescription.

Dr. Troutman's injection had made Molly Belle drowsy. Her brownish-black nose pressed upon the blanket, and her sides rose and fell as she dropped into a deep, sound sleep.

In the solitude of the quiet room, Emmanuelle set to work tidying the coffee table. She boxed up old magazines and catalogues that lay scattered in a mismatched pile beside five remote controls. Why did a man need so many remotes for one television set?

When Nicholas returned, he hung his hoodie by the door and crossed the room. Crouching, he stared at his sleeping dog.

"She's asleep and not in pain," Emmanuelle assured him. "See? Her tail is twitching. She's probably dreaming about chasing purple pigeons or flopping in the grass at the Cherish Hills Inn. When she wakes up, we'll give her the medicine."

Nicholas nodded. "And I have bad news and good news." He rolled to his feet and handed her a white paper bag. "The bad news is the kiosks were closing. The good news is I managed to plead our upsetting afternoon to my friend from The Grill Room. He was smoking a beef brisket and added coleslaw. I figured you were hungry. I also snagged a couple cups of coffee and two honey-glazed donuts."

She gave an appreciative sniff. "My mouth is watering."

He went to the kitchen and pulled a water from the fridge. "What do you want to drink?"

She followed him and put the kettle on the stove to boil. "Hot tea. Thanks."

He folded his shirtsleeves to his elbows and draped a dishtowel over his shoulder. "My place is a mess, although I used to be fairly neat."

"I think I have enough tidying here to keep me occupied."

"Yeah, for at least a year." He grinned, then grew solemn. "Since my failed engagement to a woman who—"

"You didn't fail." She reached for a thick mug in the cupboard. "Your fiancée did."

They dished out the smoked barbecue brisket and coleslaw and brought stoneware, napkins, and utensils into the living room. She placed the stoneware on the coffee table, set her napkin on her lap, and took a neat bite of brisket. Chewing, she nodded toward Molly Belle. "After she sleeps, she may be sore. Follow the directions on the prescription."

"You'll come … tomorrow?"

She reached for her tea. "I texted Dorothy to let her know what happened. She and Ryan are still in Stanley. She'll stop in tomorrow to see you and the dog."

"And you?"

"I'll be here on Monday morning, as long as you don't mind leaving the dog by herself to come get me."

"The weatherman calls for a pleasant week. Sunny and highs in the fifties. If you'd prefer to walk—"

"I never walk alone anymore, but will walk with Molly Belle." She gulped her tea and set the mug on the coffee table, and then her napkin alongside it. "However, can you drive me to the inn? It's getting late and I'm sure the innkeeper will be worried. Besides, you have his vehicle."

"I phoned Tom, and he knows Molly Belle is fine. He assured me he isn't leaving the inn tonight." He rested his hand lightly on hers. "Please stay a while longer. You haven't finished your brisket, and I could use the company."

Hesitantly, she replaced her napkin in her lap.

Nicholas relished his meal as if he hadn't eaten in a week although she nibbled and pecked at hers. After they finished, he lifted his water for a last pull while she cupped her mug and stared out the narrow window. A splash of light streaked across the black velvet sky.

"You realize we're in full view of your neighbors." She grinned at him over her mug. "One of them is cruising into their driveway."

"Dorothy has reminded me on a weekly basis about buying curtains."

Still holding her mug, she wandered to the window and considered the quiet night covering the sleepy town. The room stilled to a comfortable silence.

"I've been waiting for a beautiful woman to come along who can help me choose the right ones," he said. "Fortunately, I've known her all along."

She pivoted, catching his wicked grin and look of interest as his gaze focused on her face. Her pulse leapt in a disconcerting combination of anticipation and panic.

"Emmanuelle." His voice grew quiet. "I can hardly kiss you when you're standing on the other side of the room."

"Nicholas, we hardly know each other."

"A year ago, we talked regularly. Our bond was strong. Let's be honest. We both know it still is."

She walked to the couch and set down her mug. He set down his water. Their gazes held, the quiet punctuated by the dog's light snores.

Her thoughts scattered. She rearranged them into a semblance of reason. "A year ago we had a common purpose —ensuring your sister made a full recovery."

"Are things so different?" Gently, his fingers curved around her nape, soothing, stroking. "I'll help you make a full recovery from whatever you're struggling with." He bent his head slowly, and his lips met hers with sweet tenderness.

For a moment, she went rigid.

"I'm attracted to you, Emmanuelle," he murmured. "Always have been. I'm here for you."

Her body reacted in a dizzying sensation of emotions she couldn't explain. She didn't want to respond to him. Or perhaps she did because her reaction felt so natural. Trusting a man, feeling safe and cared for in his arms … She'd thought those feelings happened to other people.

Tentatively, she reached her arms around his neck and returned the kiss.

His mouth deepened as he fit her response to his own. He kissed her fully, insistently, boundlessly, creating a knot of pure awareness in her stomach. The longer his mouth pressed to hers, the more vibrant the sensations became. It was as if a new person had taken the place of the broken Emmanuelle. The new Emmanuelle was sincere and receptive, the former hesitant and uneasy, avoiding any connection with a man.

A sharp woof broke them apart.

Molly Belle lifted her head and regarded them. Before Nicholas could get to her, she laid her head down and went to sleep.

Emmanuelle's lips twitched. "Her injection is wearing off."

He settled on the couch and watched Emmanuelle, his gaze heated. "Shall we continue? We left off at—"

"Your dog may wake up again."

"I'll take my chances." His arms slipped around her, and she reveled in the pleasure of his hard mouth pressed on hers. She kissed him back while his warm hands shifted protectively around her.

Ages later, he lifted his head and cradled her face. Affection smoldered in his hazel eyes. "You came into my life at exactly the right time."

Molly Belle stirred, twitched, woofed to no one in particular, then plunked her nose back on the blanket.

He chuckled. "I think I have a love-hate relationship with that dog." With a sigh, he lowered his hands from Emmanuelle's face. He forked a last bite of coleslaw, leaned against the couch, and stretched out his legs. "Stay a while longer. Please. I'll be sure you make it back to the inn before midnight, Cinderella."

Across the inches of the couch separating them, she met his stare. His striking features were full of hope, almost boyish.

He was an honest man. Genuine and steadfast, his every movement capable, yet easy-going.

"All right, but only because you said 'please,' Prince Charming."

He reached out and gathered her to him. "Remember the night we watched television together when we were Skyping?"

"How did you ever persuade me to stream a documentary

about the Hubble telescope when I had a concert to prepare for the next day?"

He threw back his head and laughed. So good-natured, so familiar. "You should thank me because you learned several new outer-space terms. And all the planets—Mercury, Venus, Earth—"

She laid her hand on his arm. "I'm a musician, not an astronaut."

"Where is your harp, by the way? In New York?"

She kept her features blank and tried to make her voice impassive. "My harp is gone."

His expression was thoughtful as he obviously sensed her bleak mood. A beat passed.

"One of my favorite memories," he said, keeping her in his arms, "is the night you played the harp for me. 'Danny Boy.' Remember? I'd had an argument with Alice, and you said music would soothe me, so you lit candles and darkened your apartment. You had told me your harp was accented in twenty-three karat gold. I remember it shimmered in the candlelight each time you plucked a string. Truly, Emmanuelle, you looked like an angel, and it gave me goose-bumps." He traced her cheekbone with his forefinger.

"You sang while I played," Emmanuelle said. She'd clung to the memory of those shared times, although she'd known he was engaged and never pressed him for anything other than friendship.

Not long afterward, Dorothy had gotten out of rehab for opiate addiction, and Emmanuelle had met George, the wealthy hotel magnate.

And George had taken away her harp. Her pride. Her life.

CHAPTER 7

*N*icholas felt like he danced through the following week, and he wasn't a man who'd ever managed more than a two-step.

Molly Belle improved every day. She had reclaimed her sleeping spot at the foot of his bed, ate regularly, and reveled in her short daily walks with Emmanuelle. She'd even taught the dog to "sit" by holding a treat near the dog's nose. Once Molly Belle was sitting, she'd repeat the command, give the dog the treat, and shower her with affection and praise. She'd repeated the same sequence throughout each day, then demonstrated Molly Belle's progress for Nicholas each evening.

She'd taken Molly Belle to a shop a few doors down from his place and selected a fresh pine wreath, simple and unadorned, that she'd hung on his front door. On another occasion, she purchased curtains in a dazzling shade of lipstick-red and hung them on his bare living room windows. The effect was homey, warm, and Christmassy.

She'd also experimented with cooking new dishes. Thanks to Ryan's *Southern Charms* cookbook, Nicholas never knew quite what to expect for dinner. He only knew an exotic, savory meal waited for him when he got home.

In the evenings, he and Emmanuelle dined in his cozy kitchen, on a wooden table tucked beside a snowy window, polishing off spaghetti carbonara and thick slices of buttery bread accompanied by oven-fried pickles.

"Surprise me," he'd tell her each morning after she'd arrived.

And she did.

He enjoyed her companionship, her considerate nature, the way her dimples flashed whenever she was amused. He hadn't found a word to put to his feelings, especially since he hadn't wanted to become romantically involved with a woman after his breakup with Alice.

With Emmanuelle, though, the word *love* came to mind.

On the last day of the work week, Nicholas issued his customary thank you to her as soon as he strode through his apartment door. Molly Belle wriggled with delight, bounded to his side and greeted him with a continuous train of wet doggy kisses.

He scrubbed a hand along the dog's ears.

Emmanuelle was seated on the couch, intent on studying a page from Ryan's cookbook.

"I've been thinking about dinner all day," he said. He'd been thinking about her too, although he didn't mention that part. For a celebratory end-of-the-week supper, Emmanuelle had declared she was experimenting with a different fix on a traditional Christmas recipe—roasted turkey and sweet potatoes garnished with a fancy topping Nicholas had forgotten the name of.

He slid his gun from his holster, took off his badge. "How was your day?"

"Busy. Despite her size, Molly Belle thinks she's a lap dog." Emmanuelle kept her head down, busy flipping pages.

"And Dorothy and Ryan invited us for Christmas dinner so I tried a new dessert recipe tonight too."

He breathed in a lungful of smoky air just as the smoke alarm went off. "Is something burning?"

"Oh, no!" The cookbook fell from her lap as she jumped to her feet. "I forgot to set the timer."

They sprinted toward the kitchen. The dog whined and raced in the opposite direction, scratching at the door to be let out.

"I was testing a fruitcake recipe," Emmanuelle said as he opened a kitchen window to let out the smoke, and then turned off the alarm.

Not a dreaded fruitcake. Since Nicholas was fairly intelligent, he kept the comment to himself as he retrieved the burnt cake from the oven and set it on the counter. He commiserated with Emmanuelle, sighed, and tried to look regretful. He wanted to joke about the fruitcake making a good doorstop and wisely changed his mind.

"The cake can't be salvaged, so I'll phone for pizza delivery," he said. "Sound good?"

"If you stopped to look around, you'd see I cooked a twelve-pound turkey and sweet potatoes. Is pizza your fix for whatever comes your way?"

"There's no such thing as bad pizza. So ...yes." He lifted the foil off the potatoes and pointed accusingly. "What's this white stuff on top?"

"Goat cheese and scallions."

"Sounds awful ..." He caught her scowl. ... "fancy." He congratulated himself for thinking so quickly on his feet. "Sounds awful fancy. Do you think I'll like it?"

"Fifty-fifty."

He suppressed a chuckle. She looked positively intoxicating, even with her heart-shaped mouth twisted into a grimace as she beheld the burnt cake.

He left the kitchen to check on the dog, who'd resumed her place at the foot of his bed.

When he returned to the kitchen, he drew off the hairband she'd used to secure her hair when she cooked, brought her closer, and embraced her for a lengthy kiss. "We're beginning to sound as if we're a couple, and I like the sound of it."

She drew an unsteady breath and dropped her gaze, but not before he noticed the warmth kindling in her vivid blue eyes, the flush of heat tinting her creamy complexion a soft pink.

"We can't be a couple."

"Why not?"

She kept her gaze rooted on his bare wood floor. "Because I won't be a burden to you." She placed her arm between them, an effective wedge.

He'd half expected her reaction.

Anything to do with Molly Belle's care prompted an easy conversation. So did the latest recipe in the cookbook. Or classical music, especially her favorite composer, Beethoven. She responded to his kisses, molding herself to him. But any talk of a serious relationship put her off-balance.

He drew her to the couch and took a seat beside her. In an attempt to lighten the mood, he teasingly bumped her shoulder with his. "Tomorrow is Molly Belle's vet appointment. I'm hoping you'll go with me."

"Absolutely."

He smiled, relieved. He'd come to rely on her for emotional support.

"Afterward," he went on, "I'd like to buy a Christmas tree. My apartment is begging for a dose of holiday cheer, so are you up for a stop at a tree farm outside of town? In the past I've cut my own tree." He gestured to the dog. "Because she's still recovering, we'll buy a precut tree."

"Perfect." Her smile was luminous and lit his small apartment with merriment.

The attraction sizzled between them. Soon, he thought, when she was ready, she'd tell him her trepidation, and he'd assure her she was safe. Mutually, they'd dismiss her worries. She was in Cherish where life was secure. He'd keep her out of harm's way—whether real or imagined.

Trying to tamp down his eagerness, he reached into his shirt pocket and withdrew a small box wrapped in gold paper with a red satin ribbon. "Thank you, Emmanuelle, for everything you've done for me this week. On my lunch hour today, I stopped at Musically Yours and bought you something." He held the box out to her.

Lightly, she touched her hand to his. "Nicholas, you didn't have to buy me anything. I wanted to take care of Molly Belle."

His senses buzzed, alive to the brush of her fingertips, the thickened skin where calluses had formed. Once she had told him she was proud of those calluses, a badge for practicing long hours to pursue her dream of becoming a professional harpist.

And she had.

He'd taken her suggestion to give God his attention and had begun praying every night. Lately, he'd lifted a plea that she'd make Cherish her permanent home.

She could build a life here. *They* could build a future together.

He slipped an arm around her waist, delighting in her nearness, staring at her for a long moment. "I wanted to buy you a gift. It was my pleasure."

"Nicholas …" She ran a hand through her unruly blonde curls. Her chin trembled. Although they'd known each other for over a year, she grew unexpectedly shy.

"Please open it." He stilled her hand and kissed her

temple. He was giving her what he could. He wanted to give her so much more.

Nodding brightly, she rapidly undid the paper and unlatched a plain gray box. A tiny harp dangling from a solid-gold chain shot emerald green and diamond prisms across his plain white ceiling.

"The harp charm is from Ireland, from Dublin. I wanted an Irish harp fit for the most gifted woman I've ever known." He brushed his knuckles over her flawless cheek, brushed away a stray tear.

"Happy tears," she said.

He nodded. "Our conversation from the other day about the night you played 'Danny Boy' brought back good memories. I want this necklace to do the same."

"It brought back good memories for me too." She fingered the necklace. Her eyes shimmered a soft blue velvet. "I haven't bought a piece of clothing or jewelry for myself in months. Thank you."

"I looked for a twenty-three-karat necklace to match your harp, but this was the best I could afford. My salary as a deputy sheriff isn't much, though I plan to work my way up to a position of management." He drew her to him and she rested her cheek against his chest. "Someday I'll buy you a real harp."

He spoke above her, breathing in her floral perfume, citrus and violets and expectation.

"Money isn't important," she said. "I know this gift is from your heart."

She was splendid. She made him feel alive again, brought him out of his sadness. After his fiancée had left him, he'd grieved, focusing on his scars. But a new emotion was rising over the scars, allowing him to become again the man he once was—one of faith, free from cynicism, free to open his heart once more.

They avoided eye contact. The moment held too much emotion for her, for him.

"I know how much your harp meant to you," he murmured. "You once let me in on a secret, that your parents surprised you with a harp for your twelfth birthday. They'd saved money for years to buy the best. A Lyon and Healy harp, correct?"

"You remembered." Her tears came hard, sudden, and she let them.

He soothed her, crooning, rocking her. "You're not alone anymore, Emmanuelle."

Any further conversation was forgotten as she wept. When she withdrew, she wiped at her eyes with the handkerchief he provided. "I'm sorry. I mean, crying was uncalled for and I put you in an awkward—"

"Don't apologize. You're the best thing that's ever happened to me." He swept wisps of hair from her nape and secured the delicate gold chain around her throat, then ushered her to the bathroom mirror. "Dorothy assured me you'd fall in love with this necklace."

At first, Emmanuelle kept her gaze downcast before staring at herself. Carefully, she slid a finger along the fine chain and then found the exquisite detailing of the harp. "I haven't worn anything this pretty in many months. Thanks to you, I'm beginning to feel like a woman again. Someone who matters." Her smile sparkled in the mirror reflection.

He stood behind her and rested his hands on her shoulders. "You matter very, very much. More than you can ever imagine."

He stared at her, a vision of beauty with the heirloom-quality necklace shimmering against her creamy skin above her navy-blue cashmere sweater. At that moment he knew. It had returned, his love for a woman.

Only this time it was real.

CHAPTER 8

*A*fter Dr. Troutman's nod of approval, Nicholas and Emmanuelle set off for the Christmas tree farm. Molly Belle waited in Nicholas's car while they chose the last fir tree on the lot. The tree wasn't perfectly shaped; in fact, it wasn't shaped at all. Nicholas named the tree Charlie Brown since the branches jutted out in random angles.

"Every underdog needs a loving home," he declared, and Emmanuelle wholeheartedly agreed.

One of the employees at the farm shook the tree to remove any loose needles, then wrapped it for transport. A short drive later, Emmanuelle and Nicholas hoisted the scraggly tree up his flight of stairs and into his apartment.

"The tree looks better already," she said as Nicholas secured the tree in a sturdy metal stand. "It's just begging for lots of care and plenty of water. And we'll trim your whole apartment to resemble an old-fashioned Christmas. Ryan's book features all sorts of inspiring ideas."

Nicholas pushed himself to his feet after pouring water into the base of the tree stand. "I thought it was a cookbook focused on recipes."

"Recipes and decorating tips. And there's a thought-provoking article on empowering women that provides tips on how to keep safe in dangerous circumstances. The entire book is highly motivating."

"Quite the cookbook," he observed.

They referenced a "traditional Christmas" article as a guide and spent the afternoon decorating. Using heavy embroidery floss, they strung popcorn and cranberries. Nicholas found a set of multicolored lights stuffed in his hall closet. He began at the tree trunk and moved upward, wrapping the lights taut by weaving them from side to side.

"There isn't much of a tree to light," he said with a laugh. "The branches are beyond sparse!"

"I'm always drawn to these types of trees." She stepped back to assess the tree. "In the end, it's all about hope, isn't it?"

"True. And few people are as hopeful as Charlie Brown."

"Multicolored lights remind me of happy times with my family in Remsen. Call me nostalgic and old-fashioned."

"Then I'm old-fashioned too. Nothing is better than colored lights on a green pine tree to get you in the mood for Christmas."

"Last year, my ex wanted white lights and neon-blue bulbs on the tree he'd purchased for his swanky condo in a high-rise. I argued for colored lights. He didn't agree, of course, saying white lights were chic and modern. I like modern." She hesitated, combed nervous fingers through her hair. "No that's wrong. I just told him that."

"You lied?"

"I had no choice. He had two switches, calm or angry. I knew better than to disagree and kept my opinion to myself. He'd trained me like we're training Molly Belle—to obey commands." She watched the dog, resting on a blanket in the corner. The dog returned her stare with steady, shining eyes.

54

"I understand my former situation now," she went on. "It's easier at a distance."

"What's your ex's name?"

She took a moment to adjust her fire-red tunic, fussing and fidgeting, as if the tunic didn't fit correctly over her jeans. "George."

"That's it? George? George who?"

"Just George." She shrugged, shivered. Slight, but he saw it.

"Where's George now?"

Another shrug. She looked around, rubbed her hands together. "I assume he's in New York."

Her ex had evidently hurt her, and the realization brought anger bubbling to Nicholas's throat. When he found him, *and he would*, he'd silence George with a good stiff jab and a command of his own. *Stay away from Emmanuelle.*

He wrapped an arm around her shoulders and she leaned into him. Each time they were with each other, his need to protect her grew stronger.

He turned to the next page in the book to change the subject. She might get too upset if they continued discussing her ex. "The next round of decorating is to find red and green bulbs for our quirky tree. Do you prefer glass bulbs or—"

"I prefer family vintage bulbs and pinecones and silver tinsel. But ..." She dug in her tote bag and drew out a tiny angel ornament, brandishing it in the air. "I've carried this with me ever since I left New York. The clerk at the airport told me it was a good luck charm. It belongs on your tree."

"*Our* tree," he corrected her, and hung the ornament on a thin lower branch. "All this decorating warrants a celebration, so let's call out for pizza."

"Again? Is pizza your remedy for everything?"

With a laugh, he pulled his phone from his jeans pocket

and placed an order for a large cheese and pepperoni pizza, with a side of barbecue for Emmanuelle.

After pocketing his phone, he took her hands. "Let's wait for the delivery on the porch steps. The weather is mild, so we can go outside without jackets." He glanced at Molly Belle, sleeping soundly, then eased open the door.

They sat on the stoop. It was one of those inviting South Carolina evenings, when the sun had warmed everything in its path, including his front porch.

The view of his charming cul-de-sac lit with strings of festive lights, the nearby clip-clop of a horse-drawn carriage, filled him with gratitude. He imagined the residents inside their homes, savoring steaming cups of hot cocoa, sitting beside their cozy fireplaces.

From a few streets away came the last strains of "We Three Kings." Sung, he surmised, by the Cherish Church ladies' caroling group. He grinned, envisioning the women, young and elderly, dressed in their traditional Victorian costumes, complete with big bonnets and hand muffs.

The day had been perfect. Ending the evening with Emmanuelle by his side brought a quiet, joyous peace, and he whispered a prayer of thanksgiving. Tenderly, he pressed a kiss on her palms. "Two weeks from today is the Musically Yours holiday concert," he said. "Ryan is leading the elementary school chorus in a Christmas carol singalong and then singing a couple solos."

She rested her cheek on his shoulder. "Cherish is like a picture out of a Christmas card."

He chuckled and went back to appreciating the street decorations. Several neighbors had run animated light displays in a scalloped pattern along their fences.

Yes, this was the ideal town to live, to work, to raise a family.

He put an arm around her and she snuggled nearer, the

warmth of her body reaching out to his. He could get used to this. A delightful woman, her breathing soft and even, whose slight body had grown heavier because she was … sleeping?

He grinned. She'd fallen asleep quickly, even quicker than he usually did. Between taking care of his dog and creating nightly meals fit for a food connoisseur, she was clearly exhausted. He considered her profile, her small turned-up nose, the light sprinkling of freckles on her cheeks. Several times during the past week, he'd caught her staring at her cell phone as it rang. She never answered a call, and a few times her face had turned bone-white when she'd glimpsed the screen.

"Unknown caller," she always said, dropping the phone back into her tote bag. Whenever he pressed for details, she just chewed her bottom lip and stubbornly stayed silent.

He reached into his pocket for his phone and canceled the pizza. No sense in waking her when the delivery person arrived. Surely that frozen pizza was sitting somewhere in his freezer.

From inside the apartment, Molly Belle barked.

Emmanuelle woke with a start and rubbed her eyes. She peered at him, darted a peek at her watch. "Sorry, I didn't realize I dozed. I haven't rested well in several months."

"Because of George?"

A noticeable gap hung in the air as she scanned the street and its bright decorations. Distractedly, she nodded.

He went to brush pine needles from her shoulder and she flinched. He let out a whistled sigh and pulled back his hand. "Don't. You insult me when you do that."

"Do what?"

"Treat me as if I'm your ex. Just because I raise my hand doesn't mean I'm going to hit you." He deliberated, but only for a second. "What's really going on with you?"

"Too much." She eased up, then sat back down. "Nicholas,

I can't give you the relationship you want. I'm not the right woman for you."

"How do you know?"

She closed her eyes. Tears escaped. "Because you're a good man and my life is complicated."

"I like complicated."

"No, no, you don't." She opened her eyes, a deep shimmery blue. They stared at each other.

"It's odd," he mused.

"What?"

"The fact you're a harpist and you don't have a harp. Did you sell it?"

"My harp was smashed to pieces." She didn't pause for his sympathy, didn't bury her face in her hands. "George destroyed it."

"Why?"

He hadn't meant to ask the question because he knew the answer. As a law enforcement officer, he'd come across men like George. Domestic violence was the leading cause of injury to women. He'd read the statistics, recognized an abuser's behaviors and characteristics. After the honeymoon phase, they became controlling and jealous, and oftentimes sought to isolate their partner.

"Why?" Emmanuelle repeated. "Why would a man who supposedly cared for me take away something I loved, something so meaningful? To break me, I suppose." She shook her head; she'd answered her own question. "He knew precisely which buttons to press. He was exceptionally charming and people were attracted to him. Me included."

Nicholas's anger was sharp. He pulled it in. "How did you meet him?"

"His secretary booked me to play the harp for one of his office functions, the grand opening of his tenth boutique hotel in the New York area." Her voice caught. "After we became a couple, he always reminded me I was beneath him and how thankful I should be an important man like him was interested in someone like me … someone who was little more than a street performer."

"You know that's not true. You're a skilled professional."

She trailed her fingers along the edge of the porch railing and let out a sigh.

"When are you deserting me for New York?" he asked.

"I'm not deserting you. I happen to live there." She smiled and broke off, apparently waiting for his rejoinder. When he didn't offer one, she added, "I don't have a definite date in mind. Dorothy offered me a job at her music conservatory. I've considered finding a place in town and teaching harp lessons." She shrugged and blew out a breath. "Although I know it's better if I keep moving."

The last part of her answer didn't register because he'd fixated on the first part. His heart had leapt when she'd mentioned living in Cherish.

"Is he the reason you came here? Is he the reason you choose to keep running?"

"I have no choice and I'm not running." Her fingers nervously worked the hem of her tunic before she propped her chin in her hands. "Okay, yes, maybe I am. If George O'Donnell finds me, I don't know what he'll do."

George O'Donnell. Piercing rage sliced Nicholas like a knife. "He won't do anything to harm you. I'll make sure of it."

"You don't know him. He's well-off and powerful."

He joined her cold hands with his warm ones. "And I'm in law enforcement."

"That's why I'm afraid. If you go after him, you'll get hurt. He operates in influential circles with big-city types."

"In our quiet town, you'll be safe. You must know I'll always protect you."

"Our town," she repeated.

"Yes. And our life."

"Nicholas?" A smile ghosted her lips as an errant tear streamed down her cheek. "Will you do something for me?"

He gazed at her enchanting face, her over-bright eyes. He would protect her with his life.

"Anything," he said.

"Will you hold me for a minute?"

CHAPTER 9

*I*n the ensuing two weeks Emmanuelle slept poorly, despite the inn's exquisitely appointed room and her luxurious queen-sized bed. Nightmares chased her and were always the same: the dim outline of a man with flat black eyebrows above dull gray eyes, trailing her every move.

George O'Donnell.

She'd scramble through unnamed woods while the flash of something vicious, and corrupt, and overpowering, followed her. The nightmare always ended the same, with her weeping and running farther and farther away from Cherish.

She'd wake beneath her cozy coverlet, her heart hammering, searching the room for something recognizable. Country-green walls, the hand-stitched quilt draped over a rocking chair, the braided rug covering the wide-plank pine floor, helped steady her breathing.

"Only a nightmare," she'd murmur, wiping her sweaty brow. "Vivid, horrible, and not real."

She'd focus out the window at the sprinkling of stars

against the black velvet sky. Then she'd close her eyes and think about Nicholas—his kindness, his easy-going manner, his self-assured confidence. Efficient and calm, whether tidying his home or ministering to Molly Belle, dealing with dangerous circumstances on duty or holding her as if she were a china doll. He was all man, all kindness, all compassion.

"In our quiet town, you'll be safe. You must know I'll always protect you," he'd said.

Only then, imagining his capable arms around her, could she seek the peace of slumber.

* * *

BY THE THIRD week of December, Cherish had become a jubilant fairyland, a kaleidoscope of Yuletide hues. Parades were held every weekend, and quaint mom-and-pop stores were decked out in magical window dressings. Children and adults alike stopped and gaped, mesmerized in child-like fascination.

Illuminated by tiny white lights, Emmanuelle's comfy inn, with its snow-covered roof and wisps of smoke billowing from the chimney, looked like a postcard image of Christmas town, USA.

Tom had taken a liking to Molly Belle and allowed her inside, provided she stayed in the foyer and didn't jump on any of the patrons. Unfortunately, the third day she was allowed in, Molly Belle knocked a teenage boy over when she'd leapt on the boy's legs. Despite Nicholas's explanations that the dog was still a puppy with a playful, silly personality, Tom banished Molly Belle to the porch. Both hands braced on his polished wood desk, he'd leaned forward until his cheaters slid down his nose and declared she wasn't allowed inside until she graduated from dog obedience school.

Considering Nicholas had abandoned the idea of obedience school until Molly Belle was fully recovered, Emmanuelle was certain the dog wouldn't be entering the inn anytime soon.

A cold front had brought snow to Cherish, a white dusting that topped off the winter-wonderland. As the snow fell softly, day after day, Emmanuelle's mood became more hopeful. She spent her time at Nicholas's apartment caring for Molly Belle and cooking delectable meals—a flaky crusted chicken pot pie brimming with roasted chicken and baby carrots one night, a sweet winter corn-bread with a splash of jalapeno the next. Oftentimes, she'd bake a tray of Christmas cookies, oozing chocolate chips, warm from the oven. As she cooked, she'd tune the radio to a Christian holiday station and hum along to every Christmas carol.

In the middle of the afternoon, she'd leash Molly Belle for a walk. Few things outshone walking a devoted dog who loved going outside for a squirrel-chasing adventure, especially when sunlight warmed Emmanuelle's cheeks and bracing air brought remembrances of Christmas in Remsen.

At Dorothy's prodding, the two women spent an evening shopping. Emmanuelle purchased a pair of shiny gold earrings to complement her harp necklace, plus a rose-tinted lip gloss. There was something so feminine about earrings and lip gloss, Dorothy said, that made a woman feel attractive. Regarding her reflection in the shop's mirror, Emmanuelle agreed. She'd caught her hair at the nape and secured it with a lace bow, the result a messy bun highlighted by escaping corkscrews of blonde hair.

She'd also painted two opposite walls of Nicholas's living room in a golden-yellow and convinced him to reupholster his couch in a deep-chocolate brown. He'd grinned his approval, and she too was pleased with the result. After

Christmas, she aimed to tackle his kitchen and paint those walls a cool mint-green.

After Christmas.

Yes, because she'd decided to live in Cherish. She hadn't told Nicholas, not yet. She'd decided to surprise him on Christmas, after they attended a church service with Dorothy and Ryan. She'd accepted Dorothy's offer to give harp lessons at the Musically Yours music conservatory and had begun formulating a plan to buy a new harp. Ryan told her that the nearby city of Stanley boasted an excellent symphony that was actively looking for a principal harpist, and encouraged her to audition. She'd agreed, the idea prompting recollections of how much she enjoyed performing.

On the Saturday of the holiday concert in Cherish, Emmanuelle spent the morning peeling potatoes and carrots for a hearty beef stew she simmered on Nicholas's stove. The weatherman had predicted snow, which had rapidly accumulated to several inches.

Nicholas had had to respond to a domestic-dispute call, and she'd gladly volunteered to stay with Molly Belle. He'd added that one of the other officers, Joseph Hannaford, would be on duty at the concert that evening. Large crowds were expected because of Ryan Edwards's performance.

Done with the stew, she surveyed the living room from the kitchen doorway. The Charlie Brown Christmas tree was delightful, brightly lit and brimming with cheer. Her angel ornament hung from one of the branches, and she laughed out loud, inhaling the scents of pine and promise.

Life was good. Very good. On an even more optimistic note, there'd been no sign of George. After she'd begun watching Molly Belle, every morning she'd received a phone call precisely at eight o'clock, a few minutes after Nicholas left for work.

Whenever she answered, no one spoke.

Once, she'd sworn she'd heard breathing on the other end. Bad connection? Most likely. She rejected her suspicions that it might be George. Merely an over-zealous telemarketer, she'd tell herself.

Still, she told Nicholas, admitting to her uneasiness. He listened thoughtfully before assuring her she was right—a telemarketer had programmed her phone number on speed-dial. After a long, thorough kiss, he assured her there was nothing to worry about.

And then, without warning, the mysterious phone calls had stopped.

As the next few days passed, the realization she was finally free from George renewed her confidence. With a strong handsome deputy by her side, friends who loved her, and a spirited dog ever near, what was there to fear? Truly, Christmas in Cherish promised a happiness she'd never dreamed.

CHAPTER 10

*A*fter they'd eaten stew for an early dinner, Nicholas drove Emmanuelle back to the inn to get ready for the evening concert. They passed tree limbs heavy with snow, bushes dusted with a fine white powder.

At the inn, she gifted Tom with a loaf of her crusty bread, prompting him to taste it. He'd chewed with his eyes closed and exclaimed, "Will you marry me, Emmanuelle?"

Before she could reply, Nicholas draped an arm on her shoulders and assured the innkeeper she was spoken for.

She floated to her room where she ran a warm shower, refreshing herself under a stream of multiple jets. The scents of her soap and shampoo—brown sugar and vanilla—reminded her of hot cinnamon rolls slathered in butter cream frosting.

Her anticipation of the evening rising, she grabbed a fluffy towel for her hair, and wrapped herself in a luxurious white robe. She padded across the wood floor of her room and deliberated on her outfit, ultimately choosing a comfortable pair of colored denims and a red cashmere sweater.

Despite his numerous concert engagements, she'd never

heard Ryan perform live, and she was looking forward to the evening.

At 7:00, a light tap on her door signaled Nicholas's arrival.

When she opened the door, he lifted her to her toes and held her. "Emmanuelle Sumter, you look gorgeous and smell like a cinnamon roll." He frequently remarked on her appearance, always complimentary, always causing her to melt, just melt.

She saw the seductive-green passion in his hazel eyes as their lips met.

"And every time I see you," he went on, "I fall more in love with you." He stated his feelings simply, without preamble or fanfare, his mouth brushing against her ear, his warm breath heating her insides.

She ran her fingers over his nape. His blond hair was thick and curled over his collared parka. His lips were smooth, his mouth perfectly shaped. His well-defined jaw and sharp cheekbones brought a chiseled handsomeness to his cover model features.

It's too soon to talk of love, she wanted to say. But it wasn't too soon, because she was falling in love with him too.

She hugged the realization close. This good-looking, conscientious man loved her, and with each heartfelt embrace, each heady kiss, her defenses were thawing. Slowly, she was shaking off her fears and yielding to him.

"Ready for an amazing concert?" he asked.

"I can't wait." She went to her closet and tugged a pink tasseled hat over her hair. "Dorothy said she'd accompany Ryan on keyboard if they can figure out how to run electrical power on stage."

"So far, they haven't," Nicholas said. As she rummaged through the closet, he added that the afternoon sun had melted much of the morning's snow, so the streets were messy tonight.

"Just let me grab my boots. Where's Molly Belle?"

"She's near the porch."

She swiveled. "Alone?"

"She's on her leash. Tom is playing with her in the snow." Nicholas struggled to keep a straight face. "He won't admit he's got a soft spot for dogs, although you and I know he does." He helped her on with her jacket and exaggeratedly hefted her tote bag from the bureau. "What do you carry in this? Lead?"

"Necessities. You know, my cell phone, wallet, loose change …"

"I wouldn't want to tote this heavy bag around."

"You would if you were a sensible woman." She laughed. "I can't be deprived of my pink lip gloss."

Still bantering, they made their way down the carpeted staircase.

As soon as they strolled onto the porch, Molly Belle scampered around them, feathery tail wagging, as if she hadn't seen them in a month. Nicholas thanked Tom and reached for the leash. Hand in hand, Emmanuelle and Nicholas stepped from the porch.

Although the morning snow had blown in quick and heavy, as Nicholas had said, most had melted under sun-kissed daytime skies. As the evening thermometer plunged, what was left had frozen, causing thin sheets of ice to gloss over the surface of the remaining snow. Tom had shoveled a generous path and covered the steps and sidewalk with rock salt.

"I've never listened to opera," Nicholas said, tucking her hand in the crook of his arm as they started for the town square. "I expect—"

"You've never heard Ryan sing?" Her lips twitched with

amusement. "Your sister is married to one of the most famous opera singers in the world!"

"Once, maybe, when we were teenagers, I overheard him singing an operatic version of Dorothy's favorite top-forty hit. I assumed he was trying to impress her. They used to sit for hours on the side porch of our house." Nicholas's deep voice vibrated with laughter. "But I'm all for the idea of a bonfire and roasting s'mores after the concert."

When they reached the square, Ryan and Dorothy gave an absent-minded wave as they arranged chairs beneath a white canvas tent. A stage had been set up alongside the ten-foot decorated Christmas tree. Various kiosks serving refreshments lined the outer edges of the square, and Nicholas briefly introduced her to his coworker, Joseph Hannaford, the officer on duty. As the crowds thickened, a fine, snowy mist began to fall.

A halcyon town awaiting Christmas, Emmanuelle mused. The entire scene was a miniature version of New York's festive theater district. Cheery memories, she thought, … until … until …

She brought a jittery hand to her forehead.

A few months after she began dating George, she wore her favorite sweater to a theater event, and had left her jacket in the restroom at intermission. When he noticed, he demanded they leave before the show was over. She assumed he was angry because she had been foolish enough to have forgotten her jacket. He was concerned, as the theater was cold, she reasoned.

She was way off the mark. He shouted at her and called her a tramp for strutting around in a clingy sweater that he deemed too provocative.

He was jealous. She got that, and even felt flattered.

At first.

The relationship deepened. She believed she was in love

with him, and he was in love with her. However, he began to erupt when she least expected, no matter how fine a line she walked. Scary remembrances of George's viciousness, his narcissistic behavior, his insincere repentance, brought a quake down her spine.

She forced the chilling memories away and glanced at the rugged man standing beside her.

She was being foolish. She was safe, the town was real, this man was real. And this was the picture she needed to carry in order to move forward in her life. The uncommonly large crowd had simply dredged up memories from her uneasy mind.

As if he'd read her thoughts, Nicholas protectively tightened his arm around her waist. "Are you all right?" His hazel gaze locked on hers.

"Yes, I was thinking about how grateful I am to be here. And I'm happy, truly happy."

"So am I." He spoke quietly, tenderly. "I love you, Emmanuelle."

She beamed up at him, this man of faith whom she'd enjoyed endless conversations with, a man who spoke plainly what was on his heart.

"I love you too, Nicholas."

He smiled at her as if she were incredibly beloved.

She sighed with contentment. Finally, her world was coming together, and she whispered a thank you to God for giving her a promising future alongside the man she loved.

As they wove through the tent to find a good seat, she scanned the tent to see where Dorothy and Ryan had gone.

An exuberant Dorothy was arranging the last row of folding chairs. Her simple, classic black sweater dress showed off every curve of her lithe figure. She'd pinned her dark hair into an understated twist at the back of her head, drawing attention to her emerald-green eyes and pearl stud earrings.

Ryan strode over to her, impressively tall with dark, compelling features, his broad shoulders filling out his navy jacket to perfection. He draped a tweed coat around Dorothy. Something she said made him laugh out loud, and he gathered her in his arms and kissed her.

Their delight in each other was so infectious that Nicholas and Emmanuelle shared a grin.

"Well?" he prompted.

"Well what?"

"Well, if everyone is kissing, then where's my kiss?"

"You're impossible. We're not performing in a concert tonight."

"I plan to sing along to every Christmas carol. Does that count?"

She chuckled. "No. Besides, we're not newlyweds."

"Not yet." A slow, roguish smile moved across his face.

She felt her blood heat from her toes to her temple. "You're thinking to kiss me here, with all these people around?" Coyly, she shook her head, teasingly discouraging him. Then with a mischievous smile, she tilted her head back, inviting a kiss.

Dr. Troutman and Scarlett entered the tent carrying two cups of coffee and a bag of chips. They spotted them, waved, and jostled through the crowd. Molly Belle yipped and tugged on her leash in her attempt at a greeting.

Her red hair springy beneath her leopard ear muffs, Scarlett offered a sparkling smile and opened her chips. She offered them to the group, then began munching.

"How's one of my favorite dogs?" Dr. Troutman rubbed Molly Belle's head as she scrabbled her front paws up his legs. He bent and examined her feet. "Just making sure there's no snow trapped in the pads."

"I've been checking," Emmanuelle said.

He sipped his coffee. "Are you two here for the concert?"

"*I* am," Emmanuelle said and then pointed to Nicholas. "He's here for the s'mores."

Dr. Troutman made a dramatic show of choking on his coffee. "Glad to see you're still in Cherish, Emmanuelle. Don't you live in New York?"

Nicholas pressed a light kiss on her forehead. "I'm trying to talk her into moving permanently to Cherish."

"Well, I could use a knowledgeable person in my office. Scarlett is a wonderful receptionist although she's going to be a little busy, now that we're engaged." His hand reached out to cover Scarlett's, but not before Emmanuelle noticed a three-stone diamond ring in a rose-gold setting on Scarlett's ring finger.

"Congratulations," Emmanuelle and Nicholas said simultaneously.

"Thank you." Scarlett's shimmery, ruby earrings swung sideways as she nodded. Enthusiasm glowing in her face, she turned to Dr. Troutman. "I love animals, but I love you more."

Emmanuelle saw the elation in the veterinarian's smile as he swung his attention back toward her. "If you're looking for a job, Emmanuelle, you can work for me anytime."

"My sister beat you to it." Nicholas said, nodding toward Dorothy. "She asked Emmanuelle to teach music lessons at her conservatory. Did you know Emmanuelle is a professional harpist?"

"I'd like to hear you play," Scarlett said.

"Someday." Emmanuelle grimaced. How's that for evasive? she upbraided herself. She was a professional harpist with no harp.

"I'm sorry. I can see from the expression on your face that

I troubled you." Scarlett swallowed a chip and snapped up another. "Dorothy mentioned you don't have a harp."

Emmanuelle stopped her grimace and turned it into a smile. "Don't apologize. Look what Nicholas bought me. Isn't it beautiful?" She drew out the harp necklace from beneath her jacket for Scarlett to admire.

"Yes, very beautiful, and very thoughtful." Scarlett eyed the necklace. "An early Christmas gift, Nicholas?"

"Nope." He laughed. "It's my gift to Emmanuelle for coming to Cherish. She's a blessing to me."

Emmanuelle's heart gave a funny lurch. Nicholas offered safety and security and he was more considerate than anyone she'd ever known. Not every man was cruel and intimidating, she reminded herself yet again. Healing from abuse was a slow road, and it took time and infinite perseverance. And she'd walk that road with the man she loved.

New beginnings.

"You make a very striking couple," Scarlett was saying. "Two good-looking blonds."

"I agree with one of your observations." With a mile-wide beam toward Emmanuelle, Nicholas said, "We'd better claim a seat, my good-looking blonde."

As people converged, aromas of chocolate fudge and honey roasted almonds lifted into the air.

"The staid doctor and his perky receptionist are engaged?" Emmanuelle asked.

"Apparently." He grinned. "He must be twice her age."

"They're charming together and I'm delighted for them."

"The vet has lived alone on his alpaca farm since his wife's passing. He's a moral Christian man and I'm glad he met someone he can share his life with."

"I hope Scarlett likes alpacas." Emmanuelle laughed. "Do they bite?"

"Not normally. And she can eat her junk food while Dr. Troutman's alpaca herd munches on green plants and grass."

They settled on seats in the last row, just in case Molly Belle spotted another dog and attempted to dash off for an impromptu romp in the snow.

When the audience quieted, the first half of the concert began with the elementary school's children's chorus. The music teacher conducted, and everyone joined in a heart-lifting rendition of "Silent Night." Before intermission, Ryan led the crowd in the "Hallelujah" chorus from Handel's *Messiah*. As tradition dictated, everyone stood.

"I've always wondered," Nicholas said under his breath, "why are we supposed to stand?"

"There are many theories, the principal one being that King George II was so overwhelmed by the 'Hallelujah' chorus that he stood up. And whenever the king stood, so did everyone else."

After a brief intermission, Ryan came on stage for the second half. His bass voice, rich and finely textured, was exactly as Dorothy had described, and Emmanuelle felt as if she couldn't breathe during his entire a cappella rendition of "Away in a Manger."

When the concert finished to thunderous clapping, whistles, and cheers, Ryan held up a hand to quell the applause and extended congratulations to the children's chorus. The children scampered back on stage, bowed low, and then grinned and waved at the audience.

Emmanuelle rose along with Nicholas and announced she'd ferret out the booths serving roasted almonds and fudge. Her nose could only take so much temptation.

He circled an arm around her shoulders. "What about our s'mores? The mayor is building the bonfire and we'll eat in a few minutes."

"I'm adopting Scarlett's motto—to embrace life and

indulge yourself. No worries. I promise I'll eat the fudge and almonds and s'mores." She sighed. "Although I won't be able to fit into the holiday skirt I brought if I keep eating at this rate. Fortunately, I also own a pair of slacks with an elastic waist."

Nicholas didn't appease her with a chuckle. Instead, his fingers tightened on her shoulders. "I'll go with you."

"Why?"

"Those suspicious phone calls you were getting …" He looked around and nodded at a busload of fans swarming around Ryan. "There're too many people here tonight."

"I'm twenty-five, not five, and I lived in New York, one of the busiest cities in the world. I can certainly navigate a crowd and get my own snacks without an escort. I've gotten over my fear of walking alone." She shook off his arm and grabbed her tote bag. "Besides, Dorothy's headed our way. Please congratulate her for me. I'll shoot ahead of this next horde and catch up with all of you in a few minutes."

He hesitated. "Are you certain you'll be okay?"

"Enough time has passed. I'm better. Really." She walked purposefully toward the food kiosks. Out from under the tent, she saw the night was black—no moon or stars, and the shimmer of snow was now a gray mist.

She wound past the busy fudge and caramel-corn stands. The stand that advertised roasted almonds was farther down, and there was no line. Actually, the stand looked deserted. Had they sold out of almonds already and closed shop?

She paused, debating what to do, and sensed someone walking up behind her. "Emmanuelle," a man said, "can you give me directions to the stage?"

She was so sure she'd imagined the familiar voice, she started walking toward the stand.

"Emmanuelle."

She froze. Her shoulders tightened, her breathing stopped. *Move*, she commanded her feet.

"Turn around, Emmanuelle."

Obediently, she did. George had always had a hold over her.

The sight of him standing so near was enough to unfreeze her. She shifted, one foot stepping back, but his gaze immediately sharpened on her. If only she could make him believe she was standing stock-still while she slowly moved backward.

"How … how did you find me?" She licked her lips and expelled a quick breath. He couldn't be here. He was locked away in a hidden compartment in her mind, in New York, at a theater festival.

"Didn't take long." He grabbed her arm. "A couple of your so-called friends mentioned you'd gone off to some back-water town in South Carolina for the holidays." He laughed derisively. "'Cherish.' I couldn't even find it on a map."

"You don't know any of my friends." She braced her body against a cold wind and tried not to inhale. He smelled of vodka and anger and day-old sweat.

Despite herself, she couldn't control the shiver that rippled through her. He noticed. She saw the satisfaction in his bloodshot gray eyes. He had foreseen this, her cowering, her clumsiness, as she fingered the straps of her tote bag.

"I hired a few musicians for my office party," he said. His fingers tightened on her arm and she flinched. "They were more than willing to help once I offered a large bonus. You starving performers are always looking for handouts."

She swallowed a terrified scream and eyed her isolated surroundings. Several long sprints lay between her and the roasted-almond stand. She could outrun him.

No, argued her practical self. He was a large man. His pace outmatched hers, and he'd overtake her. All he'd have to do was drag her into the nearby woods, and she'd be alone with him.

Adrenaline consumed her, shaping her terror into a soundless rage. She wasn't a weak, passive victim, shrinking into herself just because he spoke.

This was her town, not his.

Mentally, she reviewed the article from the *Southern Charms* cookbook. If a woman was confronted by an attacker, one of her first lines of defense was her handbag.

She lifted her chin, straightened her spine. "Well, now that you've seen for yourself I'm here, go slither back to your swanky place in New York."

Momentarily, his composure slipped, his fingers loosened. "Every day, I think about when your broken harp was hauled away. I felt so bad, I decided to buy you a new one. We'll call it my Christmas gift to you. It's expensive. You'll like it."

"Keep it. I don't want it."

His eyebrows lifted in distracted mockery. "What—"

She couldn't be afraid. She couldn't allow herself to cringe and plead, but needed to prevent her fright from taking over.

Don't back away. Use the element of surprise. He won't expect you to fight.

"I said keep it." She lifted her heavy tote bag as a club and swung directly for his face.

She was too slow. He saw the blow coming and shoved her to the ground. A dull roar filled her ears, pain firing through her body as she hit solid ice. He fell on top of her, and she fought him, biting and kicking, jabbing at his eyes, focusing all her energy on getting away.

A shiny, silver knife sliced the air and came at her throat. "I heard you've been seeing an officer in town, Emmanuelle. Did you forget? You were meant only for me."

She shut her eyes to keep out the light-headedness, seeking the safety of somewhere dark and safe and silent.

Heavy, racing footsteps cut through her dizzying thoughts.

"Drop the knife and keep your hands over your head."

"George O'Donnell, you're under arrest for aggravated assault."

Two men's voices. Nicholas. And another man. Officer Joseph Hannaford.

"Emmanuelle? Are you okay?" Nicholas's steady tone reached through her fogged thoughts. She squinted. The color had drained from his face, and even in the darkness she could see his distress.

Tears welled. "Yes, yes. I'm—I'm fine. He didn't hurt ..."

Her brave declaration was diminished by her sobbing. She couldn't contain her tears and reached out to Nicholas for comfort. She wanted to be held, wanted her apprehension quieted, wanted only him. Her legs wobbled as he helped her to her feet, and she sagged against his strong body. His gaze stayed focused on her.

George sneered at her as Officer Hannaford snapped handcuffs on him. "You won't get away with this, Emmanuelle."

She noted that he showed no remorse.

"I already did," she said flatly. "Quit following me and go back to New York. I never want to see you again."

"This one stop-light town is no fun. I was leaving anyway." He didn't look tough or threatening now, not with his hands cuffed behind his back. "Just remember, Emmanuelle. You're an insignificant nobody."

Nicholas tightened his fists. "What did you say, O'Donnell?"

"Nothing, Nicholas," she said quickly. "He can't hurt me anymore."

The slow dance of George's belittlement, his cruelty, had ended. His hurtful comments would no longer snake through her dreams because she refused to carry her resentment anymore. She'd acted with courage, and someday, with God's grace, she'd forgive George. Just not today.

"Mr. O'Donnell," Officer Hannaford said, "we've been monitoring your activities. Lots of illegal narcotics are being siphoned through your hotel deliveries into other states besides New York. Drug trafficking is a felony, a federal one when it's across state lines. And then there's the evidence of money laundering, illegal weapons, and other crimes." His gaze flicked to Emmanuelle, then zeroed in on Nicholas's clenched fists. "Why don't you bring your girl back to your apartment and cool off? I guarantee this guy will be locked away for a good many years."

*E*mmanuelle looked like a dream and cooked like a gourmet chef, Nicholas decided, taking a whiff of something heavenly as he strode into his apartment. He was greeted by Molly Belle's hopeful eyes and madly flapping tail.

He hung his pea coat by the door, took off his deputy badge, and slid the gun from his holster. With the dog on his heels, he locked the gun in his safe.

"No walks, Molly Belle," he said. "Emmanuelle texted me and I know you've been outside twice already."

Molly Belle cocked her silky ears, then followed him into the kitchen.

Nicholas feasted his gaze on Emmanuelle as she blended ingredients for a holiday fruitcake. She was dressed for Christmas Eve in a red velvet top and black pencil skirt that showed off her perfectly toned legs. She'd tied a plaid apron featuring a gingerbread man over her outfit. Her blonde hair tumbled in ringlets around her shoulders.

"Merry Christmas, angel," he said. "You're stunning." He tried not to stare, but she sure had shapely legs. He'd brought home a bouquet of red and white carnations, a festive beginning to the Christmas season, the florist had declared, when she'd snatched his credit card and rung up the sale.

No matter how hard he tried to budget, money seemed to slip out of his fingers faster than water.

"Well, thank you, Deputy Thompson," Emmanuelle said. "You're quite handsome yourself in your deputy uniform." She wiped a hand on her apron and twirled. "I was able to squeeze into this skirt after all, despite the endless barbecue sandwiches I've eaten lately. How do I look?"

"Gorgeous." He grinned approvingly, then held up the flowers.

Her face lit. "For me?"

"For Ryan and Dorothy's house," he amended. "The carnations are a Christmas dinner centerpiece, a thank you gift to them along with your … fruitcake." He gave himself a silent pat on the back for not grimacing.

He blamed his fruitcake dislike on the media, for the cake was fodder for endless jokes. His favorite was one by Johnny Carson, "There is only one fruitcake in the entire world, and people keep sending it to each other."

He didn't share that quote with Emmanuelle.

"I'm trying a new recipe," she said. "This one was passed down to Ryan by his nana."

"Yes, you'd mentioned it this morning. No *Southern Charms* recipe?"

"This one is better." Emmanuelle grinned and pressed the mixture into a baking pan. "It's so generous of your sister and Ryan to welcome us into their new home for the holidays."

The air smelled subtly of candied cherries and walnuts and dates, and Nicholas sniffed enthusiastically. Should he give fruitcake another chance? Most likely, Emmanuelle's cake would prove as tasty as all the other delicacies she'd prepared the past few weeks.

He set the bouquet on the table and brought her into his arms for a hello kiss.

"I missed you today." He nuzzled her neck. The splendidness of her, her sweet lips pressed to his, her sylphlike form leaning into him, brought him such happiness.

She wiped her hands on her apron and twined her arms around him. When he didn't release her, she shifted. "The fruitcake," she reminded him.

"Fruitcakes are invincible." He kept her close and rested his chin on her shiny blonde curls.

"Nicholas …" She extracted herself to pop the cake into the oven. "The recipe says the cake takes forty-five minutes to bake, which gives us plenty of time to arrive at Dorothy and Ryan's house by seven for dinner. The church service starts at midnight." She glanced at her watch. "It's five now."

Absently, he rubbed Molly Belle's head and eyeballed Emmanuelle as she pulled off her apron and put the flowers in a vase with water.

"Nicholas, did you hear me?"

"I think so."

"What did I say?"

"Something about Christmas dinner." He'd heard the dinner part and little else. He'd been preoccupied with her gorgeous legs.

"I brewed a pot of coffee. Do you want a cup?"

Before he answered, she brought out two mugs from his glass-front cabinet and poured.

"No donuts?" he teased, rousing her into a smile.

"On Christmas we eat fruitcake for dessert."

He sighed and scratched his head. *How could he forget?* He'd just have to keep hoping for the best.

"Emmanuelle …" From his shirt pocket, he withdrew a

neatly wrapped present tied with a white satin bow. "This is a little gift I bought for you."

She looked surprised. "You're very generous, but my wonderful harp necklace is more than enough."

Which, he'd noticed, she wore every day.

"This is another gift because it's Christmas. And because I appreciate you."

Ever since she'd arrived, his apartment had been transformed. Maybe he hadn't paid attention to the dog hair accumulating on his unswept floors before, but he'd sure appreciated it when his wooden floors gleamed.

She smiled. "I bought gifts for you too. They're wrapped and under our Charlie Brown tree. Let's open them now."

With the dog at their side and coffee cups in hand, they wandered into the living room. She clicked on her favorite Christian radio station, then brought a gold-foil-wrapped box from beneath the tree and handed it to him. "Merry Christmas, Nicholas."

They sat together on the floor, backs against the wall, and stretched out their legs. She was barefoot, free from the restrictions of her former lifestyle—one of control and fear. Now, her smile came easy, her movements unrestrained. The subdued colors of the Christmas tree lights warmed her complexion to a healthy rose hue.

Molly Belle settled beside them, patient, good, eyeing them thoughtfully with shiny black eyes.

Nicholas chuckled. He felt like a kid again, filled with the magic of the season. He felt like singing out loud when a new artist's rendition of "O Come All Ye Faithful" lilted from the radio.

"Well? Why are you waiting?" she teased. Expectantly, she watched him open her gift, an electric travel mug. "Do you like it?"

"I love it. Thank you." He shouted with laughter. "This is perfect."

She grinned. "Now that you're a deputy, you're always focused on getting a good cup of coffee. If duty calls and pulls you away from the office, your coffee won't be left cold anymore."

"Thank you. I've become attached to my coffee. And I've become even more attached to you." He pressed a kiss to her temple.

Still grinning, she reached behind the tree and produced another box, this one lighter and wrapped in the same metallic-gold foil paper.

"Two gifts?" he asked. "Why?"

"You bought me two, so now we're even." She placed the box on his lap, her expression growing serious.

He unwrapped the foil paper slowly, revealing a large jeweler's box. Then he paused, regarding her for a long moment, wondering why she'd lowered her head and seemed suddenly self-conscious. He unhooked the lid, and a silver pendant hanging from a heavy chain shone back at him.

"Read the words on the front," she encouraged. "It's a prayer."

"All right." He read aloud. "'Lord, keep my deputy safe from morning till night, give him strength in your precious light.'" He turned the pendant over. She'd personalized the back with an engraved script: "'I'm proud of you.'"

He wiped at his eyes as the emotion swept over him. He swallowed and held the pendant up to the light to admire it. "Thank you, Emmanuelle."

"You're very welcome."

He nodded toward his gift. "Now it's your turn."

Her fingers moved more slowly. She set the wrapping paper on the floor and gazed at the silver case she'd revealed.

Carefully, she unsnapped the lid. A black velvet bed held a solitaire diamond ring in a twist of fourteen-karat white gold.

She drew an unsteady breath. "It's … it's beautiful." Tears welled, falling down her cheeks. She wiped at them, laughed as she brushed the wetness away. "These are happy tears," she clarified, laughing and crying at the same time before she sank her head into his chest and gave in to the weeping.

"I know." He held her until her cry had passed. The same joy had gripped him.

Taking her left hand, he slid the diamond engagement ring onto her finger. "Will you marry me, Emmanuelle?"

She stared at her finger, stared at him. "Read the explanation on the box that came with your pendant first."

He gazed at her and pondered her reply. How had the conversation shifted to *her* gift when she wore *his* gift on her finger? If his feelings weren't in such a tangle because she was sitting so close to him, because it was Christmas, because it was so easy to love life again, he would have noticed how her bright eyes shone with anticipation.

He lifted the box and read the inside flap. "'A deputy's wife's prayer.'" He set the box down. Paused. Reflected. "Wait a minute. A *wife's* prayer?"

"I planned on making my home in Cherish, and wanted to tell you on Christmas Eve." She looked almost sheepish. "Then I decided that if you didn't ask me to marry you, I'd ask you."

"Well, my answer is yes." He smothered a laugh and tipped up her face. "What's your answer?"

"Yes, yes, yes. I love you, Nicholas Thompson."

His mouth descended on hers as she pressed closer. "I love you so much," he murmured, and then his mouth captured hers again for a breathtakingly long kiss.

When the kiss ended, she stayed in his arms.

"I've been thinking," she began, snuggling closer.

He brushed a kiss against her hair. "About what?"

"About the past few days, going over and over what happened the night of the concert. You obviously knew my relationship with George wasn't over. I didn't. And then I fought back when he attacked me. I shouldn't have."

"He's a dangerous man. You didn't realize how dangerous."

She blew out a breath. "Afterward, when I thought about how deserted it was back there, I chastised myself. I reacted foolishly for edging him on, and then trying to fight him."

"It was a knee-jerk reaction. You were threatened. You didn't realize how serious the situation would become, and so quickly. Officer Hannaford and I had been running a long background check on George O'Donnell ever since you told me his last name, so I was at fault. I knew how dangerous he was and I should never have let you go off alone."

"I only walked across the square to buy almonds." She sighed. "Although I've been blaming myself. I'm good at that."

"Don't." He kissed her again. "If anyone is responsible, it's me. I knew that George was involved in illegal activities."

She nodded. "And then I thought, through the bad came the good. Because of you—because of me—because of us, I've taken my power back. I didn't deserve his violence, and I felt so bitter and resentful when I arrived in Cherish. I've prayed a lot, and I finally realized if I kept feeling that way, that meant he still controlled me. So, I've let go of it. New beginnings, thanks to the grace of God."

Nicholas knuckled a tear from the corner of her eye.

She'd confronted her shame, her anger at herself, and realized God had helped her through the storm.

Love was here, love was now. Love was the magic of the

season. They were standing on the edge of Christmas, waiting for the new year and their new life to begin.

For an eternity, they sat together on the floor, his arms enveloping her and holding her close.

* * *

NICHOLAS AWOKE to the sound of Molly Belle's whining as she darted across the living room. The shriek of the smoke alarm had him staring blindly ahead. Smoke rolled out of the kitchen.

"Emmanuelle." He shook her awake. "Are you keeping tabs on the time?"

"Yes, it's—" She gaped at her watch. "It's nearly seven o'clock!"

They raced to the kitchen just in time to extract a burnt fruitcake from the oven.

He shut off the smoke alarm. She winced at the cake.

"Oh no." She blew out a breath. "I hope I have enough ingredients left over to bake another one."

"You mean you're going to try to bake another fruitcake?"

She scanned the counter. "Unfortunately, it's too late tonight."

"Well, there's always tomorrow, although none of the stores will be open on Christmas, so we'll just have to wait."

He tried to sound regretful and knew he didn't.

He opened a kitchen window to let out the smoke and inhaled crisp winter air. A neighbor was inching his car into the driveway, wheels spinning, windshield wipers flapping like a wild bird's wings. Fresh snow was falling to the ground, hugging the landscape in a burst of white potential.

"We may not be going anywhere tonight," Emmanuelle murmured. She stood beside him, peering outside the window.

"What will we eat for Christmas dinner?" he asked.

"Burnt fruitcake and coffee?"

"I'll call Dorothy. Once the roads are plowed, we should be able to get to their house and then attend the midnight church service."

He hugged her. The exquisite feeling of her warm body next to his, made his heart beat stronger. He'd been bitter, just like her. In his bitterness, he hadn't wanted to change. He'd preferred to feed on his own loneliness and feel sorry for himself. And then, God had blessed him with Emmanuelle. He'd brought her into his life at the perfect time.

She was his family now, along with Dorothy and Ryan. And Molly Belle, who'd trotted into the kitchen, plopped beneath the kitchen table and curiously eyed the burnt fruitcake.

By the window, Nicholas kissed Emmanuelle, a kiss full of love and promise. "I love you, Emmanuelle."

Her eyes were wet with tears. "I love you too."

"And I'll take a lifetime to prove it to you, right here in Cherish," he said.

"You don't have to prove anything. I know the man you are, and that's why I love you."

Truly, whatever came their way, they could handle it. His faith had been tested, but these were lessons. He'd bounced back from sadness and adversity. They'd both bounced back.

Because God had them covered. Together and always.

With Emmanuelle in his arms, they were ready to face life's challenges.

And this was a Christmas to cherish.

THE END

A NOTE FROM JOSIE

Dear Friends,

Thank you for reading, *A Christmas To Cherish,* set in the charming fictional town of Cherish, South Carolina.

I've always enjoyed writing about small town life, and Christmas is a special time of year.

Because I am a musician and even played the harp for a while, my heroine, Emmanuelle, is a professional harpist.

The hero, Nicholas, is the heroine's brother in *A Love Song To Cherish,* and I wanted him to have his own happily ever after.

If you loved this romance as much as I loved writing it, please help other people find *A Christmas To Cherish* by posting your review.

A Christmas To Cherish is available in ebook, paperback, Large Print paperback, Hardcover, and audiobook.

My Spotify Play List for A Christmas To Cherish is here.

NANA'S FRUITCAKE RECIPE

Ingredients:

4 eggs
    1 cup flour
    2 teaspoons baking powder
    1 pound candied pineapple
    1 pound pitted dates
    1 pound candied cherries
    8 cups walnuts

Instructions:

Pour flour and baking powder into a large paper bag, shake to mix, then add fruits and nuts. Shake well to coat all pieces with flour.

In a large bowl, beat eggs. Pour the fruits and nuts mixture into the egg mixture and use your hand to mix well. Coat all pieces. Grease a small baking pan and press the mixture firmly into the pan. Bake approximately 45 minutes at 350 degrees or until golden brown.

Enjoy!

JOSIE RIVIERA

PUPPIES

FOR CHRISTMAS

A Christmas PUPPY TO Cherish

PRAISE AND AWARDS

USA TODAY bestselling author

Top 35 Amazon Bestseller Animal Fiction

CHAPTER 1

*M*axwell Archer gave up. The harmonica wasn't there.

He might as well walk the short distance from his rental home in Cherish, South Carolina, to Musically Yours, the local music store. The store was reputed to be the finest in town. Likewise, it was also the only music store in the small town.

Open suitcases lay on the floor in the compact, plain living room of his rental. Further cluttering the room was a confusion of chirping budgies, oversized birdcages, and a stack of research notes piled beside his computer. He definitely needed some air.

Momentarily diverted by Angel, a silvery green budgie who chattered, "God bless us, every one," over and over, Max shrugged on his olive-green twill jacket, uttered a brief good-bye, and headed out the door.

He'd recited numerous words to his parakeets. The key to teaching a parakeet to talk was repetition, but "God bless us, every one," was the only phrase Angel repeated. She was a rescue bird, and her previous owner had been an elderly woman who apparently had watched Charles Dickens's, *A Christmas Carol*, on television many times.

The other two parakeets—one timid, the other bolder—squawked, chirped, and carried on between themselves.

As Max strolled, a brisk December breeze invigorated him, and he paused to regard the poignantly familiar mom and pop shops. Whitney's, the ice cream store, and Big Brothers Big Sisters, where he'd spent many afternoons after school finishing his homework. The brick building looked the same.

At twelve years old, Max had delivered the *Sunday Sentinel* to all the businesses along Main Street, accompanied by a racing dog his foster family, the Monroes, had owned. He remembered that dog. He loved that dog. A Labrador husky named Tinsel.

He couldn't contain his smile as he reminisced.

The calendar showed December fifth, and downtown was in the process of being transformed into a Yuletide fairyland. Numerous workers scurried past him, draping tiny white lights on bushes and sprinkling artificial snow over miniature pine trees.

Through the years, he'd indulged in visions of settling here in Cherish. He had envisioned a prestigious house on the prosperous outskirts and living out his days wealthy and respected.

Three decades had passed, and he hadn't accumulated wealth in any sense of the word. In fact, his last year's research project had been stalled because of insufficient funding.

And respected? In academic circles, perhaps. He fingered the bow tie beneath his chin—his acknowledgement to the realm of academic nerds, in which he was a charter member.

In any event, his appointment to the ornithology department of a large university in Jacksonville, Florida, began January first.

As he stepped inside the music store, a slim woman with dark hair and striking green eyes greeted him.

"May I help you?" she asked.

He nodded toward the frosted-glass front window decorated with treble clef signs, animated polar bears, and a model train weaving around an ice-covered mountain scene. "Nice." He made a comical face. "The motifs enhance the window with a …"

She raised an eyebrow. "Festive touch?"

"Complete with tiny icicles." He moved inside, toward a shelf crammed with key holders and picked up a key holder shaped like an amplifier. Clever. However, he doubted he was allowed to hammer nails into his temporary rental house.

He sighed and surveyed the tidy store. "Do you sell harmonicas?" he asked.

"Yes. A wide assortment." The woman nodded toward a side wall. "Is this for a Christmas gift?"

"For myself. I lost my harmonica during my move." He rubbed his shoulders and unzipped his jacket. Though his rental was furnished, his limbs ached from lifting heavy bird cages and suitcases. He was an academic, not a body-builder.

In addition, his brain was flooded with information. He'd been embedded in research the entire morning when he should have been unpacking. The hours flew by whenever he examined data and he frequently lost track of time.

"Any particular brand or style?" she was asking.

"Fenders. Key of C."

"I'll show you our bestseller, which comes with a vented plastic case." She wended around numerous aisles, located a gold-edged case on a display shelf, and handed it to him.

"Here's our most popular model. A twenty-tone diatonic harmonica in the key of C."

"An exact replacement for the one I lost." He ran his fingers along the case. "Thanks."

A sudden, booming symphony burst through the speakers, and they both jumped.

"Sorry," the woman said. "The background music in the store constantly needs adjustment." With a self-conscious grin, she dashed to the counter and lowered the volume. "Beethoven will do that."

"Do what?

"Startle customers with crashing chords." She darted him a sideways glance. "I haven't seen you before, by the way."

Well, that didn't take long, he thought. A stranger in a small town called for questions from the local shop owner.

"I lived here for a brief spell when I attended junior high school," he said. "I arrived yesterday after an almost three-decade absence."

She didn't press for additional information, and he didn't elaborate.

"Are you here permanently?" she asked.

"Only for December. Then I'm off to my dream job in Florida." Again, he massaged his nape. Was it from the move or stress? "My name is Max, by the way. Maxwell Archer."

"Hi, Max. I'm Dorothy Edwards. My husband, Ryan, and I own this store and we sell music, instruments, and fun novelties. We also offer lessons if you're ever interested."

"Which instruments?"

"Harp, voice, guitar and piano." She hailed an entering customer with a warm smile. "Joanna, are you here for your harp lesson with Ms. Emmanuelle?"

The little girl nodded.

"She's waiting in her studio."

"Thanks. Is the puppy here? Ms. Emmanuelle mentioned that he might be."

"He's in the back."

"Yay!" The girl's face brightened. "Sorry, I'm late." She clutched her music to her chest and hurried past them.

"Joanna attends Big Brothers Big Sisters," Dorothy said. "Are you familiar with the organization?"

"Yes."

Uncertain where the conversation might be leading, Max looked away. The last subject he cared to discuss was the Big Brothers program. He remembered it well. Fond memories surfaced. Some not so fond as well, but those weren't because of the excellent program.

"Scarlett, who is married to Joseph Slater, is heavily involved," Dorothy went on. "Emmanuelle is providing Joanna with free instruction and a harp. Joseph is a well-known worship singer and songwriter. He's also on our staff when he isn't touring."

"I've never heard of him," Max said.

"Do you listen to contemporary Christian music?"

"Never." Max dismissed her inquiry with a wave. "Does anyone teach harmonica? I play for fun, not professionally, but always appreciate any tips."

"Sorry, we don't. Try YouTube," she joked.

He had. He did. On a shoe-string academic budget, self-taught lessons suited Max perfectly. Learning had little to do with musicality, and more to do with determination, goal-setting, and an appreciation for music.

Dorothy set the harmonica on the counter. "What brings you here, Max?"

"I study budgies and how they mimic birdsongs and music." He smiled and handed her his credit card.

She rang up the order. "The two are related?"

"Absolutely. To quote a noted philosopher, 'birds vocalize conventional scales.'"

"Interesting."

Interesting? The fact was more than interesting.

"You studied birds in college?" she asked.

"Yes. I earned a master's degree from a New York City university affiliated with the Audubon Society."

"Is New York City home for you?"

"I don't have a permanent home. I drove down from New York to Cherish yesterday."

"A ten-hour trip," she commiserated. "My husband travels to Atlanta for opera rehearsals, and the four hours back and forth is exhausting."

"My trip was quite an adventure—to put it mildly, especially with three parakeets, all my possessions stuffed into two suitcases and a canvas backpack." He grimaced as he recalled the harrowing journey through the icy Virginia mountains.

"The birds stayed in their cages?"

"I can't imagine them flying around my van while I drive. I secured their cages with seat belts." Max leaned forward, warming to the conversation. "For safety reasons, I always remove the mirrors, bells, and swings, and placed their wooden perches close to the bottom of their cages. And I keep bottled water handy for refilling their cups."

"Good to know." Dorothy shot him a tongue-in-cheek smile. "Not that I ever plan on purchasing a pet. My brother, Nicholas, owns Molly Belle, an overgrown pup who gets into everything. That dog cured me of owning any animals."

Max chuckled. "In some respects, birds are easier than dogs."

"Nicholas is trying to find a home for a puppy that showed up at the sheriff's station a couple days ago. Are you interested?"

"What type of dog?"

"He's guessing a mixed breed—a toy poodle and York-shire Terrier."

"A Yorkipoo."

"Maybe. He's a real cutie, brown with silvery-white markings." She paused. "Wait. I'll be right back."

Dorothy emerged two minutes later clasping a puppy to her chest. She set him down and the puppy bound forward in little jumps, then stuck his nose under the counter. Furiously, he tugged on a pencil that had fallen.

"No, no. He loves to chew." At the sound of Dorothy's voice, the little ball of fur rushed headlong down an aisle, apparently unheeding of her calls. He turned a corner and almost lost his balance. Dorothy scooped him up and brought him over to Max. He licked Max's outstretched fingers as he petted him.

"He's a cute pup, isn't he?" Dorothy asked.

"He's also a bundle of charming, unrestrained energy."

"Any chance—"

"Sorry." Max shook his head. "I'm only in town for a month." Plus, he'd vowed never to own a dog again. He'd missed Tinsel too much after he'd been placed with another foster family.

Dorothy returned the puppy to the back room, then placed Max's harmonica and a complimentary candy cane in a bag. "I'm sorry it's such a short stay, but this town is welcoming, especially during the Christmas season."

Max expected he'd enjoy spending December in Cherish. The lease on his apartment in New York had ended, and he'd preferred to travel in early December rather than January.

"Are you a musician?" she asked, offering an irrepressible grin. "Naturally you are—considering you're in a music store purchasing a harmonica. Ryan and I are—"

"Concert artists."

She handed the bag to him. "I'm a pianist."

"And Ryan is an opera singer."

She tipped her head. "How did you know?"

"My friend Gerry Adams lives in Perrytown. He often shops in your store."

Unlike many of the undergraduate students Max taught his online Joy of Birdwatching class to, Gerry had been interested and engaged. Most of Max's students selected his course as an easy elective.

Not Gerry. In his fifties, he'd developed an increasing appreciation for Max's expertise that had led to a friendly rapport between the two men. Gerry had become a sort of guru, offering guidance and awareness on another subject that interested Max: music.

"I know him." A smile dawned on Dorothy's face. "Gerry sings in the choir at Memorial Street Church."

No comment on the church part, though Max had recognized the wooden sign mounted above the store's entrance.

Proverbs 19:21.

He once knew the proverb, but could no longer recall the words.

Dorothy cast her gaze heavenward. "'Many are the plans in a person's heart, but it is the Lord's purpose that prevails,'" she recited.

Max kept silent.

Memories of sitting in a stiff pew during Sunday services came back in a blink. He'd tried, but he'd never pleased God as a child. He never pleased God as an adult, either. Where was the path to peace God promised? It remained elusive.

The successes Max had achieved hadn't been enough. Thus, at the age of twenty-five, he'd given up on religion.

As far as his career, he sometimes wondered if he was on the right path. Was his research nothing more than a "fluffy" elective for uninterested college freshmen? Society seemed to think along those lines, and reports through the academic grapevine whispered that ornithology programs were soon to be scrapped.

Sure, Max was appreciated—which was the reason why he was in hamster-wheel performance mode—to continue proving himself to his colleagues.

"Gerry and I are in a band," he replied, when he realized Dorothy waited for him to say something. "We rehearse online."

"Online?" Her brow furrowed.

"You're a professional, so you expect frequent in-person rehearsals. But our band rehearses virtually every week. Technology is marvelous, isn't it?"

"Not as rewarding as live rehearsals, though."

Max had to agree. "There's a likelihood Gerry and I will perform this month, if we can find a venue."

"Inquire at The Garden Terrace restaurant. The owners book entertainment on Friday evenings. In addition, I'd be delighted to host you here at the store. Do you have any CDs for sale?"

"You're kidding, right?"

"What's the name of your band?"

"The Bearded Elves."

"Hmm. Neither of you sports a beard."

"We change our name with the season."

She grinned. "When February hits, you'll become …"

"The Bearded Valentines. But I won't be here in February. My work takes me all over the US, and I'm headed to Florida in January."

"Well, I look forward to hearing you perform this month."

"Thanks. Gerry encouraged me to rent a place in Cherish. He believes all this down-home goodness is beneficial for me."

"You're on a vacation the entire month?"

"I'm rarely on vacation."

"No wife or children?" Pointedly, she peered at his left hand.

"Neither. You're looking at a forty-year-old bachelor."

She granted a conspiratorial smile. "The right woman will come along and change your mind."

"I doubt it. Women can be ... exasperating."

She chuckled. "Will you travel to New York for Christmas?"

"I'll spend Christmas day with Gerry, his wife, Melissa, and their newborn colicky son. They're first-time parents."

Dorothy rolled her eyes. "So I've heard."

Besides Gerry, there was no one else, Max thought. Unless Max's foster brother, John, who resided in a faraway Portuguese village, counted.

It didn't matter. The season had lost its meaning eons ago. December twenty-fifth was just another day that passed in the flicker of an eye.

Dorothy's fixed smile didn't vacillate. She seemed the sort who put immense emphasis on the holidays.

He shifted. "I'm grateful for the opportunity to hunker down with my research this month."

At Dorothy's quizzical glance, he added, "On birds."

"Along with performing a live gig or two."

"Gerry and I aren't expert musicians like you and your husband, or that Slater worship singer guy. Our specialty is performing at roadside diners for a free meal."

"I well remember those days." She shook her head. "Since you'll be working here for the month, do you need any assistance with your research?"

"Can you recommend someone who could go birding with me tomorrow morning? I'd appreciate a guide."

Dorothy studied him. "I picture you in a forest, somewhere more suited to your rugged looks, rather than writing papers. You must spend a great deal of time outdoors."

"I try." He pushed a hand through his thick hair. When had he last gotten it cut? "The Carolinas have various bird species I'd like to listen to."

"Your parakeets will truly mimic other birds?"

"Optimistically, although I haven't had much luck with them imitating anything."

Except "God bless us, every one."

"I know the ideal woman," Dorothy said.

"She likes nature?"

"Absolutely, and she's passionate about hiking." A gleam of mischief shone in Dorothy's eyes. "She works at Thumbs Up, a local florist, but might be off tomorrow. I'll text her."

"What's her name?"

"Sarah Hartman." Dorothy snatched a cell phone from beneath the counter. "She dropped out of college to care for her elderly aunt, then went on to pursue a degree in floral design."

"How old is she?"

"Sarah turned thirty last month. She's the type who juggles a half dozen projects, numerous details, and never gets frustrated. And …" Dorothy paused to accentuate the words. "Her flower arrangements are exquisite."

He'd never purchased store-bought flowers in his life. The most magnificent blossoms—miniature red roses, deep violets, and pale blue ivy—spilled alongside brooks or grew wild in a field.

A response flew across Dorothy's phone screen. "Sarah confirmed she's not working until tomorrow afternoon," Dorothy read. "She had plans but is happy to change them. What's your address, Max?"

"I rented a house a couple blocks from here. It's 8 Poplar Lane. Tell her I'll bring the hiking essentials."

Dorothy typed into her phone, then delivered the response. "She'll pick you up in the morning."

"A hiker and a florist is an attractive combination."

"Oh, and she's plenty more. Animals love her. The cat at the greenhouse that handles mice won't let anyone near her except Sarah. Likewise, dogs practically grovel at her feet." Dorothy glanced up. "Remember Molly Belle?"

"Your brother's unruly dog?"

Dorothy choked a giggle. "She adores everyone and is beyond energetic, although remarkably calm and obedient around Sarah."

"Does Sarah own any pets?"

"Are you giving away birds?"

"I'd never part with my parakeets. Angel is the oldest, and she's been with me for several years." He lifted a quizzical brow. "What about Sarah?"

"She owns a few animals."

"Is she married?" He didn't want an irate husband or boyfriend on his tail for going birdwatching with Sarah.

"She's coming off a sorry relationship, but you'll discover she's a stunner."

Another word for mantrap. He understood the type well after dating a flirtatious woman who'd been beautiful enough to be on the cover of *Vogue* but who abruptly ended their month of dating with a cursory text.

From that point forward, he'd avoided any romantic overtures from beautiful women. They were interested in a guy's money and power. As soon as they realized Max had neither, they hightailed it out of his life.

"You'll learn all about her tomorrow." Dorothy peered at the phone screen, grinned, then snapped it shut. "She drives a yellow pickup truck and said she'll see you at eight."

CHAPTER 2

The following day, Max rose before dawn to wash and dry the parakeets' food bowls and water bottles, then placed a slice of kiwi in their cages. Angel, a female, occupied her own cage, while the two males shared a cage.

"God bless us, every one," Angel chirped.

Max covered three sides of the wrought-iron cage and faced her on the open side. Over and over, he enunciated, "Angel. Angel. Angel."

"God bless us, every one," Angel repeated.

"You can say that entire sentence, but you can't pronounce your own name?" He threw his hands up and surveyed the other two parakeets. The blue-winged room-mates perched on their respective swings, then burst into a flurry of activity for no apparent reason, effectively distracting Angel.

And thus, the lesson was over.

Max choked on a laugh. Some things never changed.

Regardless, he was in jovial spirits. Although his new bed was lumpy and the bedspread a musty chenille, he had slept well and left his window open a crack. The whisper of a floral-scented breeze had provided him with a comfortable, peaceful slumber.

He flicked a fatigued glance at his handwritten notes, twenty pages and counting, spread out on the computer desk. His suitcases still sat on the floor, waiting to be unpacked. He'd rummaged through them for a clean pair of jeans, a blue button-down shirt, boots, and his favorite bow tie.

A half hour after he'd showered and passed on shaving because he couldn't find his razor, he heard an engine and peered out the window.

A yellow pickup idled in the driveway. The truck boasted reindeer antlers attached to the windows and a red nose on the front grill.

The woman in the driver's seat caught his stare and waved, her smile bright and pleasant.

Sarah Hartman, he assumed. Punctual at eight o'clock in the morning.

Admirable. They were off to a promising start.

He had filled a thermos with fresh coffee and stuffed thermal cups, peanut-butter banana sandwiches, and his favorite brand of frosted sugar cookies in a bag. Hoisting a backpack over his shoulders, he headed out the door.

He opened the passenger door, smiling in at her. "Sarah, right?" he said. He put the food bag and his backpack in the back seat, then slid onto the passenger seat.

"Correct." She nodded to him. "And you're Max?"

"Indeed. Max Archer." He set his thermos in the truck's oversized cup holder. "And you're driving Rudolph."

She laughed, gentle and musical. "I love Christmas."

"Let me guess, you're a sentimental movie junkie too." He gestured to her glittery pine tree earrings and the white snowflake steering wheel cover.

"Sentimental movies are the best." She tilted her head, studying him with sea-green eyes. "You look exactly the way Dorothy described."

"Not a reindeer covered in snowflakes, I hope?"

She swallowed a chuckle. "No."

"How did Dorothy describe me?"

Sarah stared at his lips. "She said you had dark hair, silvery-gray eyes, wore a bow tie and would probably have a backpack."

"A battered and weathered one." He twisted and motioned to his backpack, its ripped seam fixed with duct tape. "Today, it's filled with necessities—bottles of water, a first-aid kit, binoculars, and my fully charged phone."

She nodded. "Sounds like you've got everything you need."

"Yes. I've brought my microphone and recorder too. To record birdsongs, I'll demonstrate the setup when we arrive at the mountain."

"Okay."

"Are you carrying a cellphone?" he asked.

"I always carry one for emergencies, but I also use my phone camera to take photos."

"Photos of wildlife?"

"Mostly deer, although I can never get closer than fifteen feet before they bolt."

"Deer aren't always the sweet, docile animals you may imagine. Be careful around them."

"I am."

Those green eyes fringed with thick russet lashes, and her creamy complexion, enhanced by light freckles across her nose, stopped him from responding with anything other than "Good."

She continued to watch him, and he returned her stare.

This beautiful, intelligent woman hadn't been scooped up by a guy?

Wearing a hooded red jacket, gloves, and brown hiking boots, she was small and slim. He estimated no taller than five feet. He found himself staring at her delicate lips before his gaze wandered down to the silver cross necklace around her slender neck.

Preoccupied with an attraction he hadn't expected, he picked up his thermos. "Another requirement for a morning outing is caffeine. Do you like black coffee?"

She nodded.

"Then we share commonalities—coffee and hiking. I also brought a package of cookies. They're store-bought because I'm not a baker. The cookies, not the coffee." He returned his thermos to the holder. "Juniper Mountain is our first stop."

"There's another?"

"Crandall's Mountain, depending on our time frame."

"Okay. My morning is free," she replied.

"Mine too."

With a quick bob of her head, she backed out of the driveway.

He stretched out his legs. "It will be good to go for a long hike. I arrived in town yesterday, driving down from New York. I'm here for the month, then heading for a job in Florida."

Another nod. She probably already knew that because of chatty Dorothy.

Because he liked to have music playing, he asked her if he could switch on the radio. She hesitated and then said yes, and he scanned the stations, on a quest for something other than a holiday tune. He settled on Jon Bon Jovi singing "Please Come Home For Christmas." Not typically merry, but more of an expressive classic.

Satisfied, Max drew out his cellphone. "Do you need directions to the mountain?"

She twisted. "Say that again?"

"Directions?" He spoke louder.

"No. I've hiked Juniper for years. It's part of the Carolina state park systems."

"I mapped the distance to Crandall's, because the mountains are within a few miles of each other."

Another glance. He repeated that Juniper and Crandall were near each other.

Each time he talked, she swiveled to look at him. At one point, he almost advised her to watch the road, not him.

He lowered the volume on the radio. Possibly, music distracted her when she drove.

"I brought a knapsack," she said after a few silent minutes. "It's on the back seat."

Don't turn around to show me, Max silently implored.

He didn't initiate any further dialogue, spending the time glancing sideways at her appealing profile.

After they arrived at Juniper Mountain and she parked, they got out of the truck and he poured two cups of coffee, handing her one. He grabbed a swallow, pleased the coffee was still hot, and scanned their surroundings.

Today might provide a breakthrough in his research, an ultimate realization of success. That is, if his parakeets cooperated and actually repeated the birdsongs.

He gazed at the gorgeous woman beside him, leaning against her truck, and smiled. Surely, Sarah would bring good fortune.

When they finished their coffees, they detoured to the visitor center and procured a map. Sarah lingered at a Christmas ornament display, sputtering in disbelief when the park ranger stated that the store was sold out of a particular ornament featuring a bear, hiker boots and the inscription, "Take a hike."

She pointed to an exhibit on the wall. "The ornament is hanging right there and will go perfect on my holiday tree."

"Those are display items only and can't be sold," the ranger responded. "More should arrive by the end of the month. Check back."

She stuffed her gloves in her pockets and tapped her fingers on the counter. "By then, Christmas will be over."

Eager to lighten the mood, Max steered her out the exit to a wooden bench. "Let's study the map. There are eleven trails." He beckoned her to sit and settled beside her, indicating a twisty pathway. "The Maple Tree route is strenuous with rocky terrain and unsuitable for beginners."

"Fortunately, I'm not a beginner," she replied matter-of-factly.

"Neither am I."

"Maple Tree isn't difficult, but I recommend ..." She ran her finger along a trail marked Oak. "This one passes through Walnut Forest, down to the Nanchee River's edge, up through a meadow, and finishes on a grassy path leading back to the visitor center."

She peered at him for a deciding opinion.

Based on the fact she'd resided in Cherish for many years, Max readily approved.

With her so close, her scent reminded him of an elusive flowery fragrance, similar to the breeze floating through his window last night. Rosewood, perhaps. Peaceful and serene.

He liked that. He liked *her*.

Their gazes merged, and he couldn't stop staring. She was stunning—high cheekbones and a flawless complexion—the type of beauty that prompted people to gape.

"You're the expert in these parts, Sarah." Max thought he spoke, but he wasn't certain, because the world had become unfocused, and she was at the center. He moved his index finger alongside hers, along the map, a light brush of fingertips.

And the attraction. His heart did a backflip.

He forced himself to concentrate on the map and swallowed. Surely, she felt it too.

An easy smile worked its way across her features.

Was she interested in him?

With any luck, she was.

At the same instant his brain shouted no, no, no. He was here for research purposes, and Sarah Hartman was a romantic complication he could ill afford. He had enough conflicts in his life—a stressful job, and no relationship at all with religion. Her necklace signified she was a Christian, and before he knew it, she might be declaring, "'This is the day that the Lord has made.'"

He'd believed that psalm once upon a time. Not anymore.

He pulled his extra pair of binoculars from his backpack and handed them to her, then hung his own around his neck. Next, he retrieved his recording device, a pocket-sized digital recorder and the microphone.

She rose. He automatically stood too.

"Your gear is more sophisticated than I envisioned."

"After years of trial and error, I finally realized my equipment had to be top of the line." He plugged the module into a mini jack cable. "The shotgun microphone has a powering module containing a battery."

She gazed at him with wide eyes and a wider smile. "I'm impressed with you and your work, Max."

"I'm impressed by you too," he replied.

"I haven't done anything remarkable."

He pressed his fingers on her forearm, lightly, to make his point. "There aren't many women who'd change their plans to assist a newcomer in town."

"I'm always happy to help."

He told himself to finish readying the equipment rather than gaze at her lovely, upturned face. He covered the microphone with a wind sock. "This reduces the noise created by the wind."

She acknowledged his description with a nod.

He scanned the sky, checking the angle of the sun. The haze was beginning to clear, gray clouds giving way to shades of pink and lavender. "Sunny days are ideal, but overcast is also fine," he said.

In the wash of the morning light, her complexion glowed. "Birding is a first for me."

"I was under the impression you're an animal lover."

"I am. Usually, I bring my dogs here."

"How many?"

"I have two dogs."

He noted her smile. "Is something amusing, Sarah?"

"I was thinking you're remarkably efficient and obviously an expert in your profession. I admire a man who makes things look easy and effortless."

Her compliment caught him off balance. He uttered a heartfelt, "Birds are my life and my career."

A December breeze rustled the trees and blew her shiny hair across her face. He smoothed an auburn lock from her cheek, and she stepped back out of his range.

"In any case …" He cleared his throat and passed her a protein bar.

"Is this lunch?"

"I packed sandwiches. This is a snack."

Before he could say anything else, she whispered a prayer, asking God to bless their food, Max's career, and the picturesque day.

Max scratched his neck. Nothing made him feel more like

a fraud than thanking an imagined God. For what? A protein bar? A clear day?

God had never granted any of Max's requests.

Nevertheless, he bent his head and studied the protein bar's wrapper while Sarah prayed.

After finishing with an amen, she said, "I love animals too," as if their conversation hadn't been stalled by prayer.

His response was a dull nod.

She nodded to the knapsack on her shoulders. "Are you interested in what's inside?"

He took a bite of the protein bar. "Sure."

"I have sunscreen and used tea bags."

At his questioning look, she clarified, "Tea bags are a natural alternative to commercial products and will ease the sting of bug bites. Or, for instance, if you walk into a poison ivy plant."

"A person doesn't walk into a poison ivy plant."

"Sure they do. At least, I have."

He grinned. "We're both protected and covered." He surveyed her hooded jacket and jeans. For a petite woman, her legs were long and shapely.

"A slight brush of poison ivy leaves on your skin is all it takes for a rash," she said.

"I'll protect you."

She wrinkled her nose. "From poison ivy?"

"From anything." Protectiveness for her stirred inside him, an unforeseen response. He'd blurted the words aloud before forming the thought in his mind.

Her dubious gaze leveled on him.

"You don't believe me?" he asked.

"We hardly know each other, and I certainly don't need protecting. In addition, I packed bear repellent."

"I doubt we'll come across any bears."

"Let's hope not, but just in case." She withdrew a soup can

from her knapsack and shook it. "It's full of pebbles and makes a handy noisemaker."

"A bear weighs a lot more than we do, and we can't outrun one. Bear that in mind." He chuckled. "Pun intended."

The joke seemed to slide past her. "I've read about bear encounters," she answered. "There are certain rules to remember, such as to speak calmly, not make direct eye contact, and never run."

"If your handy deterrent doesn't scare away a bear, the loud noise will no doubt encourage any birds in the area to take flight."

"That's not a good thing if you're trying to record bird-songs," she replied with a grin.

They burst out laughing, then started down a gravel trail.

He stood on the forest's edge and watched for motion. "Look. Listen. There's a golden-winged warbler in the trees." He raised his binoculars and encouraged Sarah to do the same.

She regarded him blankly.

He held up his microphone and began recording. "The warbler has suffered the steepest decline of any songbird."

"Why?"

"Loss of habitat for breeding."

A sharp *chip* and a melodic *warble* diverted him. He signaled toward a metal-gray and yellow bird hopping between bushes in a cluster of thick ferns.

"You're hearing an adult male Canada warbler," he said.

"Oh."

Oh? *Oh?*

"Some people pish to encourage birdsong." He imitated the sound. "I don't. I've found birds will come out no matter what and I wait for their natural behavior."

As they continued along the path, he was absorbed in recording and figuring out what birds he heard, and Sarah offered no help in identifying any of them. Every few minutes, the hushed air was fragmented by a high-pitched cry, and Max stopped to record.

Well into their walk, an outbreak of wings sounded louder than the crunch of leaves beneath their feet. Before he raised his binoculars, a bird flew out of range and into the brush. Max skimmed the shorter branches to find the bird, disregarding a group of energetic high school students breezing by with their teacher guide.

A second stir of motion in his peripheral vision had Max rushing to record.

Each clue necessitated an intermission, an awaiting, a heeding.

The appeal of ornithology. Search and find.

Max had become engrossed in the study of birds when Mr. Lenny, a foster parent, had brought him birding. He was a kind man with wavy gray hair and tortoise-rimmed eyeglasses. He was the only adult who'd shown a true interest in Max, and they started a tradition of birding every Saturday morning. For a child with precious few traditions, the man was a father figure. Lenny had made a lasting impression, inspiring a young boy who had no real home.

A woodpecker ripping through the brush, accompanied by three cardinals singing *cheer, cheer, cheer,* snapped Max out of his reminiscing. He spun and monitored their calls, tip-toeing through the undergrowth, peering above and below.

Sarah, on the other hand, seemed anxious to move on. She pointed her binoculars skyward and rarely spoke.

That is until they reached the Nanchee River's edge.

"An ideal spot for a picnic." Max nodded to the waterfall beyond and fished in his bag for sandwiches.

The weather had changed, and clouds covered the sky.

"I'll keep my cellphone handy," Sarah remarked, "in case I see a deer."

A crash came from somewhere he couldn't pinpoint. Max whirled around, searching for the source, and glimpsed a large animal emerging from the river.

"I can finally take a close-up photo of a deer," Sarah declared. She stepped toward the river, but slipped on a patch of wet grass and clung to his hand.

It wasn't a deer, Max thought. A deer would shy away.

It was a bear. A wandering yearling male by Max's estimate.

The bear started for them on all fours.

Sarah's breath burst—an inhale, an exhale.

Seconds froze.

"Where's your deterrent?" Max abandoned his equipment and drew her close. She grabbed her knapsack and pulled out the soup can.

The bear came up on hind legs, almost eye to eye with them, and with one hand, Max flung his peanut butter sandwiches, the cookies, and the protein bars as far as he could. Sarah shook the can, yelled, and tossed it near the bear.

The bear backed away, then turned and ran.

Sarah licked her trembling lips, her eyes damp. "Thank you, God."

Max kept his arm around her tight shoulders and provided a reassuring squeeze. His heartbeat raced, his mouth dry. "We're safe."

"These things happen in books and movies. Not to real people." She attempted a feeble stab at humor.

Despite her ashen complexion, he was impressed she'd lost none of her composure and had reacted quickly. Still, her rounded green eyes shone luminous beneath her russet, delicate eyebrows.

Max didn't have a boatload of experience with women, but he'd lived with enough foster sisters to know when a female was on the brink of tears. Sarah bravely tried to hold them at bay, blinking ferociously.

He wavered between his male instinct to sidestep any prospect of a sobbing woman—or the reasonable desire to offer support.

Her lips parted, her smile sluggish. "Countless questions are running through my mind," she said quietly.

"Let's begin with the most important. Are you okay?"

"Yes." He heard the quiver in her tone. "We've established we're both fine."

He lifted her chin. "Let's celebrate how grateful we are."

"By prayer?"

"A consideration for a Christian, I assume, but I thought of something more like this." He brought her closer. Unhurried, he kissed her.

Her expressive eyes gazed into his. When she veered, his hands tightened, and his mouth moved more firmly.

"Max."

"Hmm?" he murmured.

The air was hushed, the only sound the babbling river.

She slid her fingers up the collar of his jacket. "Nothing." Hesitant, she returned his kiss.

Max got so caught up in kissing Sarah, a moment went by before boisterous talking penetrated his brain. He lifted his head and glimpsed the same high schoolers from earlier.

With a self-conscious shift, Sarah pulled from his grasp. "I see we have company," she said.

"Right." *And at a most inopportune moment.*

He darted a glance at his watch, retrieved his equipment, and pushed out a sigh. "I suppose we should head back."

As they retraced their steps, Sarah glanced up at him. "Max, I can't believe …"

"I wanted to kiss you as soon as I saw you this morning," he said.

She bit her lip. "Did we do everything right?"

"The kiss was perfect."

A rosy blush tinted her cheeks. "I'm referring to the bear."

He chuckled. "All I remember is throwing food at him."

"Thank you for protecting me."

He hadn't, really. If anything, *she* had protected *him*, protected them *both*, with her bear deterrent.

"Thank *you*." He reached for her hand, soft and delicate, and a rush of emotion made him smile.

In silence, they returned to her truck.

Still dazed by the whirl of emotions between their fear and the resulting kiss, they spoke little on the drive back to Cherish. Max didn't bring up hiking Crandall's Mountain, and he kept the radio off.

When she pulled into the driveway of his home, he didn't encourage her to join him birding again. Nor did he invite her inside—something he had considered along the entire route.

"The sandwiches are gone," he said. "Sorry. No lunch."

"We could have been lunch for the bear."

"Thankfully, we weren't. Besides, he was young and not very aggressive."

"Even when he charged straight for us?"

"He's undoubtedly partying right now, devouring cookies and sandwiches and protein bars with his friends." Max tried a laugh, then sobered. "Sorry you didn't get a picture of a deer."

"I took a rapid sequence of photos with my cellphone."

"Did they come out?"

"I haven't had the opportunity to check yet."

"You had time. I knew we were safe all along," Max declared.

"Uh, huh." She became absorbed in tracing the pattern of

snowflakes on her steering wheel. "As long as the bear didn't swat the ground with his front paw."

"Or snort," Max countered.

"Or lunge."

He answered with a smile. She was lovely, amiable, and attractive, and his instinctive reaction was to lean over and kiss her again.

However, other instincts warned to keep his distance. A short-term romance didn't benefit anyone, and Sarah deserved more. With his relentless studies, travel, and limited financial resources, he had little to offer her.

He told himself he was wed to his profession, as a girl-friend from long ago had once accused him.

The mood in the truck became quieter.

Let's face it, he reasoned. Sarah wasn't excited about his profession, anyway. She'd responded to his interest with little more than a few nods. Birding was his passion, and he wanted someone to share his enthusiasm.

Satisfied with his decision, he grabbed his backpack and opened the passenger door. "Thanks for the ride and for being my guide. Have a marvelous afternoon."

Their experience would be remembered as a memorable exploration. A couple hikers who scored a birding, or rather, a bear adventure.

And their kiss? Yes, there was that. Delightful, tender, and exquisite.

Like Sarah.

CHAPTER 3

*a*fter dropping Max off, Sarah stopped by her home to tend to her animals before continuing on to Thumbs Up, the nursery/garden center where she worked.

To her intense relief, the garden center's parking lot was nearly empty. Many customers, particularly older gardeners, preferred to shop for plants in the morning. She blew out a thankful breath. She needed the quiet to revisit her moments with Max.

She'd admired his home when she drove up to the neat and tidy rental, encouraged that he didn't have a bird perched on his shoulder as she'd half imagined.

Dorothy had texted Sarah the previous evening, detailing Max's plans. He didn't intend to stay in Cherish forever—only a month to explore the area for information supporting his research.

December is an unusual month for research, Sarah had texted, *considering the holidays*.

Apparently, any close family is nonexistent, Dorothy replied. *Plus, I asked if he was married and he isn't.*

Sarah could scarcely believe that the brilliant, handsome

man, his muscular physique filling out his twill jacket, was so approachable.

On closer range, his eyes, brimming with kindness, shone light silver beneath dark, straight eyebrows. His hair was thick and longish, and she was tempted to brush back the waves that constantly fell across his forehead.

Of course, she didn't. They hardly knew each other.

Besides his intellect (she'd looked up his profile on an ornithology university website), he was amicable, humorous and thoughtful. She made the blunder of staring at him often to hear his words more clearly, and her gaze had been drawn to his firm mouth.

Then the kiss had happened.

Oh my, such a kiss! At first, she'd been tentative and self-conscious at their closeness. His mouth had sought hers with cool expertise, then persistence, then increasing claim. Her heart had responded in rapid, thudding beats.

If the teenagers hadn't entered the scene, would she still be kissing him?

Her cheeks warmed. They must have seen her and Max together.

Almost unwillingly, Max had lifted his head to end the kiss.

A kiss she never should have allowed. What an imprudent, impulsive thing for her to do—in the middle of a public state park.

Yet, his lips had been persuasive and tender.

A part of her insisted she should have ended the kiss first. The other part maintained that she and Max had shared a distressing incident. Subsequently, their mutual fright had drawn them closer.

When the bear came upon them, Max had held her. He'd kept his promise, prepared to protect her.

Once they had begun the hike, Max had been fixated on

his work. For her, the birdcalls that excited him had been faint and distant.

Why?

Why couldn't she hear the birds Max was obviously eager to record? He was so in tune with them.

Lately, she'd found that if she didn't watch people's lips while they spoke, she sometimes missed what they said.

Regardless, she appreciated Max's spontaneity, fairly bouncing on his toes as he dashed through the brush. She was accustomed to sitting on the sidelines. Her loud, raucous, older brothers had consistently stolen the spotlight, and her parents often overlooked her.

She fingered the silver cross on her neck.

Max gave the impression of being uncomfortable when she offered a prayer before eating, whereas she was a Christian and faith was important to her. By his quick exit when she'd taken him home, he obviously wasn't interested in her, anyway.

As she always did in moments of confusion, she turned to God to set her course.

The psalmist in Proverbs 4:23 had written, "Above all else, guard your heart, for everything you do flows from it."

She'd had her heart broken by a budding architect. Their relationship had ended quickly, although she'd wept for days. Since then, her emotions were precarious at best.

Nonetheless, she'd vowed to reset her path after that painful experience. Her heart wouldn't be broken a second time. Not even by Max.

Her eyes squeezed shut, and she uttered a prayer. "God, set me free from my reservations and uncertainty. Please show me the way." She always felt better after praying. Her God was a big God, bigger than her hurts and disappointments.

Taking an easy breath, she exited her truck and pushed

opened the nursery's heavy steel doors.

"Good afternoon, Sarah." Bonnie Ellerman, a coworker, tapped Sarah on the shoulder. "You're fifteen minutes early. I'm on register today, and you're working the floor. The amaryllis flowers are thriving, and timing the bulbs to bloom for Christmas worked like a charm. No wonder the garden center relies on your expertise. You have a magical green thumb."

"Hardly magical." Sarah tied a blue employee apron around her waist. "If the rest period for the amaryllis begins in late summer, the bulbs will respond. Customers appreciate the extensive blooms, thus it's worth all the planning."

Sarah picked up a warehouse broom to sweep soil off the concrete floor. She tackled the chores she disliked first, before arranging the pink, white, and red poinsettia plants for Memorial Street Church.

An unexpected thickness formed in her throat as she gazed at the tastefully decorated Christmas trees lining an entire side wall. The prospect of returning home to spend another night by herself during the Christmas season … during any season … Well, she yearned for more.

To cheer herself up, she organized a Christmas gift list in her mind. Uncle Gerry, her great-uncle in Perrytown, played guitar. Accordingly, a gift from Musically Yours would be ideal.

An insistent voice in Sarah's ear interrupted her thoughts as Dorothy Edwards came into view.

"Hello," Dorothy said. "I stopped by to purchase a pink poinsettia plant for Musically Yours." Dorothy grinned mischievously, and Sarah knew at once that Dorothy had come into the nursery for more than a poinsettia.

"Who's minding your music store?" Sarah asked with a chuckle.

"Emmanuelle." Dorothy changed the poinsettia from one

arm to the other. "So, how was your hike together?"

Sarah quirked an eyebrow. "With …"

"Maxwell Archer."

"Enjoyable."

"That's it?"

"That's it." A wry smile touched Sarah's lips as she navigated the subject back to Dorothy. "Is Ryan in Atlanta?"

"He's preparing for a classical concert there. He's the lead in a chamber choir and singing a sacred text in Latin. The concert will be live-streamed next weekend." Dorothy paused. "You know I love gushing about my husband's accomplishments, but now I want to find out about your date details."

"Hiking a mountain is hardly a date." Sarah attempted to compose her features and disguise her attraction to Max. He was so different from the architect she'd dated, who'd had arrogant qualities and a slight build. Max, on the other hand, exuded strong masculinity. He was also smart, passionate about his work and gentlemanly.

And the kiss.

The sigh-worthy kiss.

Animated chatter from customers swirled nearer, blending with the clink of a clay pot as Bonnie handed Sarah a paperwhite narcissus and requested a price check.

Dorothy trailed Sarah to the stand of blossoming paperwhites. "What are your thoughts regarding Max?"

Sarah focused on Dorothy's mouth in order to lip-read.

She'd been ignoring the polite remarks from friends about having her hearing checked. A woman of thirty was *not* hard of hearing. For the time being, she'd employ all the tools at her disposal, and one was lipreading.

"He seems nice," she replied.

"Nice. Nice?' Dorothy flung a hand to her hip. "What sort of description is *nice* for a handsome, well-versed man?"

"He's well-versed on birds." Sarah gave Dorothy a good-natured shove. "Period."

Well, no, that should probably be a comma. He was also well-versed on kindness. Similarly, he's sweet and understanding, with a romantic nature she hadn't anticipated.

"I can tell by your reddened cheeks there's more to the story." Dorothy smothered a laugh. "You're attracted to him."

"He's polite and humorous." Sarah's gaze veered to Bonnie, who was frantically signaling another employee over to the narcissus plants.

Sarah's attention swung back to Dorothy.

"Am I right?" Dorothy asked, grinning.

"Maybe."

"I knew it!" Dorothy's expression went from happy to happier.

"My reactions are mixed. He's brilliant, yes—"

"Plus, he's an animal lover, just like you."

"Let's not forget he's taking a position at a Florida university in January."

"Yes, yes." Dorothy moved to the side to allow the employee to pass. "You actually start working here at one, right?"

Sarah nodded.

"So, we have a couple more minutes. Have you considered adopting the adorable dog that Nicholas and the Cherish sheriff department are caring for? An officer is complaining they are on call 24/7. The dog has a tremendous appetite and eats a lot of puppy chow."

"Have they named him yet?"

"They're waiting for the right person to adopt him. We all agree you are the perfect new owner."

"Who are we?"

"Me, Nicholas, and Emmanuelle."

"I adopted two abandoned dogs, two cats, a goldfish and a

hamster," Sarah said. "Plus, my house is a one-story bungalow."

"You'll adore him when you see him."

"I'm touched, and would love to help … but I can't."

Dorothy sighed. "Notify Nicholas if you change your mind. Deal?"

"Deal."

"One more thing." Dorothy glanced at her watch at the same time Sarah did.

"Go on."

Dorothy pulled in a breath. "One of the reasons Max decided to stay in Cherish this month is because he's friends with Gerry."

Sarah stumbled back a step. "My great-uncle Gerry?"

"The men play in a band together. Max told me when he was in my store yesterday to buy a harmonica."

"Uncle Gerry never discussed Max before. How long have they been friends?"

Dorothy winked. "Ask Max."

With that, Dorothy waltzed to the cash register with her blooming pink poinsettia.

Sarah was left staring at the paperwhite in her hand, trying to remember Bonnie's request. Was the flower supposed to be restocked or bedecked with a ribbon?

No, no. A price check. But another worker had taken care of it.

Sarah stifled a quiet moan. Her focus was fractured. And all because of a man named Maxwell Archer. A sensitive, fascinating and accomplished man.

And then another thought formed.

Perhaps, just perhaps, she could enlist her great-uncle's help to meet Max again.

With a radiant smile and a lively step, Sarah clocked into work at exactly one o'clock.

CHAPTER 4

a week later, Max strode into his living room and ducked as Angel flew by. He allowed the parakeets to fly at least an hour a day and kept the doors and windows closed for their safety. The routine kept them healthy and happy because they needed to explore. He'd limited their time the first week, in order for them to get used to the unfamiliar environment of the rental.

For now, the roommates were back in their cages, which left only Angel perching on a curtain rod. He'd trained the budgies to return to their cages, but Angel sometimes preferred not to.

Earlier, Max had compiled his notes and organized the pages in a computer file. He'd worked eighteen-hour days all week, although emailing his file to the ornithology department in Florida hadn't produced the desired accolades. The university had demanded additional bird recordings—particularly of his budgies repeating the birdsongs.

Except his birds hadn't responded or repeated any of the songs.

After Max received the university's reply, he didn't trust

himself to respond. His ideal job. How could the department question him?

Perhaps he was in the wrong profession after all. Published studies demanded reliable facts, and budgies, as well as birds in general, were unpredictable.

Budgies mimicked humans and the sounds of their mates. However, their response to his recordings had brought distress and frustration. They peered around, attempting to establish where the birdsongs came from. When they failed to locate their perceived new friends whom they suspected were close by, they became anxious.

Max contemplated his options.

He wouldn't return to New York City, and the Florida university position didn't seem as appealing anymore, considering the head of the ornithology group wanted Max to work round the clock for little pay.

At any rate, another hike to Juniper Mountain was in Max's forecast. He considered contacting Sarah and asking her to accompany him.

During the past seven days, he'd given the morning they'd spent together deeper consideration. He remembered her face going pale when the bear charged. He also recalled how sweet she was, and how fearless. He admired her beauty, but was more intrigued by her modest and steady presence. She'd bravely held back frightened tears after scaring off the bear.

Society sometimes displayed a cynical indifference to the wonders of nature, but Sarah appreciated the unspoiled forest. He had recognized the romantic interest whenever she gazed at him, and it melted him with surprising tenderness as he recalled their affectionate kiss.

And how did he repay her kindness after she'd given up her morning to hike with him?

Why, he'd departed with a quick, "Thanks for the ride and for being my guide. Have a marvelous afternoon."

Who said such words after sharing a morning with a beautiful woman?

Apparently, he did.

He rubbed a hand over his face. After their tender kiss, what must she think of him? Their hours shouldn't have ended with such finality. He blamed his cool farewell on the fact that he was weary after the lengthy drive, his move, and endless unpacking.

Nevertheless, he needed to rectify any misunderstanding because she fascinated him.

But how?

He lifted a cup of wassail to his lips and swallowed, and a familiar comfort surged through him. Years earlier, Mr. Lenny's wife, Amanda, had mixed homemade wassail using ingredients on hand—apple, orange, and cranberry juice.

Ultimately, Max had come to realize those long-ago times of assembling in Lenny's cheery kitchen drinking wassail with him, his wife, and their son, John, had resulted in Max's fantasy of heart-warming holidays surrounded by loved ones.

That fantasy never materialized. Still, he felt a sense of allegiance and gratitude to Lenny that exceeded every other emotion. Which was why, he supposed, he drank wassail.

A few short months after Max's placement with Lenny and his family, Max had been returned to his birth mother's care until she was hospitalized with liver disease. By then, the water and electricity in their apartment had been shut off. He never learned what happened to his father, who had never been a part of Max's life.

A loud knock on the front door sounded, and Gerry's voice bellowed, "Anyone home?"

"Just me and a bird flying around the living room."

A snicker. "You've been around birds so long you learned to fly?"

"Hang on while I catch Angel."

"Will it take a while?"

"Anywhere from five minutes to an hour, depending on if she cooperates."

A loud guffaw. "The weather is comfortable and I'll wait on the porch. I brought you a housewarming gift. A bottle of blackberry brandy."

"Really? I don't normally drink brandy ... but thanks."

From experience, Max knew coaxing Angel to her cage was no easy task. Parakeets were flock animals, and keenly aware of a person's body language. They were, after all, low man on the food chain and had learned to be cautious.

Max chatted quietly and walked nonchalantly, coaxing her down from the curtain rod. After he picked her up, he held his hand lightly over her wings and carried her to her cage.

A half hour later, he and Gerry sat in Max's tiny kitchen drinking cups of wassail. Gerry poured a shot of blackberry brandy into his cup, claiming he needed something to calm his nerves, being a spanking new father and all.

Max declined the brandy. He wanted to keep his wits about him while he engaged with the birds. Tonight, he planned on playing the harmonica—perhaps a scale followed by a soulful ballade. Maybe they would mimic the musical sounds.

He leaned back in his stool as Gerry brought him up to date on living with a newborn and how he embraced father-hood in his fifties. Then Gerry poured himself another shot.

Max's initial thought upon seeing his friend in person for the first time in years was that Gerry's hair had turned a bushy stark-white—whiter than it appeared on screen—framing a robust, pink-cheeked face. His glacial-blue eyes were piercing, yet friendly. His once crusty exterior had softened.

By day, Gerry worked in a pet store in Perrytown. By night, his passion was music. Over the course of their Internet jam sessions, Max discovered that Gerry had a powerful bass voice, and his guitar skills were disciplined and focused.

Gerry raised his cup for a toast. "To the Bearded Elves. Forever may we sing."

"Forever may we sing … anywhere?" Max clinked cups.

"An opportunity will present itself."

"Dorothy Edwards suggested The Garden Terrace."

"We'll check it out." Gerry ran his tongue over his lips. "Hey, this is tasty wassail for a bachelor."

"Wassail is my holiday indulgence. I learned how to make it from my foster mother and father."

Max tapped a relaxed fist against his heart. "They were the epitome of kindness."

"I've known you many years, my bird singing comrade. You don't celebrate Christmas. Wassail is Christmas."

Amused, Max drank a final gulp. He too appreciated the irony of savoring wassail, rather than, say, a cold beer. Avoiding answering Gerry, he looked into the living room. The parakeets were busy quibbling with their toys and preening.

Gerry took the hint. "Any luck with the birds repeating your recorded songs?" he asked.

"None, even though I play different tracks for them every day."

"Maybe your birds would respond well if there was another animal around. I hear there is an adorable puppy in need of a home."

"A puppy galloping through my legs every morning, and keeping me up half the night?" Max shook his head. "This house is a rental, and a puppy is known to chew everything in sight. I already bumped up the place when I lugged my suitcases inside."

"My wife and I have discussed pet ownership, but newbie parenting is enough for now." Gerry commiserated with a nod, then gestured to the parakeets. "What do they mimic?"

Max shrugged. "Nothing."

As if on cue, Angel blurted loud and clear, "God bless us, every one."

Gerry swiveled on his stool. "Is that your bird?"

"You're hearing Angel's favorite, and only, sentence."

"Ho, ho, ho. You own a budgie who celebrates the holidays." Gerry chuckled. "Have you seen the Cherish town square transformation?"

"Too busy."

"Those little wooden houses lined up around the ten-foot Christmas tree resemble a Norman Rockwell village when lit at night. There's also a craft fair selling local wares. My wife prefers cranberry-scented candles and pine-smelling soaps."

"It's going to be challenging to shop with a newborn."

Gerry linked his hands behind his head. "Barring the matter that neither of us has slept more than three hours since little Freddie's birth, my answer is yes, it will be. Are you up for any babysitting?"

"Perhaps when he's a little older. He cries a lot?"

"He's colicky." Gerry stared into his cup, then at Max. "I thought you always wanted children."

"Someday. In the meantime, call me when he turns five."

As Gerry rambled about the egalitarian share of chores in his marriage, Max's thoughts gravitated to his research. Should he expand his study to include cardinals? A recent article by a colleague had supported a claim to include natural-history habitats, and cardinals were the state bird in neighboring North Carolina. Perhaps the Jacksonville university would be more attentive if Max's study included additional birds.

He massaged his nape. Shouldn't the ache be gone? He'd moved in a while ago.

Stress, a little voice nudged.

No. An adamant no. Stress is a motivator.

In the meantime, didn't the department head realize Max couldn't *force* his budges to talk?

"Seen the live reindeer at the children's petting zoo?" Gerry asked.

Max's musings gravitated to Sarah. She loved taking photos of deer.

Aware his friend regarded him, Max shook his head. "No time." With a weary sigh, Max picked up their cups and rinsed them in the sink. Then he led Gerry into the living room. "I'll let the birds fly around if that's okay."

"Suits me. I let my cat roam throughout my house."

"Just don't bring your cat to my house when the birds are out."

"You'll meet my new baby before you ever see my cat. I can bring little Freddie over anytime."

"Looking forward to it," Max murmured.

At the far end of the room, beyond a scarred wooden coffee table, stood a cushioned sofa and a side chair. Two large cages were hung at chest level on the opposite wall, situated near the window so the birds could see outside.

Gerry pushed his hands into his jean pockets. "I identified the recordings you sent—a golden-winged warbler and a Canada warbler."

"You're correct. You were always a top-notch student."

Gerry knew his birds. He could have found the information using birding apps, but a conscientious and deliberate Gerry most likely had done his research.

"All the birds were recorded at Juniper Mountain?" he asked.

"Yes. And the setting is superb." With an airy wave of his hand, Max gestured toward the threadbare sofa for his buddy to get comfortable, then opened the doors to the bird cages. "I enlisted the help of a local guide."

"Who?" Gerry took a seat, shooing away a bird that quickly decided to roost there. "A park ranger?"

"A woman named Sarah Hartman. She lives in Cherish and—"

"Sarah Hartman? Sarah is my great-niece."

Max stared in surprise. "You never mentioned that."

"Why would I? Our conversations center on birds and music. So, what's the consensus?" He sounded so matter-of-fact that Max grinned.

"About Sarah?"

"Who else?"

"She's lovely. Absolutely lovely." *Okay, yes, that was an understatement.* His vision of her lustrous hair cascading over her shoulders, the red highlights glistening in the sun, served as a reminder of her beauty. "And plucky. We had a close encounter with a bear and she was magnificent."

"A real live bear?"

"Big and breathing, but Sarah's quick thinking came to our rescue. She's marvelous under pressure."

"Sounds like her. She's a wunderkind with animals."

"I've heard."

Gerry leaned in. "Can I tell you something about her I've noticed lately?"

"Should you betray her confidence?"

"It's more of a speculation shared by me and a number of her friends. We believe she has a hearing deficiency she's denying."

Thoughtfully, Max nodded. That would explain her

occasional hesitancy to speak and the way she kept looking at him when she was driving, as if she had trouble hearing him.

He felt a clutching in his heart. He, more than anyone, should understand. Not exactly the same, but Mr. Lenny had worn a hearing aid, saying it helped him listen and communicate—mainly in noisy situations.

Max waited while Gerry went into the kitchen and refilled a fresh cup—all brandy and no wassail.

When he returned, he stopped short and regarded Max for a suspiciously long time. "Well?" he prodded.

"Well, what?"

Gerry took a quick swallow of brandy. "Did you and my divine niece get along?"

Max cleared his throat. "Of course." He turned, a clear sign he wasn't willing to make any small talk when it came to his feelings toward Sarah. Some subjects were personal, and she was special.

"Alrighty then." Gerry's laughter rippled through the room. "Next topic. Church."

"Let's close that topic before you begin." Max flipped open his computer, scanning the files, calculating how successfully he could change the church subject without Gerry asking a thousand questions.

"Let me reword. Not church, necessarily, but the Cherish church *choir*." Gerry hesitated for emphasis, his tone growing insistent as he touched on the real issue. "A strong baritone voice is needed for our cantata. The choir is performing at the six o'clock service on Christmas Eve."

"If you're hinting for me to join, I haven't set foot in a church in years."

He'd attended as a child, since Mr. Lenny had served at the local church as an associate pastor, but Max had gotten away from anything religious once he heard of Mr. Lenny's death. None of his other foster families, nor his birth mother, had favored religion.

"Come once to rehearsal, Max, and see if you're a decent fit. I think you are, though it's your call. The choir members are good people and—"

"No one's refuting their goodness."

"Then help us out." Gerry extended a sheepish smile.

"Isn't Ryan Edwards your main singer?"

"Normally, although he's conducting the choir on Christmas Eve. And right now, he's in Atlanta rehearsing. Another member is stepping in for the next couple of weeks."

Max hesitated, ready to cut off any additional arguments from Gerry with a shake of his head.

"You're here for Christmas, correct?" Gerry asked. "And staying through New Year's."

"I am. However—"

"You'll recognize the traditional hymns: 'Away in a Manger,' etc. You'll catch on quick. You're a fine note-reader."

Max's eyebrows furrowed. His friend knew he wasn't a churchgoer, yet he was asking him to sing in a church choir. He considered Gerry's earnest expression as his mind scrambled for an excuse. At a loss for how to decline, he returned to the computer files.

"Did I mention Sarah is usually at the church when we rehearse?" Gerry added. "She designs and arranges the altar flowers. Sure looks pretty all decked out in red with green velvet ribbons."

"The church or your great-niece?"

Gerry winked. "Both."

Max sprang to his feet. "When are the rehearsals?"

"Thursday evenings at seven o'clock."

"Sarah is usually there?"

"Usually."

"I'll give the choir a try."

"I thought so." Gerry sent Max a knowing grin. "Oh, and bring your harmonica."

"Why?"

"The finale is a rousing rendition of 'We Wish You A Merry Christmas.' I'm playing guitar and a harmonica would be a nice touch."

"What about Joseph Slater? He's a professional guitarist."

"He and his wife, Scarlett, are flying to Australia next week for a worship conference. They asked me to step in."

"No one else plays harmonica in this town?"

"None that I know of. Consider it an honor to be asked. I wanted to add a sixteen-measure solo at the end."

Max digested this and considered reverting to his earlier decision. Singing in the choir was one thing. Playing the harmonica in front of Ryan Edwards, a world-renowned opera singer, was quite another. He opened his mouth, but Gerry interrupted.

"The other day, Sarah mentioned hanging wreaths on all the church windows on Thursday night."

Max chuckled. "I'll bring my harmonica."

Gerry drained his cup. "I knew you wouldn't let the baritone section down."

CHAPTER 5

*H*armonica tucked in his pocket, and his favorite bow tie in place, Max arrived at the white-painted Memorial Street Church on Thursday evening. Night had darkened the winter sky, forming a blanket of black velvet, and the steeple soared proud and magnificent against it.

An outdoor nativity scene took center stage. The life-size creche included the Holy Family, two white lambs, kings and shepherds, and a wooden stable.

Gas street lamps were wrapped in fragrant pine boughs, and a trembling wind rustled the tree branches.

Inside, an assemblage of youthful and older men and women were taking their places on the risers, and a small group of women hung wreaths on the arched church windows.

Looking around, he spotted Sarah balanced on the third rung of a stepladder.

He strode over to her and tapped her on the back. "Good evening, Sarah."

She whirled and almost fell into his arms. A burst of

delight lit her face, and everything around him—the stained glass depicting Bible scenes, the whiffs of incense and candles, the other people's voices—faded away. The intensity of her gaze did funny things to his insides. Regardless of the way their last time together had ended, she looked pleased to see him.

"Max!" She clung to the sides of the ladder for support. "I chatted with my uncle Gerry this week and he claimed you're singing in the church choir."

"Temporarily," Max corrected.

"You're also in a band with him?"

"The Bearded Elves." Max steadied the ladder as she climbed down.

"The Bearded Elves? That's … different."

"Don't get hung up on the name. It will change soon."

She tilted her head to the side.

"When you're *not* a number one hit band, you're granted some flexibility." He grinned. "Wait until February. You'll see."

But then, he wouldn't be here in February, which left him with a sense of sadness.

She didn't reply, accepting his explanation without question, not even with the prompt of "What happens in February?"

Then again, maybe she hadn't heard him.

"Uncle Gerry raved about your superb baritone voice and perfect pitch," she said instead.

"He's biased since he was an undergrad student in my bird-watching class." Max removed his jacket and placed it on a pew. "Besides, doesn't every choir member sing in tune?"

"I'm not certain. Based on my great-uncle's comments, some don't." Sarah stepped to a side table and gathered red spray roses and luxuriant ivy, creating an elegant bouquet in a green glass vase. "The choir is all volunteer. These folks aren't professional except for Ryan Edwards and a few of the others."

Max turned her to face him. "Are you brave, Sarah?"

She looked startled by his unexpected question. "I try."

"You're the most courageous woman I've ever known."

Her cheeks pinkened. "Thanks."

"I intend to explore Crandall's Mountain next weekend. Will you join me? I hesitated inviting you, considering our adventure last week."

"You mean, because of the bear?"

"Because of me. I apologize for my rudeness. We didn't part on the finest note."

"You're here now. The present is all that matters."

"Is that a yes?"

Her nod of affirmation was accompanied by a smile of delight. "Let me check my work schedule, but it sounds like fun."

She was full of life. Eager. Forgiving. And stunning. The hiking gear she'd worn the previous weekend hadn't done her justice. She'd looked anything but glamorous in a hooded jacket, snowflake gloves and boots. The woman gazing at him now was entrancing. By the light of numerous church candles, the jeweled sparkle of her emerald eyes mesmerized him.

"For the record, I like hiking more than ever," she said.

Her statement thrilled him, sending a rush of gladness straight to his heart.

Before he could reply, Gerry called him to the choir to begin the warm-up.

Max nodded at Gerry over his shoulder, then curved back to Sarah. "The rehearsal runs an hour. Will you be here when it's finished?"

"Most likely. There are thirty windows in the church."

"I'll see you after rehearsal then?"

She chewed her lip. Glanced away.

He stared at her in eager silence. "Well?"

"Sure. If I'm done beforehand, I'll wait."

The recognizable first notes of 'Joy To The World' led by the sopranos, announced the beginning of choir practice.

Max hurried to the risers and took his appointed place between Gerry and a gray-bearded man. He retrieved a hymnal and thumbed through the selections until he located the correct piece.

The uplifting lyrics and melody, published by Handel in the 1700s, plucked him backward to a tiny church, sitting on a hard wooden pew as he listened to Mr. Lenny's heartfelt sermon.

Max focused on the associate conductor for the most part during the rehearsal.

However, he often stole glances at Sarah. She wore black slacks and a shimmery candy-red sweater, and her slim figure kept drawing his attention.

Whenever she caught his gaze, she quickly looked away. However, she smiled first, and he reciprocated with a responsive grin.

The final selection called for a guitar and harmonica. The "honor" of playing a harmonica solo in front of the other musicians was one that Max would've happily forgone, but when he was done, he was satisfied with his performance.

"What's your decision?" Gerry asked once the rehearsal ended.

Max slid the harmonica into his pocket. "I'll join."

"What was the deciding factor? The beloved hymns, my brilliant persuasion, or my great-niece's presence?"

"The latter," Max assured him.

In a refined southern drawl, an elderly woman intro-duced herself as Mrs. Marge Addyson. Her gray hair was neatly coiffed, and her rouged cheeks plumped with her smile as she held out a freckled hand. "Your baritone voice is as fine as a sunny winter's day. Welcome to Cherish. I'm the associate pastor."

"Thank you, ma'am. I'm Maxwell Archer." He shook her hand, frail yet sturdy. He was surprised at the callouses.

In a deafening stage whisper that garnered the notice of the remaining choir members, Marge announced, "You're the professor birdman who went hiking with our Sarah."

Our Sarah?

Intent on sidestepping a discussion involving Sarah that might be overheard, Max replied, "I'm affiliated with an ornithology department at a university."

"Birds."

"Ornithology is a branch of zoology," he clarified, "and is a discipline involving the study of birds."

"Impressive, and a distinctive description."

"Animals are important in my life and profession."

He expected Marge to rhapsodize about the significance of pets. She did just that, but offered a particular recommendation.

"Nicholas, the town sheriff, is looking for someone to adopt a cuddly homeless puppy," Marge said. "Considering your animal expertise, you're ideal."

Although both startled and pleased by her consideration of him as a candidate, he replied, "I've already been asked by the woman who owns the music store."

"Dorothy Edwards?"

"Yes, and I declined."

"Aren't you a fan of stray mongrels?"

"I should be, because I'm one myself." He regarded her with an ironic grin. "I used to live in Cherish."

"When?"

"Three decades ago, and for a brief spell. My foster family's last name was Monroe."

"I don't recall a Monroe family, although oftentimes my memory fails me." She pursed her lips. "I'll remember something that happened a decade earlier and forget something that happened a minute ago."

By the looks of Marge Addyson's well-heeled style and demeanor, Max assumed she resided in the wealthy outskirts of town. The Monroe family had occupied the impoverished fringes.

"I'm in no position to take on the responsibility of a dog," he said. "I move around a lot and my three parakeets are a literal handful. In January, I begin my dream job in Florida. I've struggled for ages to be on the faculty of a prestigious university."

"I express the feelings of the entire town when I say I'm overjoyed you're in Cherish." Marge reached for her handbag and tugged on a pair of flowered red gloves. "Regardless of your job, I hope you're here a long, long time."

"I appreciate your hospitality."

It warmed him—this undeniable sense of community, a welcome transition from big city living.

"Our church holds services on Saturday afternoons and Sunday mornings. On Christmas Eve day and evening, we offer several services." She studied him with an astute gaze. "Christmas is an opportune season to honor our Lord."

For a split second, their exchange grew awkward. Max wasn't about to divulge his lack of faith to the elderly associate pastor in the middle of a church.

He opted not to reply, although he recognized the wisdom flowing from her heart.

"You need honest and caring people in your life," she said.

He managed a grim smile.

"Do you serve God?"

Surprised at her bluntness, he answered truthfully. "I tried the religion route when I was younger. It didn't go well. The people in my circle …" He shrugged.

"Perhaps the season has come for a different circle." She squeezed his hand, her intelligent eyes exuding care and friendship. "Press on, Max. We're all here for you in your journey."

Journey to where?

"'Thanks be to God for his indescribable gift,'" she proclaimed.

"Second Corinthians 9:15." At her lifted eyebrows and inquisitive gaze, he avoided eye contact. "My special foster father was a pastor," he said.

"Special?"

"Yes."

"Was?" She grasped her blue tweed coat draped over a music stand.

"Mr. Lenny died many years ago."

She fiddled with the silver bell brooch on her coat's lapel as she studied him. "You miss him."

"Very much." Max glanced toward Gerry, who was collecting choral music.

Gerry picked up his guitar, slicked back his white hair, and approached them. "Hi, Mrs. Addyson."

"Hello, Gerry." Marge smiled up at him. "I just asked our newest choir member if he was interested in adopting the stray pup that wandered into Nicholas's office."

"What was his answer?"

"I'm right here, Gerry." Because they were close friends, Max caught the drollness in Gerry's tone. "As much as I'd love a puppy, I can't commit."

"I refused as well because my plate is full. Sorry." Gerry flashed a guilt-ridden smile. "However, let's all go out for a celebratory drink at The Garden Terrace."

"What are we celebrating?" Max inquired.

"You joined the church choir."

"Don't you have to rush home to your new baby?" Caught between amusement and confusion, Max and Marge inquired in unison.

Gerry shot them a look filled with emotions—including self-reproach and longing. "My mother-in-law is visiting and insisted on rocking the baby to sleep. She holds the magic touch."

Max grinned. "Therefore, your and your wife's roles aren't egalitarian tonight?"

"Little Freddie giggles from head to toe whenever I make faces at him," Gerry replied. "Or raspberry kisses. I'll do both in the morning."

Mrs. Addyson left shortly afterwards, pleading tiredness, and shaking her head in refusal at the invitation. She reminded them that she was past retirement age and went to bed early.

A bang of the ornately carved doors signaled the last of the choir members filing out.

Max peered around. Sarah was hanging a final wreath on a window.

"Go ahead to the restaurant," he instructed Gerry. "We'll be along shortly."

"We?"

"I'm hoping Sarah will join us."

Gerry clapped a hand on Max's back. "I'm rooting for you, my friend. I'll inquire about a gig at the restaurant while I'm waiting."

"Do you think the management will agree?"

"Simple logic. We order a meal and they'll hire our band."

"Just because we eat there doesn't mean they'll want us to *play* there," Max countered. "Hundreds of customers dine at the restaurant every day."

"It's a start."

"Will we get paid?"

"I was thinking more along the lines of free drinks."

Max bit back a grin at the logic he didn't see at all, pulled on his jacket and hurried to Sarah.

"Perfect timing," he declared.

"For what?"

"You're finished, and I am too."

"I'm *nearly* done." She swerved around him to a table and secured buckthorn berry branches into florist foam, then arranged the branches with a trail of ivy in a copper vase.

He followed her as she set the vase near the altar. "Will you join us?" he asked.

"Where?"

"The Garden Terrace."

"It's after eight o'clock."

"Hardly late."

"There's cleanup here. In addition, I'm scheduled for a double shift tomorrow."

"I'll finish." To Max's relief, a short, heavyset woman spoke up. "Sarah, you go on and enjoy yourself with this handsome newcomer."

Max turned to her. "How do you know I'm a newcomer?"

"Cherish is a small community." The woman reached for the last two poinsettias. "Word travels fast."

"Thank you, Rosemary." Sarah's shoulders lifted as she turned to Max. "I'd like to, but—"

"Do you have any noteworthy plans on a Thursday night?"

"After I tend to my pets, I planned to catch up on some reading."

He persevered. "Did you drive here?"

"I walked. I don't live far."

"There's a chill in the air, Cinderella. Ride with me, and I guarantee you'll arrive home before midnight. Besides, I don't know where the restaurant is."

She laughed. "I'm certain you can find it without my help." In the flick of a few seconds, her mood had switched from indecision to humor, and it struck him that no matter her disposition, he appreciated her companionship.

"I have it on excellent authority you're the ideal guide," he said.

She gathered a half dozen stemmed red roses and placed them in a bucket filled with water. "From whom?"

"Me."

With a sideways smile, Sarah retrieved her jacket, then tucked her hand through his arm.

He couldn't help grinning as he escorted her out the wooden doors and down the church steps.

CHAPTER 6

*T*he Garden Terrace wasn't the restaurant Max imagined. Certainly, the Monroes hadn't been able to afford such luxuries as dining out.

He'd pictured a genteel garden, a sparkling fountain, and an abundance of plants. After all, the restaurant's name alluded to a *garden.*

Instead, he and Sarah were welcomed by lively waitresses, a boisterous clatter of dishes, and heavenly whiffs of mesquite smoked chicken. An oversized sign at the entrance stated in bold letters, "The holidays are for barbecue." Multicolored lights were strung from the ceiling and pine cones and faux red berries wound around rustic poles, accentuated by tan burlap. A keyboardist provided a background performance of "Carol of the Bells."

"This restaurant doesn't subscribe to minimalism," he joked.

"They're renowned for sugar-free lemon cake and sweet tea," Sarah told Max as he led her through the crowd and ushered her to a booth Gerry had claimed.

Somehow, Max remembered that about this restaurant.

He'd eaten a slice of the cake in his youth and had savored every bite. Another aspect of this appealing town were that things stayed the same. A time machine rewound to an era without the push and shove of big-city living.

"Sugar and sugar-free." Max helped her off with her jacket, tugged off his, and hung both on a coat hanger. "Isn't that a juxtaposition?"

"An oxymoron." Sarah teased him with a nudge. He noticed that she had watched his lips as he spoke. The restaurant was noisy and even he strained to hear their conversation. "Or rather, one cancels out the other. The calories in sugary tea—"

"Is a paradox," Gerry interrupted, indicating the guitar on his seat. He motioned them to sit across from him.

"Wrong," they contradicted him, which produced lots of laughter.

In the minutes between ordering and waiting for their meals—hot chocolate topped with marshmallows for Sarah, a slice of the sugar-free lemon cake and tea for Max, and a draft beer and two platters of French fries for Gerry—Max arrived at several important deductions.

First, Gerry wasn't, as Max earlier had presumed, merely a first-rate student, a talented musician, and a newbie father. Gerry was also candid and clever. While he inquired about Max's and Sarah's hiking adventure, he closely observed the way Max draped an arm around her shoulders.

And Sarah, with her delicate features and lilting voice, had a remarkable gift. She was charismatic, and she gave an enthusiastic account of the bear adventure, flavoring it with enough elements to engage Gerry. By doing so, she successfully avoided any reference to the kiss she and Max had shared.

Smiling at her wide-eyed gaze as she described the

babbling river, he felt inside him the stirring of a sentiment so remote, so foreign, he gasped in denial.

He was falling for her.

Not in the cards, he told himself. He was leaving in January.

Even so, the sentiment prompted him to curve a lock of shiny hair behind her ear. Her glittery gold star earrings winked back at him.

"You forgot our interruption by the teenagers," he said.

Her eyes glistened with laughter. "If they hadn't approached, we would still be ..."

"Kissing," he whispered in her ear and squeezed her shoulders, a gentle reminder in case she'd forgotten.

Oblivious to the direction of the conversation, Gerry pulled out his cellphone, concentrated on a text and frowned. "My wife," he muttered.

"Is little Freddie sleeping?" Max inquired.

"Almost." Gerry tried for a smile that said all was well, although he didn't entirely convince Max.

After their drinks and food were served, Gerry took a deep pull from his beer and set it down. "Incidentally, my friend, management agreed."

"To what?" Max handed him a bottle of ketchup and watched him smother the fries, then slid the platter to the middle of the table for all to share.

"To us performing here a couple Fridays from now." Gerry broke off a fry and chewed. "The Bearded Elves are back in business."

Max helped himself to an ample portion of fries after scarfing down his cake. He'd forgotten how much he liked lemon. "We weren't ever *in* business. Nonetheless, your news is exciting. Are they paying us?"

"Our gig is doubling as a debut audition and management is requesting familiar holiday tunes." A smile quirked Gerry's mouth. "I'll organize a playlist. We can rehearse separately, then together before our unveiling."

Sarah joined in with a chuckle. "Am I invited?"

"Absolutely. We'll perform in that far corner. There's even a dance floor." With his half-eaten fry, Gerry gestured to where the keyboardist played on a small stage.

Once their table was cleared, Gerry insisted on paying the bill, then peered at his phone and announced, "I'm heading home before my wife and her mother murder me."

"Did the baby wake up?" Max asked.

"The baby never went to sleep."

"No magic touch from your mother-in-law?"

"Our next option is to phone Merlin the Magician. Evidently, little Freddie is offended by the idea of sleeping."

Sarah surged up as quickly as Gerry did. "I should leave too." She peered at the restaurant's rustic wall clock, which showed after nine o'clock.

"Don't rush on my account." Gerry waved toward the dance floor. The keyboardist had begun a jazzy rendition of Ray Charles's "That Spirit of Christmas," and a handful of couples swirled to the rhythm.

Max slid his arm around Sarah and led her to the intimate dance floor. She was so petite, scarcely five feet tall, her head hardly reached his shoulder.

She gazed up at him with a jesting smile. "Are you the type who steps on your dance partner's feet?"

"Exactly." He chuckled, tempted to kiss the edges of her smile. "You?"

"The same, so watch out." Her laughter was mellow and melodic. He loved her ability to laugh at herself, as well as with him.

"Has anyone ever described you as a wonderful, caring man?" she asked.

"I dislike labels."

"I do too, but my intuition tells me you're a good person."

"Never tell a man he's good. Strong, maybe, or marvelous—"

She rested her head against his chest, and he whirled them around and around. Her steps were agile, gliding to the rhythm. Above them, the multi-colored lights sparkled, creating a wondrous, otherworldly effect. Her hair spun with each pivot and twist, and he kissed her forehead, her cheeks, her lips.

"What a wonderful feeling," he sang, adlibbing the lyrics, "to waltz with a precious, vivacious woman who is as sweet as a sugarplum."

As they danced, he reviewed the plan he'd conceived within the past half hour. While he lived in Cherish, he'd see her as often as possible.

Her descriptions of him—good and caring—were poignantly familiar. Mr. Lenny's wife had often called him a "caring little boy." Once, his outlook on life had shone optimistic.

His timeworn thoughts now were shadowed with the awareness that a future with a loving wife hadn't come to pass.

He blew out a labored breath.

He'd gotten over the injustice of being born to birth parents who couldn't focus on anyone except themselves.

Some children were born lucky. Other weren't.

But now he'd met Sarah.

How wonderful they could spend a few weeks together.

How awful they could only spend a few weeks together.

Seeming to sense the dipping of his mood, Sarah muttered she was sorry for stepping on his foot—she hadn't —but her comical expression portrayed her attempt to cheer him and her refreshing humor. But then she added, "I should get home."

With a nod, he maneuvered her off the dance floor and retrieved their jackets. Outside, the streets were dark and quiet. Gas lamps flickered, forming pools of warm light.

"How far do you live from the restaurant?" he asked.

"Three blocks." She turned right. "My house is in the center of town."

"I'll escort you. It'll give me a chance to walk off my fried-food coma."

Plus, it would take longer than a quick drive in his car, and he wanted to enjoy every precious minute with her. He pointed toward the town square as he heard voices rise in harmony. He recognized the "Silent Night" refrain.

"What's going on?" he asked.

Sarah hesitated. "Going on?"

"The singing."

"Oh, singing. It's carol singing," she replied. "The town's Christmas committee sponsors caroling three nights a week in December. Anyone can join. Afterwards, they serve hot apple cider and roasted chestnuts."

Now that she had mentioned it, he recognized the scorching charcoal aroma, rich and nutty, permeating the air, along with the hint of woodsy fireplaces.

Beams of silver fell around them. A full moon graced the sky, and a smattering of stars twinkled in shimmering beauty.

A chilly burst of wind tugged at their jackets.

Sarah bowed her head and closed her eyes to avoid the sting.

His gaze fell to her long, thick eyelashes, an unmistakable reddish-blond. Her copper-colored hair, as smooth as the finest silk, fell loose around her face.

"I recalled Carolina weather being warm all year round," he said, "but my remembrances are from a youngster's perspective."

"How long were you here?"

"Briefly." He shifted the subject, in no mood to upset the fine balance of a pleasant evening by being reminded of his tumultuous upbringing. "I assumed the climate was comparable to Florida."

"Do you like hot weather?"

"In all honesty, no." His reflective pause initiated a jab from his conscience. *Dream job, remember? You're moving.* "How about you?"

"I've lived here my entire life. I know everyone and am comfortable here. Still, I sometimes wish to see other places."

"Like Florida?"

"Are there more palm trees than the Carolinas?"

"Probably."

"You'll receive a pay raise with your new job?"

"Not necessarily, although I'm optimistic my research will resonate with people avid about ornithology. That is, unless my appointment is cancelled. Universities are tightening their proverbial belts, and bird study isn't at the top of their budgets." He shrugged, sighed. "If it happens, it happens."

"You work a lot of hours. It's a considerable workload." She seemed to choose her words carefully.

"Which will become heavier once I take on more responsibility."

"I'm sorry you're not a hot-weather fan."

"I don't particularly like cold weather, either. Nor do I care for synthetic snow, the kind the outdoor fairs manufacture for gala events."

"The Carolinas enjoy four distinct seasons," she replied. "I eagerly wait for snow on Christmas Day. No assurances, though. The weather here is unpredictable."

"I lived up north for years. If it doesn't snow, we're surprised."

She grinned. "In Cherish, if it *does* snow, we're amazed."

Several of the shops' single-paned windows had frosted over, and they peered through the glass, admiring one-of-a-kind gifts—a man's handmade striped red tie, a vintage green and gold pinecone necklace, and jars touting themselves as a "One-Stop Spa." An innovative store advertised a pet-friendly dog bakery, and Sarah commented on the unique toys, ranging from whimsical Merry Christmas bandanas to tail-wagging elf sweaters.

While they strolled, she was more outgoing than the day of their hike, regaling him with hilarious stories of her pets, beginning with what happened when she returned from work each day to a houseful of welcoming animals.

"My two dogs and two cats wait by the door until I arrive," she described. "Even if I leave for ten minutes to get the mail at the post office, they're under the impression I've been gone for hours, and the greeting parade begins anew."

She grew more gorgeous by the second. Her cheeks had grown rosy from the cold, her wide-set eyes sparkling a deep emerald. When she chuckled, tiny puffs of her breathing filled the air. He couldn't look away.

"My budgies are happy," he said. "They spend their days singing or talking."

"Uncle Gerry told me they haven't mimicked the bird-songs you recorded."

"Nothing yet."

Max went over the endless hours he'd spent with his birds. Why wouldn't they mimic other birdsongs or harmonica music? He reined in his frustration and focused on Sarah. "My budgies have individual temperaments. One male is timid, the other bolder, and the third, a female, speaks her mind."

"Hurray for the female. What does she say?"

Max pushed out an exasperated breath. "'God bless us, every one.'"

"From *A Christmas Carol*? Tiny Tim?"

"Exactly. She's a rescue bird. An elderly woman owned her."

"What's her name?"

"Angel." He resisted the urge to laugh. "Don't be fooled. She's the most unangelic bird of the three."

"Is unangelic a word?"

"It is now."

"We all have distinctive personalities, because God created variety and uniqueness."

"You're saying He knew what to do."

"Exactly."

"But how, Sarah? I'm not at peace with all this religious jargon."

"Don't search for peace." Her tone softened, and he felt his expression grow less rigid. "You already are at peace. God is inside you."

She expressed herself with her body, gestures, and expressions rather than a deluge of words.

He had appreciated her artistic flower arrangements at church and he knew she was hard working and industrious. Her faith in God was clear, and he sensed she possessed what Mr. Lenny had called "a new creature in Christ." Combined, these attributes contributed to her magnetic personality.

In the sparkle of twinkling lights dancing from nearby homes, the sadness in his heart diminished. Sarah carried the same unique gift—to enhance the world around her merely by her presence. She was an extraordinary, special woman.

Soon, they reached the gaily decorated Musically Yours. Although the music store was closed, they paused to admire the window display of the polar bears, treble clef signs, and model train.

How many hours, Sarah mused aloud, had it taken Dorothy and Ryan to dress up the window with such flair?

"Maybe they had help," Max said.

"From who? A polar bear?"

"Maybe Beethoven himself." Max curled his fingers around hers. Happiness lifted his spirits, and, judging by Sarah's contented sigh, the holiday atmosphere of the winsome town affected them both.

"Cherish Hills Inn also has particularly noticeable decorations. The inn is located farther up the street." Sarah gestured with her chin. "The innkeeper, Tom Canning, is a long-time resident, and strict about who he rents to."

"I tried to get a room there, but Tom wasn't keen on renting to me and my birds for the entire month of December."

"Not surprising. The inn is posh and unconducive for pets."

"Ah. That explains Tom's half-hearted response."

"What did he say?"

Max grabbed a mouthful of air and shouted, "No."

"That's why Tom doesn't have anyone currently staying at his inn. He's choosey and a stickler for elegance."

"Thank you." Max picked her up and twirled her around.

"What for?" She giggled. Wriggled.

"For sticking up for me."

"I did?"

"Yes. You stuck up for me instead of Tom."

"I'm getting dizzy. Put me down."

He continued to spin, but slower this time, holding her close. "Not until you guarantee me something."

"You expect an assurance after that?"

"Promise me you'll never change." He gazed at her amazing face, trying to ignore the flip in his pulse.

She met his stare. "Our lives, our paths, take many forms, Max."

He spoke clearly and deliberately, as he had done all evening. "Not with us."

He set her down and reached for her hand, whistling the entire last block to her house. It was set back from the road and surrounded by bare-branched trees. The front door was painted gray and bedecked with shiny pink ornaments and a garland heavy with silver tinsel.

"You're a true holiday-lover," he remarked. "I hope the porch doesn't collapse under the sheer mass of the decorations."

At her doorstep, with barking dogs and loud meows in the background, he slipped his arms around her. So close their foreheads touched, he tipped up her chin and kissed her.

She stood on her tiptoes and yielded to his hungry mouth. Her lips were plump and inviting, fitting together with his, two pieces of an intricate puzzle matching perfectly. Her hands reached up and her slim fingers tangled behind his neck.

Her enticing sweetness obliterated his concerns—an uncertain job market, his research, his turbulent past—and he savored every second of their kiss. The promise of December, creamy hot chocolate and tart lemon cake—he'd hit the jackpot when he met Sarah.

He was filled with anticipation and gladness.

And a spark that completely surprised him.

A spark of love.

CHAPTER 7

The following day, Sarah clocked in at the greenhouse at ten o'clock in the morning. Fragrant whiffs of lush evergreens never failed to bring thoughts of sparkly white lights and an array of gaily wrapped gifts.

That morning, she'd secured her flyaway hair with a green headband because it always frizzed after shampooing, even when she used her favorite rosewood shampoo. Then, she'd tugged on a cream-colored cable-knit sweater, jeans, and snowman dangle earrings.

After a wave at Bonnie, who had positioned herself at the cash register, Sarah sorted Christmas cactus. She lavished care on each showy red and white flower. Many had been overwatered, which led to root and stem rot.

While she tended to the first plant, she tried to ignore the butterflies in her chest as memories of her previous evening with Max kept surfacing.

His animated features when he chatted about his birds, his quick-witted banter, his musicality, were all part of his personality. He was bold yet vulnerable; humorous yet sensitive.

And she loved every minute she spent with him.

He'd dismissed his upcoming Florida job with a casual "if it happens, it happens" as he rubbed the dark stubble of his beard. Nonetheless, his dismissal had only confirmed that he cared about the prestigious position more than he let on.

The plants, she reminded herself. The plants.

She tended to the next one and again, her mind meandered.

The mouth-watering food and drink at The Garden Terrace, her intimate dance with Max, their leisurely stroll ending in an earth-shattering kiss—all those memories came back in a rush. Rational thought had a way of abandoning her whenever she was within two feet of him.

She pressed a finger to her lips. Was last night a first date? After all, he'd invited her to a restaurant. Or was it a second if she counted their hike on Juniper Mountain?

"Do you have any noteworthy plans on a Thursday night?" he'd asked her.

Um, no, unless scrubbing the kitchen floor and vacuuming were considered noteworthy. In any event, she was glad she'd accepted his invitation.

At the end of the evening, he'd requested her phone number and had promised to text, phone, and see her often.

He was a man, he assured her, who never reneged on his promises. True to his word, he'd texted a few minutes later, telling her how much he'd enjoyed their hours together. That text had resulted in an hour's worth of conversation.

Was his kiss the beginning of something extraordinary, something lasting?

As quickly as it came, she released the thought.

He was in Cherish for one month. He'd made that fact abundantly clear.

Nevertheless, his affectionate words and tender actions were sincere.

Weren't they? What if he didn't call or text again?

A favorite passage from the Bible, Matthew 6:34, reassured her: "Do not be anxious for tomorrow, for tomorrow will be anxious for itself."

She wondered about Max's past, because Marge Addyson had left a voice mail for Sarah that morning when Sarah was in the shower.

"I scoured the Big Brothers Big Sisters files," Marge said. "I believe I've found a photo of your Max, probably taken close to thirty years ago when he lived in Cherish with his foster family. You'll want to see it, I'm sure. I'll stop by your home … I'm assuming after six o'clock? Call me if that's not okay."

Her Max.

Sarah's heartbeat had drummed at Marge's reference, and she scarcely paid attention to the rest of Marge's words.

Wait.

Big Brothers Big Sisters.

Despite Max's brilliant mind and academic demeanor, his background apparently wasn't silver-spoon. She considered him handsome, but there was a blunt masculinity to his square jaw and muscled physique. Had he been the type of boy who'd been in many brawls?

She knew he wasn't afraid of anything.

Not even a charging bear.

By the river, his strong, chiseled arms had held her tight.

Images of a Christmas spent with him brought comfort to her lonely world, a breathlessness whenever she recalled the glimmer of interest in his gray eyes. His dark hair, a tad too long, curled at the nape, and she'd wanted to smooth the adorable cleft on his chin.

By far, he was the handsomest man to set foot in Cherish.

He's leaving, her sensible side was quick to remind. *Do you honestly want to get hurt again?*

A jarring announcement over the store's loudspeaker called for a price check. Quickly yanked back to the present, Sarah surveyed the rows of cacti, trying to recall which plants she'd tended. White blooms or red?

The nursery door opened, and a blast of wintry air hit her.

Nicholas, the town sheriff, accompanied by Molly Belle, his rambunctious golden retriever, strode toward her. Molly Belle's leash didn't prevent her from romping away from him. She knocked over a bunch of plants in her hurry to chase … nothing.

"Stop." Nicholas tugged on the leash and peered at the spilled soil on the concrete floor. "Sorry, Sarah."

"It's a fast clean-up." Sarah grinned at Molly Belle. "Are those doggy obedience classes helping?"

Nicholas shoved a hand through his blond hair. "The instructor recommended she get lots of exercise. What an understatement." His moan was part sigh, part frustration. "We take her out often, although she's easily distracted."

The dog beamed up at them with expectant black eyes, then went back to lapping the water spilled from the plants.

"Here, Molly Belle." Sarah grabbed a water bottle, foraged for an empty container, and poured water into it. "You'll find this is tastier."

Nicholas crossed his arms and turned to face her. "You're one of only a handful of people Molly Belle will listen to."

Sarah appreciated that aspect of living in a small community. Folks were now using strong, clear voices when talking to her. Needless to say, it wasn't because she had a hearing impairment, despite what her friends hinted. They merely needed to speak louder, especially when she was in a crowded place with many voices.

Perhaps another reason why Dorothy had recommended Sarah as Max's hiking companion was because she knew that Sarah preferred the quiet solitude of nature.

"Molly Belle isn't obeying your commands?" she teasingly asked Nicholas.

"Once in a while. Once in a *great* while."

Sarah laughed, wiped her hands on her employee apron, and grabbed a broom. "Are you purchasing anything in particular today?"

"I'm here for two reasons. First, my wife wants a live wreath for the front door, rather than the fake one I purchased at the grocery store."

"The wreaths are all hung outside. You passed them when you entered." Sarah swept the soil into the dustpan and discarded it. "What's the second reason?"

"I hoped to discuss the puppy who wandered into the sheriff's office—"

"We discussed the subject. My answer is no."

"Sarah, you're the ideal choice."

"I can't, Nicholas. My house is overrun with pets."

He kneaded the back of his neck. "You have two cats and a hamster."

"Plus two dogs."

"Your dogs are friendly."

"You didn't remember I owned dogs until a second ago. My Shih Tzu is ten years old and set in her ways, and the other dog is a cocker spaniel who thinks she owns me rather than the other way around. I'm confident someone will welcome the puppy as the perfect addition to their family."

"Who?" Nicholas muttered, half to himself. He tugged his phone from his pocket, scrolled through it, then drew her attention to a tiny puppy with fuzzy silver-colored fur. "Do you agree he needs a loving home for Christmas?"

"Absolutely." She scrutinized the photo. "He?"

"Yup." Nicholas eyed Molly Belle, who had secured a place on the concrete floor in a spot of sunshine. "He lacks a safe, loving environment. Here's some videos. Doesn't he look like he's ready to take on the world?"

A bouncy puppy filled the screen, a roll of fat evident under his chin. In the second video, he chased Nicholas and nipped at his pant legs. This was followed by a short bark as the puppy rolled onto his back and stared into the camera with sweet doggy eyes.

"We've had him vet checked and he's healthy. Plus, he's handled daily and exhibits a devoted personality." Nicholas pointed to the screen. "Look at that shiny coat."

"That puppy is in constant motion. Wagging his tail and wriggling all over the place."

"He's a gem, right? The vet estimated he's eight weeks old, and vaccinated him for the first series of shots."

Sarah smiled and leaned in. "Nicholas, you're persuasive, but—"

A tap on the shoulder caused her to whirl.

"Hi, Sarah." Max stepped within a foot of her. He smiled at her and scowled at Nicholas. "Am I interrupting something?"

"Max." She touched her fingers to her throat. "I didn't expect to see you today."

He shoved his hands in his pockets. His lips pressed together. "I wanted to say hello and—"

He looked sinfully handsome, and the thought crossed her mind that Nicholas might book Max, because it had to be illegal to be that good-looking. He wore black jeans that accented his toned legs and a chambray shirt. His familiar bow tie peeked beneath the olive-green twill jacket.

The time showed mid-morning—the hours when Max normally pored over research.

Yet, he was here, and her heart did a slow flip.

Max's scowl stayed on Nicholas.

"You're not interrupting a thing." Nicholas clicked his phone shut and shoved it back in his pocket.

Sarah flinched, sensing an unmistakable hostility between the two men.

"I'm glad you stopped by the store, Max." She gave an uneasy laugh and swallowed. "Let me introduce you to the Cherish town sheriff. Nicholas Thompson, meet Maxwell Archer."

At the same height, six feet tall, both men's features were similar—sharp and athletic and wary.

They shook hands, although Max treated Nicholas with chilly courtesy. He bent to pet Molly Belle. She responded with a gleeful tail wag.

"I'm Dorothy Edwards's brother," Nicholas clarified as Max straightened. "My wife, Emmanuelle, teaches harp lessons at Dorothy's store."

Max's expression eased. "You're off duty today, sheriff?" He sized up Nicholas' casual attire of khakis and a sweater, then positioned himself between Sarah and Nicholas, bracing a hand on a pole above her head. Although the men's verbal volley might have ended, Max was sending Nicholas a clear message.

He was interested in Sarah.

Because he was jealous. Jealous of *her.* The knowledge brought a wry smile.

"Nice bow tie," Nicholas said flatly.

"Thanks."

Okay, so it was unusual to wear a bow tie into a garden center, but Max was unique. The tie made him unforgettable, offering an air of distinguished academia. Although, considering his disheveled hair, he reminded her of an absent-minded professor.

"Today is my day off." Nicholas offered a scarcely

disguised smirk. "You don't, by any wild chance, break the law, Max, do you?"

"Never, sheriff. I'm new in town, and my rental is begging for a little holiday cheer." His gaze rested on Sarah. "I'm here to purchase flowers. Can you help me, Sarah?"

"Definitely."

"Dorothy mentioned our little town had acquired another fine musician," Nicholas said. "The other day, a man stopped by her store to buy a harmonica. I assume that was you?"

"I'm an average musician and a temporary resident," Max corrected.

Nicholas narrowed his gaze. "So, you're here *temporarily*."

"Yes."

Nicholas glanced at the pole where Max still braced his arm. "You won't want to get too familiar with folks, then, if you're leaving them soon." With a crisp nod, he turned toward the entrance. "Well, I'm off to grab a wreath. C'mon, Molly Belle."

The dog didn't move and stared up at Nicholas with a kindly expression.

"Come." Gently, Nicholas pulled the leash.

Again, no response.

"Up, Molly Belle." Sarah ducked beneath Max's arm and stepped over to the sunny spot where the dog sat. "Up Molly Belle. Obey your master."

Molly Belle immediately stood. Her tail wagged with so much enthusiasm her entire body shook.

"You do have a way with animals, Sarah." Nicholas extended a rueful laugh, then regarded Max. "Don't forget that she's an exceptional woman, and well-loved by everyone in this town."

Max gave Sarah a teasing wink. "I've already discovered she's extraordinary, and she's hands down the bravest woman I've ever known."

Sarah felt her cheeks flush pink. She blamed it on the heat and sun in the garden center.

As Nicholas and Molly Belle headed out the door, she set down the broom she hadn't realized she still held. "What types of plants are you looking for, Max?"

"My birds are happiest around dazzling flowers."

"The poinsettias this year are brilliant." She signaled for him to follow her. "Any particular shade?"

After he selected two vibrant red poinsettias and a purple cyclamen with upswept flowers and silver foliage, he said, "A bike was left in my rental and I rode it here. Any chance you can bring the plants by my house when you get off work?"

"I'm done at six o'clock."

He nodded. "Excellent. I'll prepare dinner for us."

"I can't." She bent to pick up Molly Belle's water dish. "I haven't decorated the inside of my house for Christmas and I planned to start hauling decorations down from the attic tonight. Although I don't know why I do both inside and outside decorating. The cats think the artificial tree is a scratching post, and the dogs chew the ornaments. And don't get me started on holiday baking. Why, the dogs will eat everything in sight and …"

She was babbling, and Max was grinning.

"Can decorating wait one more day?" he asked.

Something in his tone prompted her to study him.

A couple of customers wandered over, asking how to care for a Christmas cactus.

"My specialty," Sarah exclaimed. She cut her conversation with Max short and bustled over to show them the array of cacti. When they had chosen one and carried it to the register, Max was standing exactly where she'd left him.

She intended to refuse his invitation, but an entirely different answer emerged from her lips. "I need to stop home first."

"No problem. Say, seven o'clock?" His expression had softened. He looked pleased.

"You cook?"

"No. Fortunately, The Garden Terrace offers a delicious barbecue takeout."

"If you drive to the restaurant, you can easily swing to the nursery for your plants."

"Hmm." He shuffled his feet.

"Hmm?"

His gaze leveled on hers, the teasing evident. "I'll grant that your idea makes sense, although it ruins my excuse."

"Which is?"

"To see you tonight."

A giggle escaped her. "It would be a true calamity if your excuse was ruined."

"Is your answer a yes?"

"I'd love to have dinner with you."

Her spirits soared madly beneath the brilliance of his ready smile.

CHAPTER 8

*A*nother December night had fallen in the Carolinas, and stars emerged in the sky one by one.

When Max ushered Sarah inside his slightly messy bungalow, she immediately noticed the three colorful blue, white and green budgies near the window—two sharing one cage, the other alone in a separate cage. Mounds of scientific and bird magazines were stacked on a desk, the floor, and various shelves.

He kissed her tenderly on the cheek, thanked her for delivering the flowers, and rushed to take her coat. "Come. Sit on the sofa. It's comfortable. I made chip and dip."

Although he set the poinsettias and cyclamen on a tall pedestal table, she felt his probing silver gaze drift over her.

"I bought sandwiches, slaw, and a gingerbread cake for dessert." He gestured to the kitchen beyond. "Homemade wassail is simmering in the crock pot."

The cinnamon and apple aroma of the wassail made her mouth water. She grabbed a chip.

"I assumed you didn't cook," she said.

"I don't, but this is an easy family recipe."

Ah, so he had a family. When the subject had come up while they'd texted the night before, he'd veered to other topics—the weather, his research, his birds.

"Well, it smells delicious." She skimmed her fingers across her brown leather tote bag, which contained a precious manila envelope. When she'd stopped home after work to feed her animals and change into dark-wash jeans and a red striped sweater, Marge Addyson had met her at the door.

"Here is the photo from Big Brothers Big Sisters. Max looks young." Marge pressed the sealed manila envelope into Sarah's hands with excessive care. "He's very sweet and that worries me."

"Then or now?"

"Both. That sweet boy has become a charming, caring man."

"Why are you worried?"

"At choir rehearsal I stood across from him, and he could hardly keep his eyes off you. I wasn't sure the interest was mutual, but then I saw your return smiles. He cares for you a great deal."

"We've been friends only a short time," Sarah reminded Marge.

"But long enough. I know you, Sarah, and there's not a mean bone in your body. Do you believe in love at first sight?"

"Is there such a thing?"

"Certainly." Marge paused. "Max tries to hide it, but he's wearing his heart on his sleeve. I was at The Garden Terrace this afternoon for a bit of tea and cake, and he was there, ordering dinner for the two of you. He drove everyone crazy, asking about your favorite foods, obsessing about creating a splendid meal. It was almost as if the queen of England was coming to dine. He insisted on an exceptional holiday dessert."

"Lemon cake?"

"Gingerbread."

"He is very sweet." Sarah offered an affable grin, the kind that pacified fussy customers. Nonetheless, Marge wasn't easily placated.

"And?" Marge asked.

"I care for him a great deal too," Sarah replied. "However, he's leaving in January."

"Is he?"

"A promising career opportunity awaits him in Jacksonville. He's looking forward to it."

"Uh huh." Marge nodded perceptively. "Remember the Bible verse from Corinthians? 13:13?"

Sarah recited along with Marge. "And now these three remain: faith, hope, and love. But the greatest of these is love."

Now, standing in Max's living room, Sarah adjusted her leather tote bag.

"I finished another page of my research paper a few minutes ago," he was saying "This timing worked out well. Dinner at seven is an ideal fit for me."

"Me too."

"Do you often eat alone?" he asked.

"More often than not. You?"

"It depends." He exhaled. "Who am I kidding? I always eat alone." He ran his thumb and forefinger along the edge of a laptop computer, then firmly closed it. "Would you like to meet my uncooperative birds?"

She chuckled. "Sure."

"I want to tell you, Sarah, I'm thrilled you're here."

The question in his persuasive gray eyes was well-defined. *Do you feel the same?*

Slightly, she bobbed her head, a silent response he immediately understood.

He took her in his arms and kissed her. Long and sweet. Her eyes closed, and her breath came in a sigh. He kissed her again and again. Deeply, exquisitely, and soundly.

After the kisses, with her head against his chest, Sarah smiled. Things were so good.

But only for now.

She lived in Cherish, worked at a job she enjoyed, and embraced her church, family and friends. He was off to a promising career opportunity in Jacksonville.

She was a Christian.

He was not.

She loved Christmas.

He tolerated Christmas.

Therefore, she must steel herself for their imminent separation.

She pulled out of his arms, brushed a hand over her hair, which she'd secured in a French braid, and approached the bird cages.

The parakeets squawked as she peered inside.

"Hello, pretty birds," she said.

All three began chirping at once. Vibrant birdsongs flooded the room.

Max came beside her, looping an arm around her. "Fascinating," he said, staring at the birds.

"What's fascinating?"

"The birds. Their reaction to you. I've never seen such behavior from them before."

LATER, they dined in his tiny kitchen on scrumptious barbecue served on his finest white ceramic plates, drinking bottled water. When dinner was finished, he ushered her into the living room and switched on the overhead pendant light.

"Would you like a mug of my homemade wassail with our dessert?" he asked. "The gingerbread is from the restaurant."

"You didn't make the gingerbread too?" she joked.

"My contribution to a festive meal is wassail." He retreated to the kitchen, then returned with two steaming mugs of wassail and slices of gingerbread on a tray. The consummate host. He set the tray on the coffee table, handed her a mug, and took the other for himself. He tapped a seat beside him on the sofa, waited for her to sit, then settled so close their legs touched.

She sniffed appreciatively. Fruity, spicy aromas rising from the mug conjured images of Christmas. The perfect warm drink for a brisk winter night.

She happily sipped and nibbled. The gingerbread tasted fresh out of the oven—sugary, buttery, and delectable. She expressed her compliments aloud, then added, "You touched on the fact that wassail is a family recipe."

Max smiled, but it was distant and distracted. His forehead tensed, and he gave the impression of wrestling with her statement.

Into the beat of an uncomfortable silence, she said, "I have a surprise for you from Big Brothers Big Sisters. Marge Addyson came by my house." Sarah drew the envelope from her tote bag. "She brought this."

Max frowned and pushed his plate of half-eaten gingerbread to the side. "Which is?"

She noted the hesitation in his voice and dipped her head toward the envelope. "A photo of you when you lived in Cherish. You were … maybe twelve years old?"

He faltered. "Close enough."

"You attended Big Brothers, correct?"

"Every afternoon after school when the Monroes worked

late." He managed a sardonic laugh. "Or rather, when they forgot about me, which was often."

Knowing she might be placing him in an awkward situation, she handed him the envelope with the same care as Marge had handed it to her.

"You don't have to open it if you don't want to," Sarah said.

"I'd like to." Yet he flinched, as if gearing for a disappointment.

He shoved out a breath, then withdrew a black-and-white glossy photograph.

Sarah peered over his shoulder. "Is that you?"

He nodded. The dark-haired boy staring back at them held a stoic expression. His fingers grasped the collar of an enormous dog who stood by his side.

Her heart turned over at the boy's brave demeanor, despite the uncertainty in his eyes. She wanted to hug the photo to her chest, hug the young boy and never let him go.

"Your features haven't changed." Emotions welled inside her, although she managed to keep her tone even. "I'd recognize you anywhere with that determined expression. It's been what, over thirty years?"

Max sipped his wassail, a deceptively casual gesture. "I remember when this was taken, right around Christmas."

"Is that your dog?"

"Not mine. The Monroes." His gaze swung to the parakeets, who perched silently on their swings. "I missed that dog more than anything when I was moved to another foster family. More than I missed the Monroes. Much more."

Sarah swallowed the lump in her throat. "What type of breed was the dog?"

"A Labrador husky." Max rubbed his eyes with his forefinger.

She waited for him to continue, but he showed every sign

of being lost in troubled reflections. He stared at the photo, then looked away.

"What was the dog's name?"

"Tinsel."

She studied the photo. A young Max stood outside Big Brothers Big Sisters. His jeans were five inches too short for his long legs. He looked thin, almost undernourished. But his eyes were warm. Max's eyes.

"Want me to refresh your wassail?" he asked.

"I'm good, thanks." She held a hand over her mug. "Did you want to discuss the photo?"

"Nope. I'm a foster kid, Sarah. I moved around a lot. I had some good foster parents, and some not so good." He choked on the words. "The Monroes were not so good."

"And the family where you learned to make wassail?"

"Mr. Lenny's family."

"Where are they now?"

"He and his wife died. My foster brother, John, lives in Portugal. A few years ago, I gave up trying to stay in touch with him."

"Why?"

"What's the point? He lives so far away." Max didn't move a muscle. He cleared his throat. "Do you suppose it's in a man's best interest to suppress unhappy events, to keep them hidden from the woman he's falling in love with?"

Sarah's cheeks warmed. *Max was talking about her.* "The question is, how can that woman help a man repair those inner hurts?"

"I don't know. Sometimes I want relief from all the past pain." His face was expressionless. "My heritage, or rather, lack of heritage."

Now she understood where his resolve to make something of himself had been formed. It had started with the photo.

Or perhaps years earlier. Perhaps in other photos, in different towns with different families. Perhaps with different pets. And every single heartbreaking situation had strengthened Max with the fortitude to break free and make something of himself.

"Try prayer," she said softly.

"Been there." He linked his hands behind his head and peered at the ceiling pendant. "Done that."

"Try again."

His memories, unwelcome and agonizing, would continue to haunt him until he released them.

He dragged in a breath. "Years ago, I prayed to God to grant my foster brother a successful surgery."

"Go on."

"John only got one shot at a basketball scholarship. I knew how much it meant to Mr. Lenny."

She measured her words. "What happened?"

"God didn't listen. A week before Christmas, John's last surgery left him with a distinct limp and one leg shorter than the other."

"A physical disability." Sarah slid her fingers through Max's. The appeal, the warmth of his hand … this attraction only grew stronger each time they were together. "A handicap."

"Handicap? Ask John how much of a handicap. He didn't attend college. Now he lives in a faraway village, and I haven't seen him in years."

"How did Mr. Lenny react after the failed surgery? You obviously hold him in high esteem."

"He didn't share my anger and frustration at God. He was a pastor—a virtuous and noble man. After listening to my ranting, he reminded me that John was alive and healthy, which was all that mattered."

"Lenny was right."

"At what cost?" Max tore his hand from hers. "Why were the other athletes on John's team strong and whole? He had a promising pro basketball future."

"Lenny was a man of faith."

Max stared straight ahead. He didn't seem aware any longer that she sat beside him. "Lenny declared that John had God on his side and God was all he needed."

"You don't agree?"

"I can't shake my resentment toward a God who plays favorites."

"Try again. Try prayer," she repeated.

"Prayer will make the hurt go away?"

"God will. Reflect on the healing truths of His words every day."

Max lifted his arms and surveyed the room. "I don't see God anywhere."

"Just because you don't see Him, doesn't mean He isn't here."

His expression gradually relaxed, and her chest still ached for him. He had erected a barrier around his heart. A barrier that was impossible to breach until he put aside his resentment and anger.

Pushing up from the sofa, he carried himself stiffly as he walked to the computer.

A moment later, birdsongs floated through the room, the same songs he'd recorded during their hike.

She came to stand close and motioned to the parakeets. "They aren't repeating anything?"

"Nothing. Not even when I play my harmonica."

The single green and white budgie in a wrought iron cage flapped her elegant feathers. In a clear, bell-like voice, she said, "God bless us, everyone."

CHAPTER 9

A few hours later, Sarah headed home.

Max sat on his living room's threadbare carpet and leaned against the sofa.

She was exceptional, fascinating, and extraordinary. More than extraordinary.

The Big Brothers photo had transported him back to the land of unfulfilled dreams. Life with the Monroes had been intolerable, specifically during Max's difficult adolescence.

He wasn't certain why Marge Addyson had gone to the trouble to find that photo and then give it to Sarah. A woman of well-meaning honesty, she may have wanted him to confront past issues in order to move forward.

But he'd done that already, hadn't he? He was accomplished. He'd succeeded in establishing a noteworthy career. Besides, life-altering injustices could never be forgiven.

He shook his head, a rueful smile. His thoughts harbored the very bitterness he thought he'd overcome.

Days ago, Sarah had encouraged him to reflect on the truths of God's word.

"Start with Psalms," she had advised. "The verses will promote healing, comfort and well-being."

"All that?" he questioned.

"All that," she echoed an assurance.

He'd heeded her advice about reading the Bible, although he hadn't told her. It wasn't a subject that came up in daily conversation. Although he could have told her tonight ...

Sarah. Sarah. Sarah. They were friends, and there were times when she kept him at arms-length. But there were other times when an electrical current, a snap of lightning, flowed between them. Even when they were a few feet apart, it seemed as if they touched.

He unfolded himself and straightened. He embraced the tranquility he felt when he was with her, and their evening had passed in a blur of laughs and kisses and a hint of rose-wood perfume from her fragrant hair.

Peace was indeed a part of her, a serenity and content-ment he attributed to more than her excitement for the upcoming Christmas season. It was her Christian faith. This woman, this town, was a shift for him, when his daily life was filled with more duties than he could accomplish.

He mentioned as much to Gerry when they met a few days later for an impromptu jam session at Musically Yours. Dorothy had afforded them an after-hours studio, and the men had gratefully accepted.

A grin on his weather-beaten features, his fuzzy eyebrows raised in a tickled question, Gerry responded by saying, "So, you're in love?"

Max pulled back, disconcerted. "Who said that?"

"You did."

"When?"

"By your eyes, words and actions."

Max navigated to safer ground. "You sure you don't mind

meeting here to rehearse? The drive from Perrytown is a haul for you."

"You and I share a passion for music, and rehearsing in person is a blessing."

Max tugged out his harmonica. "I assume your wife is understanding about the hours away from little Freddie?"

"Totally. As long as I'm home by ten o'clock." Gerry set an amp on the floor, then searched for an outlet. He plugged one end of a cable into the amp, the other into the guitar. Snaps and shrill bangs followed, and Gerry switched the volume down.

Because Max lived a few blocks from the store, he had walked, admiring the decorations on the way over, likening them to a Christmas postcard.

The temperature had dropped in the past few days, and blades of grass peeked through a frost of white. Holly bushes were in vibrant red-berry bloom, and blinking red, green, and white lights were everywhere.

He passed a busy coffee shop with folks bustling in and emerging with large cups of hot chocolate topped with creamy whipped cream. Aromas of fresh brewed coffee and toasty chocolate brought scents of the season to mind. A vendor on the corner peddled roasted chestnuts in paper cones. Giggling youngsters ran by him, their laughter high-spirited over the chatter of adults. On side streets, flickering candles gleamed from residences, and vibrant lights from their evergreen trees shone from the windows.

Max never remembered decorating a pine tree, except for the year with Lenny and his family. The snapshot of that one perfect tree, the one perfect Christmas, lived forever in his mind.

When he reached Musically Yours, he was immediately immersed in the harmonies of guitar music sounding from the speakers, the cozy overhead lights, and the warmth of an excellent heating system. After greeting Gerry, who was already there, he asked what they were listening to.

"Joseph Slater's newest worship song, a contemporary Christian arrangement," Gerry noted. "He slowed the tempo, kept the instrumentals simple, and let his voice do the heavy lifting. He's an awesome vocalist."

"Awesome, indeed." Max tilted his head, and allowed the poignant lyrics to wash over him.

"'Mary Did You Know?' is one of my favorite pieces," Gerry said. "Are you aware that the composer took seven years to complete it?"

"Good things are worth the wait, time, and effort," Max replied. "And when you find something good?"

"Never let her go."

Max regarded Gerry. "I'm assuming you mean Sarah?" he asked, and then went on to talk about her in such a way that Gerry told him he was in love.

Gerry brought on a grin and didn't reply.

Focus on the music, Max told himself as Gerry finished tuning his guitar.

They decided on a playlist for their upcoming performance—a medley of carols that included, "O Christmas Tree," "Santa Claus Is Coming To Town," and the finale, "The Twelve Days of Christmas."

"A fun holiday singalong," Gerry said. "For the encore, we'll perform "All Is Well," which is uplifting and inspirational."

"You're certain we'll get enough applause for an encore?"

"Stranger things have happened," Gerry mused while he plucked his guitar. "On another note, my wife and baby are attending. My mother-in-law too."

"How's little Freddie lately?"

"I anticipate my wife's hasty exit after our first song."

"Hopefully, we won't sound that bad."

"We're fairly decent. Besides, my wife deserves a night out."

"With little Freddie," Max reminded with a grin. He pointed to an autographed album hanging on a wall, the cover depicting Joseph Slater and an acoustic guitar. "Musically Yours sure promotes this guy."

"He's a big-name artist who lives in Cherish."

"Joseph settled here," Max mused, arching a single eyebrow.

"Same goes for Ryan Edwards. Love is like a fairy-tale, at least that's what my wife parrots. Joseph met Scarlett when he was here for a music promotion. He decided to put down roots after all those years of touring and married her last year."

"Because of Scarlett, he gave up his career?"

"Hardly. Life is a compromise, my friend, and you're clearly smitten too. Are you still coming to my house on Christmas Day for dinner?"

"Unless you're having second thoughts."

"On the contrary, I'm thinking about inviting my great-niece to join us."

Max beamed. "A tremendous idea."

"I suspected you'd be receptive." Gerry smirked, then leaned back in a wooden chair he'd snagged from the student waiting area. "Now let's rock-and-roll to some favorite Christmas carols."

On the Friday evening of The Bearded Elves' debut, Sarah grabbed a seat at a round table near the band, along with Dorothy, Ryan, Gerry's wife and son and mother-in-law, Nicholas, and Emmanuelle.

She'd dressed with care for the evening—a fit and flare lace dress, strappy-leopard print heels she already wanted to kick off, and sparkly gumdrop-red earrings. She'd topped her outfit with the fine royal blue wool coat she wore on special occasions.

During the past two weeks, lighthearted conversations and dinners with Max at The Garden Terrace, their stolen kisses, their bantering texts, had become routine. Max invited her on another hike, and she'd happily accepted.

Each time they parted, he promised to see or text her the following day.

And he always did.

She should have been joyful. She was. But a heaviness weighed on her spirit because the days flew too quickly. Soon, January would arrive.

Refreshed by endless glasses of sugar-free lemonade, she sang along to the familiar carols with the others, especially during Ryan's sidesplitting rendition of "The Twelve Days Of Christmas."

As he reached the final, "And a partridge in a pear tree," his operatic voice swelled through the restaurant.

Max confirmed his ability as an excellent harmonica player. He'd been too modest, she thought. Whenever he hit an imagined wrong note, he glanced at her with a chagrined smile. The keen, honed bite of blues he produced on such an inexpensive instrument proved him a man of many talents, and pride flowed through her.

Can you believe the tunes a person can produce from such a modest instrument? he had texted a few days earlier. *Wood, two pieces of metal and minute brass reeds.*

The only thing I can play is the radio, she'd texted back in jest, despite his assurances that he would teach her how to read music.

When? she'd wanted to ask. However, she remained silent.

Wait till you hear our encore, he'd responded.

What's the name of the song?

It's an inspirational piece. It'll bring tears to your eyes.

She was seeing a side of him she hadn't envisioned beneath his polka-dotted tie, chambray shirt, and jeans—a look she'd catalogued as distinctly Max.

During each fifteen-minute break between sets, he'd made it a point to sit next to her. He drew her close, his arm draped around her shoulders in a gesture that seemed possessive, but delighted Sarah immeasurably.

After the band's first set, Melissa, the baby, and her mother left. Little Freddie had been fairly well-behaved, and Melissa and her mother had taken turns walking around the restaurant to soothe the baby.

Sarah surprised herself by offering to help. She'd never been an active participant in group situations, and had felt increasingly uncomfortable in even small crowds now—reticent to speak in case she'd misheard someone, and hesitant to ask people to repeat themselves.

In any case, she wasn't used to these feelings—the attention from Max, the joy of being among a welcoming, friendly group. This was camaraderie, sharing jubilant hours with friends and family who cared.

After the rousing rendition of "The Twelve Days of Christmas," Gerry and Max grinned and bowed to enthusiastic applause. As calls for an encore rose, Max stepped down from the small stage. Dorothy stopped him, saying something to him. Sarah couldn't see Dorothy's face, but she could see Max's, and she couldn't resist eavesdropping by reading his lips.

"January first," he seemed to be saying, "I'm eager to leave for Florida and head up an ornithology department."

January. Leave. Eager.

Sarah's stomach tightened.

She half rose in her seat. But no, she shouldn't be

surprised. He'd repeatedly cited his new Jacksonville job. His time in Cherish was temporary.

Unexpectedly weak, she braced her hands on the arms of her chair. She'd been a fool for falling for him. Hoping against hope, while knowing the romance would come to an end in January.

Questions surfaced with no answers. He was a man of his word and had accepted the university position months ago.

Nevertheless, confronting the pain of his departure brought unexpected heartache. They'd never actually discussed him leaving. It was a point in the future neither had chosen to broach.

No matter. She'd slip into the background again, a pattern she'd honed over the years. Loneliness encroached so swiftly she couldn't react, save for tugging on her shoes and scouting out the quickest path to the exit.

She'd been unmoored by the attentions of a stranger. She'd only known him a few weeks. *A few enchanted weeks.*

She swallowed hard and stood to leave as soon as Max and Gerry returned to the stage to more applause. The diners had awarded the men a standing ovation, and the enthusiastic applause soon quieted.

Max angled a glance at her with a broad smile. *Success*, he seemed to say. *Thank you for supporting me and my music.*

She grabbed her coat and turned away, then rounded to glimpse him one last time. His chin drew in, perplexed, as he lifted the harmonica to his lips.

Dorothy caught her hand. "You're leaving? What about the last song?"

"It's later than I thought." Sarah made a show of peering at her watch, aware of how quiet everyone at her table had become. However, she couldn't face another conversation with Max.

From the onset, he'd spoken the truth. Nonetheless, truth

was difficult to confront, especially when it waylaid you at the happiest moment of your life.

Nicholas stood and excused himself from the others. "Sarah, I'll walk you to the door."

"Thanks. I can manage." She veered left, away from him, struggling to keep her emotions in check.

"It's no bother. I have an ulterior motive."

They passed straggling diners, plates of food being cleared from empty tables by tired-looking waitresses, while Max's bluesy harmonica accompanied Gerry's vocals.

"'All is well all is well, ... Sing Alleluia.'"

"It'll bring tears to your eyes," Max had said.

And it did.

The lyrics were hopeful and encouraging, and Max harmonized with Gerry, his baritone voice complementing the uplifting words.

A Christian song. Max was singing a Christian song.

"What's your motive?" she asked Nicholas when they reached the entry. "The abandoned puppy?"

"Yep. And if I don't find a home for him, he'll end up in an animal shelter. It's a no-kill shelter, but still ..." His words trailed off.

She opened her mouth. Closed it. She was about to refuse when she paused. A darling puppy would be the ideal distraction for her hurt heart.

"I'll take him," she burst out.

"Sarah, thank you! Why did you change your mind?"

"I can't let a lovable puppy spend the holidays in a shelter."

"I'll bring him over to your house in a couple days." Clearly, Nicholas was uncertain whether he'd understood her. "I realize Christmas Eve is almost here ..."

"No worries. The puppy has spent too many nights alone already."

CHAPTER 10

*O*n Christmas Eve, Sarah sat alone.

Only for tonight. Tomorrow, she would drive to Perrytown to dine with her great-uncle, his wife, and little Freddie. He'd phoned her, and she'd gratefully accepted the invitation. In years past, she'd spent Christmas Day with her parents and brothers, traveling to their homes in the Carolina mountains. They'd moved away from Cherish, and she was the only one who had remained.

This year, she'd elected to stay home with her growing number of animals.

She had already attended the three o'clock church service. She'd done so purposely, in order not to run into Max, who would be singing in the choir at the six o'clock service. Right about now, he would be entering the church to get ready.

She'd returned from the service invigorated and encouraged. The sermon had touched on how God didn't free people from traumatic situations, but rather, He was there walking with them every step of the way.

Yes, she'd experienced troubles and challenges. However,

any expectations fixed on the Messiah to grant a person's peace came from within. God didn't promise an easy life, and Sarah couldn't experience peace when she had been anticipating a textbook Christmas with the man she loved.

Her mind traveled back to the loving way Max had regarded her—by the river, at the restaurant, in his home. His tenderness when he kissed her.

No. She couldn't allow him into her thoughts anymore. He belonged to the huge, widespread world of birds and his research, not the microscopic town of Cherish.

Yet she'd felt loved and protected when his lips pressed against hers—his strong arms shielding her when they'd encountered that bear.

She hadn't wanted to lose that, the sense of being cherished and safeguarded.

But Max's love was never hers to begin with.

She peered at the roly-poly puppy nestled in his crate. Already, he'd created a wealth of joy in a short period of time.

He was beginning to eat solids, and she'd continued the transition of soaking the food in warm water, then blending it to the texture of gruel. A fresh supply of water was ever present.

The past couple days, she'd brought his toys into her home first for the other animals to sniff. When the puppy arrived, the dogs ignored him except for an occasional sniff. She'd rewarded their unaggressive behavior with upbeat praise, and had placed the resident dogs' toys and food bowls in a separate location.

Likewise, the cats wandered over for a sniff, then dismissed the puppy.

Sarah's goal was to allow the animals to learn to trust each other. So far, so good.

She switched on a holiday radio station, and The Mormon Tabernacle choir sang "Adeste Fideles" in Latin.

Max would've appreciated the arrangement. He was so musical.

Sighing, she looked at the framed photo on her side table. When she had finally scrolled through the photos she'd taken with her cell phone the day of their hike, she found a wonderful one of Max. It was a profile picture. His face had been near the camera, and every handsome quality was evident—the dark stubble of his beard, his silver-gray eyes, his determined demeanor.

She'd also gotten a surprisingly good photo of the bear. She'd auto-merged them into a silly collage, the bear and Max staring at each other, eye to eye.

She'd planned to gift him the photo and had bought a wooden frame depicting the great outdoors with the words Into the Woods on it. She'd captioned the photo, "I knew we were safe all along."

Max's words.

She would never hear his voice again. She squeezed her eyes shut and took a deep breath. "I love you, Max," she murmured, vowing to rely on time and faith to heal her broken heart.

She slid the photo into a bag and placed it in a drawer in the side table.

As Max looked around the church on Christmas Eve from his vantage point on the top riser, his heart dropped. He scanned the pews—the exquisitely appointed windows and altars bedecked with the brilliant display of flowers that Sarah had arranged. But Sarah was not there.

"Surely, she'll attend church," he muttered to Gerry, as the men took their places in the baritone section.

Marge Addyson, standing near the altar, turned. "She attended the earlier service," she said.

She did? Why?

Two days ago, Sarah had left The Garden Terrace before The Bearded Elves' performance was over and without a farewell. Thereafter, Max's phone calls and voice mails had gone unanswered.

The previous morning, he'd stopped by the nursery. Her coworker, Bonnie, declared that Sarah was in the greenhouse dealing with seedlings and couldn't be disturbed.

The service ended with the cantata and Max's harmonica solo. When the service was over, he exited the church with his heart touched and his spirits lifted. The sermon had delivered a message of optimistic goodwill.

"God's son appeared in the least likely situation and to humble people," the pastor had addressed the congregation. "Forgive and let your resentments go. What will prevent your happiness is to strive for perfection in yourself and others."

Hadn't Max always sought excellence? Blame it on his upbringing, but he'd endeavored to become top-notch in his profession. But what good was that perfection without someone to love?

Unwilling to accept the end of their relationship, he strode from the church to Sarah's house. In a short time, he'd become accustomed to small-town living, where most places were within a few blocks' walking distance. He'd purchased a special present for her and held the package securely under his arm.

When he reached her house, he stood silently on her front porch. Although he didn't move, wild barking sounded from inside before he could even knock.

Then the barking ceased.

He knocked, hesitant to ring her doorbell. Okay, maybe

he shouldn't have dropped by unannounced, but what else could he do when she kept slipping away from him?

Suppose she was sleeping?

At eight o'clock on a clear and cold Christmas Eve? Sarah? Unless she wasn't home … But where …

Tiny yelps sounded. A yipping.

The door opened a crack, and a wobbly puppy shoved his nose through the opening, wagging a fluffy white tail.

Sarah scooped up the puppy, then gasped as she stood in the doorway. "Max?"

"Merry Christmas."

"How long were you standing on the porch?"

He shrugged. "A while."

"What were you doing?"

"Praying."

"Praying? What are you praying for? An extraordinary gift on Christmas Eve?"

"I'm praying for the most extraordinary of gifts. You."

Her striking green eyes glistened with tears, her features a flood of emotions. "Merry Christmas."

"May I come in?" She couldn't just stand at the door holding a puppy.

"Yes. Please."

He stepped inside and brushed a kiss across her temple. She cuddled the tiny Yorkipoo to her chest. He grinned at the pom-pom tail, the paws reminding him of a hedgehog, and the molten-brown eyes peeking beneath half-closed lids. Perhaps he wasn't a Yorkipoo …

"Apparently, Sheriff Nicholas convinced you?" Max asked as he stroked the puppy's velvety fur.

"Careful," she warned. "His teeth are like little needles." She set the puppy inside a blanketed crate. The two older dogs settled. The cats walked away.

And Sarah walked into Max's embrace.

He drew her closer, pressing his lips to hers, fearful to break the hold for fear she might disappear.

When the kiss ended, she rubbed her cheek against his jacket. "I'm glad you're here."

Her home wasn't decorated for the holidays, which surprised him, considering her festive porch.

"My fake tree and ornaments are in the attic." She seemed to read his mind. "I haven't had time."

Or rather, had she felt like him, and didn't have the heart to decorate?

She was gorgeous in a crimson cashmere sweater and form-fitting black pants. Her figure was trim with curves, a wreath of dark russet curls framed her perfect face.

"I do have appropriate holiday cookies and eggnog, if you're interested," she said. "And both were bought from the grocery store."

They shared another commonality besides coffee and hiking and a love for animals. They appreciated store-bought items when homemade wasn't an option. Or, he supposed, even if it was.

He smiled, removed his jacket, and adjusted his bow tie. For the Christmas Eve service, he'd elected to wear black dress pants and a crisp white shirt.

"Can I be direct?" he asked, after she'd taken a jug out of the refrigerator, poured him a glass of eggnog, and set out a platter of frosted vanilla sugar cookies in the shape of snowmen.

"I wouldn't expect anything else."

He placed his gift on the coffee table. He'd wrapped it in plain brown paper tied with twine, topped with a green and white parakeet ornament.

"Why did you leave the restaurant without saying good-bye?" His hand slid up her arm in a caress. "Furthermore, why were you avoiding me? Is my singing that bad?"

She smiled. "No."

"I'd like to continue seeing you."

She fixed her gaze on a point beyond him. "I can't deal with a long-distance relationship and you're leaving for Jacksonville in a week."

He heard the hurt in her tone. His gaze stayed on her.

He invited her to sit on the sofa in the living room and he settled beside her. "Who said I was moving to Jacksonville?"

"You've mentioned little else since you arrived in Cherish. The other night at The Garden Terrace when you spoke with Dorothy, you declared your eagerness to leave for Florida in January and head an ornithology department."

And then it hit him. Sarah cared about him. Deeply. So deeply, she couldn't face him leaving.

And he was delighted.

He pulled her nearer. "I said I was eager to greet the new head of the ornithology department in Florida in January."

She blinked. "I don't understand."

"I declined the position. The latest candidate is a colleague from my New York university days who's done amazing research on zebra finches. She's a workaholic and will be an excellent fit."

"So much for my lip-reading abilities. And eavesdropping." Sarah sat straighter. "You didn't accept the position?"

"No."

"I made an appointment with an audiologist to test my hearing. I've read that I won't be as fatigued at the end of the day if I haven't had to struggle with the effort of listening."

"If you indeed have a hearing loss, it should be addressed." Max smoothed his lips over her hair. "I should've been clearer about my feelings. I would've been if you hadn't vanished."

"I haven't gone anywhere."

"This project has involved numerous researchers working

around the world. My bit with budgies is only a small part of the larger study on birdsongs."

"And?"

"The paper will take a couple years to complete, especially as current research sends scientists in different directions. Which means I'm not going anywhere. I can continue my research here and will receive a full-time salary."

"You're staying in Cherish?"

"I renewed my lease on 8 Poplar Lane."

"Does this mean more hiking adventures?"

"Weekly." He grinned. "This place, and you, have allowed me to slow down and reflect. However, I will have to travel to Jacksonville twice a semester to meet with other members of the department. I'm hoping you'll accompany me."

"I'd love to."

"I'd also like to visit the university I attended in New York."

"I've never seen a big city."

"New York is filled with diversity, culture, and excitement. I'll take you to see the famous landmarks."

"I'd like that," she said softly.

"And I have a brother in Portugal."

"Yes."

"I need to reach out to him again. If he invites us to travel to Portugal to visit him, will you accompany me?"

She nodded. "Happily."

"Good." He peered upward. "Where's your attic?"

"You're looking in the right direction."

"I've only decorated a Christmas tree once in my life—with Lenny and his family."

"Is that a hint?"

"A broad hint. But first." He nodded to his gift.

Glancing at him, she unraveled the twine. In the box was

an ornament—a bear, hiker boots and the inscription, "Take a hike."

She smiled, smoothed her fingers over the words, then curled near him. "You remembered?"

"Of course. After numerous phone requests to the ranger, a shipment finally arrived."

"Thank you." She slid open a drawer in the table beside her and handed him a bag. "I'm sorry it isn't wrapped. By the time the order arrived, I assumed I'd never see you again."

"Yet here I am." He pulled the frame out of the bag and read aloud her caption. "I knew we were safe all along."

"Because we'll do life together."

For a long while, he held her. "I missed you at church tonight. Mrs. Addyson remarked on the preacher's outstanding sermon."

"Yes. I thought so too."

"I played the harmonica. The choir was beautiful."

"I'm sure they were. I'm sure you were awesome."

"You'll hear me play and sing again because I joined the choir." He tipped back his head, as if he were gazing toward heaven. "I was distracted—by my bitterness, and by life. I'm starting to realize that God is for me, not against me. My perspective was messed up, but finally, at forty, I'm seeing more clearly."

"God has always been your champion. He is never against you."

She whispered a word of praise, and Max joined in.

"Gerry declared that dinner tomorrow is at two o'clock, give or take a few hours," she said.

He returned her smile. "He told me the same. I guess it depends on little Freddie's schedule."

She hesitated. "I didn't realize you were dining there too."

"He didn't mention it?" Max chuckled. "He must've forgotten when he phoned you."

"You knew he called?"

"I stood next to him when he made the phone call."

"So, you figured between tonight and tomorrow, we'd see each other?"

"That's one of the things I love about Christmas. All this togetherness." He reached for his jacket and pulled out a handful of wildflowers from his pocket—intense violets and pale blue ivy. "These grow at the edge of town. I'm impressed that plants bloom here in the winter. I'd forgotten. In any event, I picked them for you. Sorry they're wilted."

"They're not. They're beautiful."

He muffled her protest with a deep kiss and drew her into his arms. "I can't give you much, but I'll give you my love."

"I love you too."

The puppy whimpered, and Sarah freed him from his crate and nestled him in her arms. When Max extended his hands, she placed the tiny bundle in his lap.

"What's his name?" he asked.

"Tiny Tim."

Max swallowed the thickness in his throat, the emotions overcoming him.

He drew Sarah near. She was all he needed, all he'd been searching for. The woman he loved by his side, a reverence for a God who was no longer elusive, and a significant, heartwarming Christmas.

"Merry Christmas, Max," Sarah whispered. "And God bless us, every one."

The End

AMANDA'S EASY WASSAIL

Ingredients:

2 cups apple juice
   2 cups orange juice
   2 cups cranberry juice
   2 cinnamon sticks

Add everything to a crockpot, mix, and warm until the desired temperature is reached.

For a larger batch: (almost a gallon)

AMANDA'S EASY WASSAIL

5 cups apple juice
  5 cups orange juice
  5 cups cranberry juice
  3 or 4 cinnamon sticks, as desired
  Enjoy!

A NOTE FROM JOSIE

Thank you for reading my holiday romance, A Christmas Puppy To Cherish. I hope you enjoyed this heartwarming, inspirational story. This is the fourth book in my contemporary "Cherish" series.

You don't need ears to hear God's plan. All you need is an open heart...

This story is set in the charming fictional small town of Cherish, South Carolina. The book follows A Love Song To Cherish, A Christmas To Cherish, and A Valentine To Cherish.

In A Christmas Puppy To Cherish, I introduce two new characters to our beloved mix of familiar heroes and heroines. Many of you may know that music is an important part of my life, and many of the characters are musicians.

I also researched the hero, Maxwell's, fascinating profession of ornithology. (The study of birds.)

And the heroine, Sarah, with her kind heart, is the perfect match for him.

If you loved this story as much as I loved writing it, please help *other people find it by posting your review.*

A Christmas Puppy To Cherish is available in ebook, Paperback, Hardcover, Large Print Paperback, and Audiobook.

My Spotify List for A Christmas Puppy To Cherish is here.

HOLLY'S *Gift*

SMALL-TOWN CHRISTMAS WISHES SERIES

USA TODAY BESTSELLING AUTHOR
JOSIE RIVIERA

PRAISE AND AWARDS

USA TODAY bestselling author
#1 Bestseller Religious Short Stories
#1 New Release Asian American Literature
#1 New Release Religious Short Stories

CHAPTER 1

*H*olly Kim's piano student was always dependable. Well, nearly always. But the wintry weather in Snowflake, Colorado, might have delayed her.

At least, that's what Holly assumed as she peered at her watch for the tenth time in ten minutes.

Rather than remain at her piano bench in her cozy living room, Holly took up a position by the window of her first floor apartment and surveyed the drifting snow covering the tree branches. Dusk edged the gray sky with a pink blush before the sun set, and murky clouds emerged. With less than four weeks remaining until Christmas, the forecast called for freezing temperatures.

And this Thursday was no exception.

She opened the French door separating her living room from the kitchen, then prepared a cup of tea while she waited for Jasmine.

"We prefer a white Christmas season, right, Butter-scotch?" Holly expressed her sentiments aloud to the calico cat sitting in a laundry basket in her well-scrubbed kitchen.

She'd rescued him from an animal shelter when he was a young adult. He'd been missing half an ear and crawling with fleas, but she'd nursed Butterscotch back to health.

The cat looked up from licking its white paws, but only for an instant. Apparently, paw licking took precedence over Holly's concerns.

As the water in her teapot heated, Holly's thoughts circled back to Jasmine. The child hadn't shown up for her piano lesson the previous week, either. And prior to that, Holly had had to cancel two weeks' worth of lessons for all of her students in November, as she had traveled to North Carolina to help take care of her aunt. She'd emailed all her students to notify them. So, for Jasmine, there had been no lesson in a month.

Holly knew that Emily Webster, Jasmine's mother, drove the eleven-year-old girl from their home in Snowflake to Holly's home in Pine Cone Valley every Thursday, then waited outside in her pick-up truck. She also knew that Emily was a single parent.

Despite being unfamiliar with specific aspects of the family situation, Holly had suspected for a number of months that things in the home weren't right. Jasmine and Emily seemed isolated from any other family and friends. And Jasmine, a diligent student who loved playing the piano and had taken lessons for two years, had seemed distracted and listless all Fall.

"Is anything wrong?" Holly had asked Jasmine in late September. As a professional teacher, she chose not to pry into a personal situation, even though she'd developed a genuine bond with the girl.

"Nope," came Jasmine's typical close-mouthed reply. "Everything's fine."

Yet, when it came time to pay her October tuition, Jasmine declared that she'd forgotten the check.

"Tell your mother not to worry about payment," Holly said. "I'm happy to teach you at no charge. You're a promising student, and I expect you'll become a fine pianist."

On the few instances when Holly had spoken with Emily, a withdrawn woman wearing shapeless clothes, she'd seemed rushed and hadn't met Holly's gaze. Jasmine was an only child, she'd explained.

After pouring boiling water into a ceramic mug, Holly lifted the window blinds and peered out onto her small garden. More snow, collecting quicker now.

Earlier that day, she'd baked Chinese Christmas cookies which had cooled on wire trays on her granite countertop all afternoon.

She plated a cookie, placed an herbal tea bag into her mug to brew, then flicked a glance at her watch again.

With a sigh, she stepped into the living room. She placed her mug on a garden stool she used as a side table, nibbled at the cookie, then sat at her spinet piano. A Chopin nocturne she'd memorized in college flowed easily, and her fingertips glided over the keys. The music was hauntingly beautiful, and Holly paused after the opening measures.

Each time she played a chord, she thought of Jasmine. When she finished, she gathered up the holiday sheet music she'd intended to teach her, which included a duet arrangement of "Silent Night." Unexpectedly, tears gathered in her eyes.

The living room was quiet. Too quiet. The clock on the mantel heralded the seconds with a near-silent tick.

Quiet. Something she'd avoided for weeks. Times like this.

Time to think.

About life. About sorrow. About the death of a friend.

Because of her sad thoughts, Holly picked up her cell

phone and rang her aunt Clementine in North Carolina to bolster her spirits.

In her sixties, plump and with age spots on her fragile skin, Holly surmised that Aunt Clementine would be either at her preferred vantage point—sitting on the front porch swing watching the neighbors' activities—or caring for her rescue dogs.

Her aunt answered immediately. "Holly, I recognized your caller ID. Hang on a second—" Her warmhearted voice was invariably a comfort to Holly, as was the recognizable barking of Angel, one of the current rescues, a pint-sized, skinny cocker spaniel with intelligent eyes and soft brown fur.

"Has Angel gained any weight since I left?" Holly asked.

"All she does is eat, and the vet told me that her health has done a complete about-face."

Holly recalled with crystal clarity the two weeks she'd spent with her aunt in November while Clementine had convalesced from hip surgery, and Angel's face-to-face doggy kisses and demands for belly rubs.

As if on cue, a dog barked.

"Is this a good time to talk?" Holly asked. "I'm waiting for a student and hoping she'll still show up."

Holly visualized her aunt wrapping a crocheted shawl around her shoulders, then busying herself with filling Angel's water bowl. "Anything in particular you'd like to discuss?"

"The loss of my wonderful friend."

"Charity Hart." Her aunt paused. "I'm sorry you weren't able to attend her funeral because you stayed to help me."

"I wanted you to get back on your feet." Holly said.

Aunt Clementine was a caring, giving person, much like Charity. However, unlike Charity, who'd longed for a husband and children, Aunt Clementine was a confirmed spinster.

"Besides, I love spending time in the Carolinas." Holly injected a note of levity into an otherwise somber conversation and subsequently failed when her voice caught. In the preceding days, she'd sought to suppress the high school memories, and now they were flashing before her eyes.

"I can't believe she's gone," Holly said. "Charity never uttered a bad word about anyone. When we first met, I was a little skittish after hearing about her reputation."

"Good or bad?"

"The best." Holly took another bite of her cookie, relishing the crunch of chow mein noodles and peanuts. "She cultivated relationships with everybody and wasn't focused on other people's opinions. Her giving came from her sweet heart. She did the right thing, all day, every day."

"Did she always live in Snowflake?"

"She left to attend college in Denver." Holly cradled the phone on her shoulder as she drank her tea. "But after her diagnosis, she chose to live with her mother."

And then, two weeks before Thanksgiving, Charity died.

"Don't cry for me," she'd told her mother, told her friends. "God is faithful."

"You mentioned she left no husband or children?" Aunt Clementine asked.

"She said she'd know when God placed the right man in her life."

Unlike herself, Holly thought, since she'd done the marriage part and failed miserably. Jim, her ex, was cruel and interested only in himself. He'd committed infidelity, left her and initiated the divorce. She'd been broken, fighting a loneliness so deep that she'd turned inward while she desperately tried to maintain an outward composure.

Marrying him had proved that she wasn't cut out for dating and men and happily-ever-after.

Awash with uncomfortable remembrances, she swept Jim from her mind and focused on the loss of her friend.

"Charity was a servant of God," her aunt said.

Holly nodded into the phone. "We attended Bible club together and studied scripture at our youth group. We'd sit in the front row and take notes."

"I imagine you heeded the pastor's words in respectful silence."

"Well, with a little giggling now and then," she admitted.

They were young then. Now, in their early thirties, they were still young.

"Is Pastor Tom still the pastor at Snowflake Chapel?"

"He is," Holly said, "along with the associate pastor, Manuel Cruz, and his wife, Alma. Whenever I'm the substitute pianist, I see them." Otherwise, she attended her local church in Pine Cone Valley.

At the same moment that she spoke, Holly stood and wandered to the enormous picture window overlooking the street. Outside, the ground shimmered a glistening, icy silver.

It had been a late afternoon much like this one when she'd first met Charity. In turn, Charity had introduced Holly to her friends—Caro, Taye, Sara, Nate, and Mia. They all became instant comrades for they shared a common denominator: They were all Christians. Over the years, they'd remained friends, though some had moved away.

"Holly, are you still there?" her aunt asked.

"Sorry, Aunt Clementine. I was thinking. You may not remember, but during Christmas winter break of my senior year, several of us decided to gift a special person with something we had chosen."

"And who was your special person?"

"It was a secret, which made the activity more delightful and memorable."

"Who did you choose, dear?" her aunt repeated.

"I chose you." Holly smiled, assuming she could divulge her secret after all these years. "You lived in Snowflake at the time, not far from my parents."

Her aunt chuckled.

"I bought you a picture album and filled it with photos of our family," Holly continued, "so you could recall our fun times."

Secret Angels, Charity had declared.

"I wondered who delivered that photo album wrapped in red polka-dot paper and tied with twine. The doorbell rang, but when I opened the door, no one stood there."

Holly giggled. "And now you know."

"I suspected, but was never certain. That album was filled with many precious images, and your mother and I were as close as two sisters could be."

Holly fingered the sterling silver charm bracelet she always wore, a beloved memory of her mother's thoughtfulness. Each charm signified important events in Holly's life—a piano, a flag of South Korea, and her graduation.

"Equally important was the gift of your time and interest," her aunt went on. "I can't tell you how much I appreciate your kindness."

"Nothing's changed. You were like a mother to me after my parents died."

Holly experienced another rush of sadness for another loss. Her adoptive parents had died while serving as missionaries overseas, and it wasn't supposed to happen that way. They were compassionate citizens, trying to help others.

As usual, her aunt was spot on. Time with loved ones was the most precious gift.

Time.

She should have made time to visit Charity when she got sick, Holly thought. But by the time she'd come home to Colorado, Charity had passed.

Truly, it was better to give than to receive. And Charity had offered Holly a precious gift—the gift of an irreplaceable friendship.

Walk with the wise and become wise, for a companion of fools suffers harm. Holly's favorite Scripture verse, Proverbs 13:20, came to mind. Such accurate words—the guardrails that kept her on a straight path that she largely attributed to Charity.

"I didn't keep in touch with her as much as I should have, Aunt Clementine."

"Life gets in the way sometimes. But you mentioned that Charity had moved to Denver."

"Still, we lived in the same state. We relied on social media to stay connected." Holly readied for the pep talk she assumed her aunt was about to offer.

"I understand all about young people and social media," came her aunt's response. "Everyone is connected nowadays."

Though in reality, were they? What was better than a face-to-face chat with an extraordinary friend or loved one?

"We're all busy," Charity had assured Holly when they'd video chatted one chilly evening. "The main thing is we are serving the Lord. God granted us his mercy and forgives our sins every single day. So praise him every single day."

Every single day.

But that's where the similarity ended. Yes, they were both Christians, but unlike Holly, Charity had lived up to her name and continued her charitable giving. Whereas, Holly had not.

"Thanks for chatting with me, Aunt Clementine." Holly peered at the wooden clock perched on the fireplace mantel. "I'm going to call my student. I tried last week when Jasmine missed her lesson, but wasn't able to reach her and left a message. She's my last lesson for tonight."

"Good luck. I love you, dear," Aunt Clementine said.

"I love you too. I'll phone again soon."

Holly clicked off and walked over to her desk by the piano. The certified letter from Green and Sons Law Firm lay open, the first page exactly where she had left it.

In Charity's handwriting, she'd added a note along with the letter:

"Dear Holly, please use this $1500 check to give someone special a wonderful Christmas. Remember all those fun times in high school? Create that magic again. For me."

Consequently, Holly had phoned Don, the lawyer at the firm, who confirmed that each of their friends had received the same amount of money.

In their conversation, Don reminded Holly that if she didn't wish to disperse her check, she had the option to refuse and the firm would donate the money to a worthy cause.

So far, Holly had done nothing except for that quick call to the lawyer's office saying she'd received the check while staying in North Carolina with her aunt. Since returning, she'd let the check sit on her desk and neglected it, as if acknowledging the letter would make her friend's death absolute.

Should she keep it? Because she certainly had no charitable cause in mind.

Another glance at her watch confirmed that Jasmine was now thirty minutes late.

The girl wasn't just late. She wasn't going to show up.

With a worried frown, Holly scrolled through her student contacts and tapped in the number Jasmine had given her when the girl first enrolled for lessons.

"This number is not in service," came the recorded message. "Please check the number and dial again."

Odd, because the number had been in service the previous week.

Holly took a deep pained breath. She should have known something was wrong. *She should have known.*

She doubled through her contacts until she found Jasmine's address.

"I'll drive into Snowflake," she announced to Butterscotch as she headed for the kitchen. She gulped a last mouthful of tea and set her mug in the stainless steel sink.

In the foyer, she surveyed herself in the mirror and tamed her straight black hair into a semblance of a style. She'd worn navy slacks, a white chenille sweater, and brown leather loafers for teaching. Now she switched her loafers for knee-high boots and drew on a crimson-red wool coat, a knitted green beanie, and gloves.

Her stomach churned as worst-case scenarios raced through her mind. Suppose something had happened to Jasmine and her mother?

Holly expelled a breath, grabbed her car keys and rushed out the door into a bitter cold evening.

CHAPTER 2

nder fifty minutes later, Holly reached Snowflake. As always, her windshield wipers carved out a clear spot for her to peep through, and she handled her four-wheel-drive Jeep with proficiency. Fortunately, the weather had calmed by the time she arrived, and only a thin layer of slush coated the roads and walkways. She'd adhered to the speed limits, although she preferred to drive fast, with the adventurous assertiveness and bold disregard of peril that was uniquely part of her parents' legacy. Similarly, they'd loved watching NASCAR on television.

However, she reserved her stock-car racing passion for when she visited Aunt Clementine in North Carolina, and attended live events.

She typed Jasmine's address into her phone's GPS and soon discovered there was no such address.

Disconnected phone number. Fake street address.

Holly envisioned Jasmine's round angelic face, her blond curls arranged into two pigtails. Whenever Holly complimented her piano playing, the girl would blush to the roots of her hair.

Well, the address might be fake, but the wonderfully artistic child was real.

So, where was she?

Holly clutched the neckline of her coat and took a deep breath to calm herself.

"Snowflake Homeless Shelter," she said aloud. She'd volunteered at the shelter with friends from church and knew it was located near Blue Spruce Plaza. It had been set up for single mothers and families who needed emergency, temporary shelter.

She brushed the snow off her Jeep with the foam brush she kept in the glove compartment, then hopped back inside. As she drove closer to the town center, she admired the stores festively adorned for Christmas. Lampposts on Main Street were graced with red satin bows and wreaths, and white lights twinkled from boutiques and mom-and-pop shops.

She hung a left and pulled to the curb of the homeless shelter a few minutes later.

Her boots clicked on the shoveled concrete sidewalk as she walked to the entrance. A pavilion was piled with plastic garbage bags crammed with personal possessions and damaged, street-worn luggage. She opted for the wheelchair ramp and shook snow from her coat sleeves.

When she entered the shelter, turmoil greeted her. The smell of cheap industrial cleaner made her hang back. Women, many holding young children, were grouped near an enclosure where an employee worked. A woman in a wheelchair waited silently in the hallway, and a handful of orange tabby kittens looped through the crowd.

At the far end of the lobby rose an undecorated five-foot Scotch pine.

Two men, a slightly hunched, heavyset man with gray

hair and a tall good-looking man she guessed to be in his thirties, hardly spared her a second look. Nonetheless, they seemed the most official, so she waited for them to acknowledge her.

"Stand in line over there, miss," the heavyset man said to her. "You'll get a ticket for some clothing and a bed, and a list of shelter rules."

Holly shook her head. "Sir, I'm not here for—"

"Apologies if you're hungry," he said with a harried glance. "Ask a staff member to unlock the refrigerator. We have bottled water, tuna, or peanut butter and jelly sandwiches."

"I've eaten dinner, thanks," Holly replied. "I'm looking for someone."

"You'll be able to find that someone real soon." He glared at the younger man, his blue gaze sparking. "All the residents have been asked to leave."

"Why?" She stepped back. "It's freezing cold out there."

"I've lived here all my life, miss, and am conscious about a Colorado winter and the danger it presents. Nonetheless, tell that to Tim, our hotshot inspector. He thinks we're in the middle of July." Lou stroked his stringy white mustache and scowled.

"Lou, I'm not the bad guy here." Tim seemed to hold his irritation in check with an apologetic exhale. Absentmindedly, he pushed a lock of wavy-brown hair off his forehead and granted Holly a slight smile.

She didn't expect to be attracted to a man in a place like this, with its utter chaos and people swarming everywhere.

But she was.

A glimmer of concern in his deep brown eyes gave her pause. Self-consciously, she worried her knitted beanie with her gloved hands. She'd yanked it off when she'd entered the building and consequently assumed her hair was a staticky mess, the ends sticking straight out in all directions. Adding to her disheveled appearance, she knew any lip gloss she'd applied that morning had faded.

And still, he regarded her with interest.

"Hello," he said.

"Hi." She looped the straps of her purse over her shoulder and offered a faint smile.

Normally, she was unimpressed by extraordinarily handsome men. In her experience, they were oftentimes hollow and superficial, or, like her ex-husband, self-absorbed. But this man threw her totally off balance, because his voice sounded soothing in the disorder that surrounded them.

He towered over her, his muscular shoulders impeding everything but her view of him.

And for some reason, he looked vaguely familiar.

"I told you, Tim," Lou was saying. "All the permits, including the electricity, should be in order."

Tim shook his head. "I'm forced to execute city regulations. You realize that. If this problem isn't taken care of it could lead to a fire hazard."

"I can't turn all these homeless people away. Where are they supposed to go?" Lou pivoted and pointed to the Scotch pine in the corner. "What about the tree-trimming party? The children are looking forward to decorating for Christmas."

"Fortunately, you have the weekend. While everyone is decorating, begin making arrangements at the hotels here in town," Tim responded. "There's the Blue Jay Motel and Rocky Mountain Bed and Breakfast."

"For thirty single women and their children?" Lou asked harshly. "The bed and breakfast has six rooms."

"I know the owner, Theresa Rose."

"So do I, and she's usually fully booked," Lou countered. "I suppose you expect the motel to accommodate everyone?"

"Of course not." Tim tapped a forefinger on his lower lip. "How about the Snowflake Inn?"

Lou cast a long-suffering scowl. "All eight suites?"

"There's the Blue Spruce Apartments."

"You mean the Blue Spruce *rented* apartments?"

Tim reacted as if he'd been punched in the stomach. He leaned over and made a pleading gesture with his hands.

"I'm sorry," he said to Lou, although his expression was set.

"Make way," an EMT shouted, steering a gurney into the hallway.

Holly hustled to the side to let them through.

"What's going on?" she asked the woman in the wheelchair. Her boots were hardly worn, and Holly surmised they'd been donated.

"Lou had to call for an ambulance a little bit ago. Old lady Alley fell off her bunk bed again." The woman put a fistful of coins into the vending machine and tugged out a bag of chips. She grinned, displaying a row of missing teeth. "She's a longer term resident and claimed the top bunk in a semiprivate room. Last time this happened, she split her head on the concrete floor." She wheeled to the window and gawked at the ambulance stationed at the curb, its blinking lights steadily flashing through the shelter's windows.

Holly trained her attention back to the two men.

"Who will pay for all these rooms?" Lou pointed a gnarled finger at Tim.

"Look, I don't want to quarrel. If there was something I could do, I would do it," Tim shot back. "But as it stands now, the shelter needs to close."

"Impossible."

"It won't be forever, just until we get this problem sorted. That's the best I can do."

"Then your best isn't good enough."

"I wish I could offer more," Tim replied in a chillingly polite manner. "But I can't."

CHAPTER 3

*T*imothy Stewart watched Lou stalk down the hallway. Again and again, he'd deflected Lou's questions because he didn't have an answer. He'd expected to sway Lou's animosity by explaining the residents' safety and the city of Snowflake's concerns.

It had been to no avail.

"I'm phoning Mayor Hardy," Lou muttered over his shoulder, half to himself.

"I said I was sorry twice now," Tim replied loudly, but not loudly enough, since Lou didn't swing around.

For the second time, Tim regarded the beautiful Asian woman standing near the vending machine. Too stressed to do anything else, he shoved his hands into his jean pockets. "I'm truly sorry about this," he said to no one in particular.

Apparently overhearing him, she nodded. "Now that's another apology."

He pushed his hair back with a shaking hand. "Do you need something, miss …?" He heard the impatience in his tone, which he blamed on fatigue and the pressure of a wearying day.

"No, I assume *you're* certainly not the one who can help."

Great. Just great. More blame.

Lou's words continued to hammer into Tim's brain. Even his best wasn't good enough.

He stretched a wool cap over his ears, conscious that the woman was staring at him. Her dark almond-shaped eyes were magnificent, her cheekbones prominent.

And she was extremely attractive.

He shook his head. She was certainly a complication he didn't need.

In order to avoid her stare, his gaze flitted to the window. The ambulance threw on the siren and sped away.

People were hurt all the time, physically and emotionally. Which hurt worst?

With no other place to look, he met her stare. "Lou is a friend," he explained.

Why he suddenly felt that he should clarify anything to anyone, especially a stranger, was beyond him.

"Right. I can see you are best buddies." Her mouth held the hint of a smile.

Debating whether to grin or scowl, he summed up his indecision by offering a rueful shrug.

He was supposed to have clocked out of work two hours ago, yet he'd stayed, unsuccessfully trying to fix the shelter's electric problem. He was an inspector, not an electrician, he'd finally reminded himself when, frustrated, he'd given up.

And now, as a result for his concern, he was being chastised by an attractive homeless woman.

"Were you waiting for a bed, miss?" Tim gestured to the line by the glass enclosure, all impatient to be checked in. Viewing the foyer, he noted a woman in a wheelchair munching on a bag of chips.

Holiday stockings were piled high on a table against a wall, along with a miniature Christmas card village. A kitten wound around his legs, and he picked it up to stroke the velvety fur.

"Your friend already asked me." The attractive woman said, as her gaze met his. "I don't need a bed or a meal. I'm searching for a mother and her daughter."

For a lengthy moment, Tim truly assessed her, and consequently, two things hit him at once.

First, she had a wonderful smile, and second, her soft, gorgeous eyes were brimming with … bemusement.

Since gazing at her was infinitely better than worrying about the homeless shelter and a decision he couldn't control, he preferred to gaze at her. There was a vivaciousness about her, the way her silky straight black hair hung loose around her face. And her profile, the pert, turned-up nose, her shoulders rigidly set, were all adorable.

He doubted she'd appreciate his observations.

"May I ask your age?" he inquired, then cringed at his audacity for asking such a question.

She flashed a smile. "I'm almost thirty-three. Why?"

"You don't look a day over twenty-one."

"My birthday is January first." She flavored her response with levity. "So, I'll look older in a month."

He grinned. "A New Year's baby?"

"I am, yes."

She didn't appear to be the average shelter resident, but because of his past, he knew well how appearances were deceiving. His mother hadn't looked like she lived in a homeless shelter, either. And she'd made certain that she and Tim were always clean and tidy.

"Who might have information concerning this woman and her daughter?" the woman asked.

"Speak to Lou." Tim shifted. "He pretty much runs things around here."

"Lou is facing bigger problems these days." She gazed out

the window where a few women stood and Tim followed her gaze. To fight off the cold, the women shivered and clutched thin coats to their shoulders.

"Right." With an exasperated sigh, Tim set down the kitten. "Bigger problems."

"Finding rooms for all these people in one weekend is a big undertaking."

"I'm well aware of the situation." As a result of him creating it, although he'd only been following orders. "Why are you looking for this mother and daughter?"

"Because I want to help them."

"Is this a good Christmas deed or something?" he asked. "The shelter is already supported by generous private donations."

"Hmm. If you look around, we can both agree the donations apparently aren't generous enough."

"The contributions are reliable and support the day-to-day expenses." He ignored her killing frown. Apparently his explanation wasn't helping the situation. "Though rewiring a place this old will cost thousands of dollars."

"How about prayer?" she asked.

"How about it?"

"Prayer will help."

He lifted an eyebrow. "How about money? Money will really help."

"You sound like a cynic. Some call it an escape so that they don't get wounded."

"So now you're analyzing me?"

"Hardly. I'm just stating a fact." She surveyed the people waiting. "All I'm suggesting is to have faith too."

Faith. God. When was the last time anyone had mentioned either to him? Probably his grandmother when he was a child. But it was more comfortable believing in nothing, and that was the way he intended to keep things.

Consequently, he was never hurt. He'd learned early on that if he relied only on himself, at least he could depend on someone.

She was evidently waiting for a reply, so he extended his right hand. "I'm Tim."

"I gathered."

"Tim Stewart." His hand was still outstretched, yet she wavered. He pressed his lips together. "And you are?"

"Holly. Holly Kim."

"You're Asian?"

She smiled. "Yes."

"Chinese?"

"Korean. We have a rounder face."

The way she watched him, with gentleness in her strikingly expressive eyes, caused him to stand still. His mother had never looked at him with such consideration. Similarly, neither had his girlfriend of the past six months.

"You live here in Snowflake?" he inquired.

A blink of a hesitation before Holly responded. "I live in Pine Cone Valley."

"About an hour away, right?"

"Under an hour, depending on how fast you drive."

"I can't imagine someone like you would ever buck the speed limit." He shot her a look of amusement. "You don't seem the type."

"And what type is that, Tim?"

A biased stereotype. He expected a blue-eyed blond wearing a tight skirt to drive fast cars, not a demure Asian woman. Noting Holly's scowl, he wisely didn't express his sentiments aloud.

"I meant—I'm a type." He congratulated himself for shifting the topic so effortlessly.

"Oh, really. What type is that?"

"I suppose I *am* a cynic when it comes to faith and religion." He offered a contrite head shake, then zipped up his navy-blue quilted parka. "But for the record, I don't have the patience for God."

"Did God take too long to answer your prayers?"

"I don't know. He's never answered any."

"Perhaps faith will produce patience so that you can trust again."

"For instance, you mean trust in God?" he countered. "Or trust in others?"

"Both."

"Right." His shrug meant just the opposite. *Wrong.*

He had sent endless prayers to heaven throughout his adolescence, asking God to change his family's situation. Instead, Tim and his mother had slept beneath bridges when the shelters in Denver were full. Free weekly newspapers served as their blankets.

Of course that was when they weren't joy riding on country roads with her so-called buddies who were forever intent on partying. If the scene involved booze, his mother was the first to arrive, oftentimes with Tim in tow.

"I understand," Holly said.

His gaze narrowed on her smile. He had the edgy feeling that she was one of those people who might try to convert him to her way of thinking. An evangelist—someone who fancied Gospel preaching and spreading the Good Word.

"Well? Is there a way I can locate them?" Behind her beautiful face was a determination that caught him off guard.

"All the women and children are housed down the hall," he said even as his radar went up. Once, his mother had mistakenly depended on individuals who claimed they wanted to help her and her son. "Call the shelter later. Or, if you wait, things should quiet in an hour."

Her shoulders stiffened. He hadn't meant to sound curt, but the day had been long and disheartening.

"Call who?" she asked.

"The shelter, miss—"

"Holly," she reminded him.

"Holly, I'm one of two building inspectors in Snowflake. I don't work here. Their exact hours are posted somewhere."

"I assume they welcome visitors day and night." She rubbed the middle of her forehead. "So the shelter really must close?"

"Yes." He steered them to an out of the way corner. "I don't make the rules, I just enforce them."

"No need to get defensive, Mr. ..."

Had he been defensive? He exhaled. *Yeah, probably.*

"Tim. Tim Stewart," he said. Was he really that forgettable? Who else walked away from a promising acting career?

Someone who was disillusioned.

He'd certainly felt that way when he was young—invisible in a sea of high school students as he and his mother moved from place to place. Ten schools in as many years, and being the new kid wasn't fun, especially as he entered adolescence.

"What happened?" Holly asked. "Why wasn't anyone aware of this electrical problem sooner?"

He was surprised her tone wasn't incriminating, especially since he'd been so abrupt with her. His gaze lingered on her lovely features. Her complexion was slightly golden, her high cheekbones flushed. Her lips were full, a deep vivid pink.

Slight and slim, she couldn't weigh more than a hundred pounds soaking wet.

And as he continued staring, he was utterly, inexplicably drawn to her.

In the silence, she waited for an explanation.

His hands dropped to his sides. "The electricity isn't up to code," he replied.

She nodded. "Go on."

His phone pinged, indicating an incoming text. He withdrew it from his pocket, assuming it was Felicia, his on-again, off-again girlfriend. He glanced at the screen. Sure enough, she was asking why he hadn't picked her up for dinner yet.

Soon. Tied up at work, he rapidly texted, then jammed the phone back in his pocket.

"Sorry," he said to Holly. "You were asking?"

"About the electricity for the building."

"The shelter lost power twice this week, and the ancient wiring presents a safety hazard."

She peered around. "Then all the more reason for me to find the family."

Lou stomped over. "You still here, Mr. Hot Shot Movie Star Inspector?"

"I was just leaving," Tim replied.

"Movie star?" Holly looked up at him. "I thought I recognized you."

"It was many years ago, and it was actually a television series." Tim dismissed her question by gesturing to Lou. "As I said, here's the guy to talk to if he can spare a minute."

Holly turned to Lou. "I'm Holly Kim. I'm aware this is a bad time, but I'm looking for—"

"Miss Kim, I'm so sorry I haven't been to my piano lessons." A girl about eleven years old raced to Holly and threw her skinny arms around Holly's waist. Her huge green eyes reminded Tim of a street urchin. "My mother lost your phone number."

"Jasmine, I'm so relieved you are here." Holly crouched down and cupped the little girl's face in her hands. "I was beyond worried. I called the number your mother had given me, then went to your address and—"

A woman with pinched cheeks and sunken gray eyes, her

mousey-brown hair scraped back by a tortoise-colored plastic clasp, hurried down the hall. She gripped a self-improvement book close to her chest. She looked anxious, as if she never was able to catch up with life and couldn't quite handle it.

Tim recognized the look, for he'd seen it often enough on his mother's face. This woman had an addiction, most likely alcohol.

"Miss Kim, I apologize." The woman advanced toward Holly. "My truck wouldn't start tonight."

"I'm just glad you're okay, Emily," Miss Kim replied.

"Mommy." Jasmine tugged at her mother's sleeve. "We don't have a truck anymore. Remember at Sunday morning service the pastor told us not to lie?"

"Yes, yes." Emily's voice was quick and impatient. "I'm not perfect, you know."

Tim dawdled by the doorway, pretending to check his phone as he readied to leave. Yes, he was eavesdropping, but he couldn't help himself.

Thus, Miss Holly Kim was a piano teacher, and she obviously had an indisputable attachment to the young girl. And she didn't live in Snowflake.

He was familiar with Pine Cone Valley, recalling that the town boasted an excellent coffee shop rivaling the Cozy Coffee Shop in Snowflake. Maybe he could invite her for coffee and a sandwich sometime.

And why would he do that? Inwardly, he reined in his thoughts.

Complications, complications.

"Tim," Lou called. "Is there any other way?"

"I wish there were, Lou." He blew out a frustrated breath. "To sum everything up, I'll be back first thing Monday to close the place."

He glanced toward the entrance. At least the good-natured giggling between two teenage residents, both wearing similar flannel shirts and torn jeans, took his mind off the problem for a moment.

"Thanks for nothing," Lou muttered, stamping away again.

So now what?

Tim lingered by the doorway. Should he say good-bye to Holly, mumble a "nice to have met you," or just leave the building?

He'd been curt with her but he'd apologized, hadn't he?

Umm, no, in fact, he hadn't. And the tension he'd felt all evening had spun an attraction to her he couldn't explain.

Really, tension could do that?

In his case, yes. Or rather, the real reason. He simply wanted to see her again.

He hung back, but merely for a second before he strode to her. She was conversing with Jasmine's mother, while Jasmine munched on a handful of chips the woman in the wheelchair shared with her.

"Holly?" He tapped her on the shoulder.

She excused herself from the conversation and curved to him. "Yes?"

"Can I call you?"

She blinked. "What?"

"Call you. You know, so that we can go out on a date."

"A date? Why?"

"I thought maybe we could go for coffee or something." He was talking like an idiot. Again, he reminded himself he'd had a very long day.

"Why?" she repeated.

"You do drink coffee, don't you?"

"Every morning. But only in the mornings."

"Are you dating anyone?"

"No. Not that it's any of your business." She combed a hand through her hair. "Are you?"

"Am I what?"

"Dating anyone?"

His conscience chattered for no reason, because he and Felicia had an understanding. No long-term commitments.

"I'm not the Grinch who stole Christmas," he said, "if that's what's holding you back."

"You're not grouchy?"

"Hardly ever."

She seemed to be holding in a smile. "So you don't live in a cave?"

"I've never stolen a Christmas, or any other item in my life."

Even at their lowest point, when he and his mother were desperate for a hot meal, at least they hadn't lifted any items out of the convenience stores they'd slipped in to escape a freezing winter's night.

"Thanks, but I'm not interested." Holly's reply was quick, dousing his enthusiasm.

"Why not?"

"I don't date."

A gorgeous woman like her?

Despite the facts that their paths might not cross again and her life was in the next town over, he was interested in getting to know her better. Nonetheless, after the crushing reality of being raised by a neglectful mother, he only dated women who didn't demand more than he could give.

Then again, Holly didn't seem like that kind of woman.

"I can call you," he heard himself saying. "Or text, if you give me your number."

"No call, no coffee, no texts. Understand?"

All right then. This was a set-down he couldn't refute.

He hid his disappointment behind a brief grin. "I understand, loud and clear." He should say more, something sharp and witty, something flippant, but words eluded him. Because in truth, he felt hurt and disheartened.

"Well, good night." He acknowledged the girl's mother and then noticed how Jasmine eyed the vending machine longingly.

He made his way to her. "Hold out your hand," he instructed.

She lifted her freckled face and chortled as he placed a fistful of loose change in her hand.

"Enjoy." He tousled her blond bangs that hung over her eyes. "Buy whatever you want.

She cast a furtive peep at her mother. "Can I get candy?"

"Yes," Emily replied, "since we've eaten supper already. Though don't eat it all at once."

"Yay! I love caramels!" As the change clinked into the machine, Jasmine whirled to give Tim a high-five. "Thanks, Mr. ...."

"Stewart. Tim Stewart."

The woman in the wheelchair backed up, and he automatically gave her a hand, straightening her toward the hallway that led to the residents' rooms. Behind him, he overheard his name whispered, and not in a flattering way. Puzzled, worried glances were cast at him. Apparently word traveled fast, because he was already slated as the guy who was shutting down the place right before Christmas.

With an offhand nod, he turned toward the door and almost collided with a resident shuffling across the lobby.

He spun to find Holly watching him. He bid her and her friends a cordial good night and added a brief smile.

She smiled back, but the smile didn't reach her eyes.

She didn't want him to call her, since she didn't want to date him, or anyone by the sounds of it. She didn't like coffee in the afternoon, or phone calls, or texts.

So that was settled.

He'd never had to pursue a woman before and he wouldn't start now, especially with one who wasn't interested.

He tugged on his wool tweed cap and wound a cranberry-colored scarf around his neck. Many had called him a fool when he'd headed for California as soon as he'd graduated from high school.

Sure, it was a year later than everyone else, but that he blamed on his constant moves. The main thing was, despite the years in between, he'd persevered.

And then, the poor kid from nowhere had landed an acting role.

Therefore, when had adversity ever stopped him?

"I hope to see you again, Holly," he called out.

She opened her mouth to reply, but he strode out the entrance, past the women smoking, the young twenty-some-things making their way inside, the piles of plastic bags jammed with folks' lives. He nodded at the police officer patrolling the area and kept walking.

Again, his cell phone pinged with an incoming text.

This time he ignored it.

CHAPTER 4

*A*fter she returned to her apartment later that evening, Holly set Charity's letter on the garden stool in the living room.

With a mug of steaming chamomile tea and a slice of toast slathered with butter, she settled on her tufted couch with Butterscotch curled at her side.

When her landlord had granted permission, she'd wallpapered the room in faux, natural-looking grass cloth that sported a knotted, woven design. On the fireplace mantel, she'd tilted an antique beveled mirror picked up at the This and That Shop, a variety store in town. Beside the fireplace, she'd tucked a sizable, lush fern into a wicker basket, and a fabric-covered box near the piano hid an overflow of music.

Someday, she'd purchase her own place and decorate it exactly the way she preferred. But for now, since it was December, she'd draped a green garland along the mantel and added a splash of red spray paint to pinecones arranged in a clear glass bowl on her kitchen counter. On Christmas Eve, she'd set up a spindly artificial tree, then attend the six o'clock church service in Snowflake.

She made a note to herself to purchase a new tree topper. The year before, the previous one had shattered.

And then would come Christmas Day.

Since her divorce she'd spent it alone, a prospect she never looked forward to.

To chat about her eventful evening at the shelter, she phoned Aunt Clementine, who answered on the second ring.

"Hello, Holly," her aunt said. "Is anything the matter?"

"No, why?" Holly bit into her toast and chewed.

"You don't usually call me twice in one day."

"Are you busy?"

"A little."

Holly went along with her aunt, assuming she was joking. Typically at this hour she was snuggled on her flowered recliner watching her favorite game show, a rescue dog or two nestled at her feet.

"I called to tell you that this was easier than I imagined," Holly said.

"What was easier?"

Holly smiled. "How best to use the fifteen hundred dollars Charity gave me. I found a special charitable cause."

"That's the way the Lord works. Don't wear yourself out looking for something that God will place right in front of you."

A muted male voice resounded through the phone.

"Is anyone with you?" Holly asked.

Silence for a beat.

"Aunt Clementine?"

"Justin Kildred is here." Her aunt cleared her throat. "We're watching a game show together."

"The man who volunteered in the reception area the day you were admitted?" A vision of the portly elderly man with wiry white hair and a friendly, hearty chuckle, prompted Holly to smirk.

"The very same. While I was in the hospital, he came to my room and visited me, and before I was discharged, he asked for my number. He told me it took him a few days to gather up his courage to ask me out."

"And she was worth the wait," Justin called out in the background.

Holly gaped into the phone. "When did this all happen?"

"We went on our first date soon after you left, a celebration because of the good report I received from the doctor. And Justin brought me a bouquet of white roses. You know how much I love flowers. And white roses signify new beginnings."

"How romantic." Holly chuckled. "And more important, I'm thrilled about how quickly you convalesced."

"My faith is my greatest report, for God always puts us in the best place for our needs."

"Which includes placing you in the hospital so you could meet Justin?" Holly envisioned her aunt blushing like a sixteen-year-old girl. "You never spoke about him once during all our recent phone conversations."

"I figured you were heartbroken over losing your friend and needed the chance to talk about your friendship."

"Charity wouldn't want us to grieve, although I can't help myself." With a choked laugh, Holly curved her hand across Butterscotch's back and was rewarded with a low purr. "She wished everyone a long and happy life."

"Maybe God was bringing forth new life in her wishes," Aunt Clementine quietly said. "His timing is always perfect."

New life. New beginnings.

Her aunt was finally finding love, and Christmastime made it even more special. She'd lived her entire life alone, and she certainly hadn't been looking for love. But so what? Love at any age was praiseworthy.

Holly picked up Charity's letter and clutched it close to

her chest. It was tear-stained and raveled at the corners. Through Charity, God had given Holly and her friends an assignment. Surely God would see them through and provide assistance.

"Tell me about your special cause," her aunt prompted.

"It all happened so quickly." Holly set down the letter, wrapped her fingers snugly around her mug, and took a sip of the earthy chamomile tea. Then she explained what had happened at the shelter and her conversation with Tim. "Perhaps I'll use the fifteen hundred dollars to find a place for Jasmine and her mother, Emily, to stay."

"How long will that amount last to cover their rent?"

"Only a few months."

"So what about the other people at the shelter?" her aunt asked quietly.

"You're right." With a sigh, Holly set down her mug. "Of course that isn't the best use for the money. I considered donating it to the shelter for the rewiring, but I'm certain that money wouldn't even come close to the required amount."

"Then start a fund-raiser to make up the difference."

"Like what, for instance? A bake sale?"

"You're a musician, aren't you?" Holly visualized her aunt —the lines in her face, the caring heart that held infinite wisdom. "Ask your students to perform a holiday piano recital and solicit donations at the door."

"And where would I hold this recital?" Holly reached for a blank piece of notepaper and a pen she always kept close by. "The wintry weather is unpredictable for an outside performance."

"Why don't you talk to that building inspector and throw around your ideas? What's his name?"

"Tim Stewart." The memory of his tousled brown hair and deep, velvety voice when he apologized for being forced to close the shelter, had a curious effect on Holly's heartbeat.

"Surely he can refer you to an electrician," her aunt said. "Or that other man … Lou. Can he help?"

"I tried to talk with Lou after I spoke with Jasmine and Emily, but he brushed me off. A few minutes later, he announced he was coming down with the flu and left. He suggested speaking with his assistant, which I did."

"And?"

"He was chatty but useless." Holly scribbled on the notepad, then fixated on her pen. "Basically, he encouraged me to do whatever I want, declaring all the while that nothing will save the shelter."

"Sounds like he was hardly helpful." Her aunt pushed out a heavy sigh. "So, find out where Tim's office is located. He's your guy."

Her guy? Hah! Not if Holly wanted a man who truly cared about helping people instead of displacing them.

"Tim didn't seem inclined to offer a solution," she said.

"What about dating him?" A whisper of mirth from her aunt kept pace with Justin's low belly laugh.

"Date him?" Holly sat up straighter. "Why? I've created a happy life here in Pine Cone Valley. I love my students and music and—"

Even as she refuted her aunt, the word swirled in her brain. *Dating.*

She put the phone on speaker, padded to the piano and braced her hands on the fall board. Dating was for others, not for her.

But how many years had she dreamed about having someone love her, an amazing guy she could love in return? A man to share her life with.

No, no, no. Tim was the bad guy, and she'd married one bad guy.

"I'm not the Grinch who stole Christmas, if that's what's holding you back," he'd said.

Holly went to the couch and plucked up her list, blank save for the scribbles.

Picking up the pen, she wrote while saying aloud, "I'm waiting until God makes it clear I've made the right choice in finding someone extraordinary."

"You should start going out and experiencing life again. You haven't dated since your divorce."

"I'm far from a hermit, Aunt Clementine." Holly drew in a quiet breath. "I'm just not interested, that's all."

"Two years is a long time."

"I'm not desperate, and I won't date a guy who throws homeless women and children onto the street."

"He's hardly done that, dear. And may I remind you that you said he apologized. Tomorrow is Friday. Go see him. From what you've described, he's eager to help."

"He's the opposite of eager."

"Interested then. Let's just say he's interested."

Her aunt didn't elaborate, and Holly didn't press her. A half dozen times, her mind quarreled that she should tell Aunt Clementine about Tim Stewart being an actor—and that he was ruggedly appealing and charismatic. But her aunt hadn't remarked on his name being recognizable, although, in all fairness, she was probably preoccupied with Justin.

The prospect of their romance made Holly smile.

Justin and Aunt Clementine were proving that it was never too late to find love.

CHAPTER 5

The following morning, Holly dressed in a turtleneck sweater and formfitting jeans, then tugged on her coat and snagged her leather bucket handbag over her shoulder. Instead of a wool beanie, she fitted a pair of leopard earmuffs over her ears and freshly washed hair.

Brisk air embraced her as she exited her apartment. A radiant sun cast sparkles on the icicles, a shiny twinkle on the picturesque landscape of mountains and valleys.

After setting her GPS for the building inspectors' offices in Snowflake, she started her Jeep on the snow-rutted side street, then veered onto the main highway. The road had been plowed, and she drove quickly to Snowflake.

The day's piano lessons didn't begin until early evening, which allowed time to brainstorm solutions with Tim. Or so she hoped.

When she reached his office, she parked at the curb. A plain boxwood wreath was fixed to the entry door, and Holly envisioned attaching pinecones, red berries, and moss, so that the holiday colors would be highlighted. She'd always had a flair for decorating.

In the office foyer, she inhaled a mixture of old cigarette smoke, a flowery fragrance, and stale coffee.

A receptionist sat behind an oversized mahogany desk and greeted her. The woman looked like she'd done everything she could to fight the aging process—tightening her face with plastic surgery, dying her hair a garish red, and applying a pair of spiky black false eyelashes. The result made her appear older, not younger.

"Timothy Stewart, please," Holly said.

"He's out on a call." The woman squinted up at Holly over pink reading glasses. "Do you have an appointment?"

"No. I met him last evening at the homeless shelter and wished to talk to him about my—"

"Henry, Tim's assistant is here," the receptionist interrupted. "Do you want to see him instead?"

"Certainly." At least, Holly thought, there was someone in the office.

The receptionist ushered Holly down the hall and pointed to a tiny cubicle.

Henry, with thinning hair dyed an iridescent purple, offered Holly a seat across from the messiest desk she'd ever seen.

"I heard about the homeless shelter, but I'll try to reach Tim for you as he's more familiar with the problem." Henry punched a number into his cellphone and kept up a stream of one-sided conversation. "I grew up in New York City, but wanted the tranquility of a small town so I relocated here. Did you know that New York has a population of over eight million?"

"That's a hefty percentage in comparison to—"

"Then I went through a complicated divorce and—" He set down the phone. "Tim isn't picking up."

"Well, thanks, anyway." Holly stood before he could begin his nonstop chatter again. "At least you tried. I'll come back after lunch." She slung her handbag over her shoulder and headed into the hallway, spotting a memorable broad-shouldered man with dark wavy hair. Tim's cheeks were reddened from the outside air, which only enhanced his chiseled good looks.

"Miss Kim. What a delightful surprise." An enigmatic smile swept across his face as he surveyed her, from the top of her earmuffs to the toes of her brown leather boots. He carried a cup of steaming coffee in one hand and his gloves in the other. "The receptionist said you were here to discuss the homeless shelter." He checked his watch. "But you should have made an appointment."

"This was spur of the moment and ..." Holly trailed off. He was obviously preoccupied. "Can you spare a few minutes?"

"For you? Certainly. Come into my office." He grinned and gestured to a door down the hall. "I assume you don't want coffee, since it's almost noon. You only drink coffee in the morning, right?"

"Your memory is outstanding."

"I've been told that before, but I'll let you in on a secret. I remember only certain things ... or certain people." He lifted his cup. "Can I get you anything?"

"I'm fine, thanks."

He flashed another grin and she was surprised by its warmth. She recalled that same devastating grin when it had spun across countless television screens, bringing up the heat level of every woman who'd watched him. But after a couple seasons, he'd abruptly left the business and disappeared.

So, he'd decided to settle in Snowflake to become a ... building inspector?

Rather than guessing his reasons for leaving a lucrative acting profession, she inched into his outdated paneled office and met his steady gaze.

He nudged the door closed behind them, set his coffee and gloves on a narrow dilapidated desk that had seen better days, then pulled out a chair for her. Papers were piled high, and half-empty coffee cups furthered the clutter.

He removed his parka, scarf and wool cap. His wrinkled, white button-down shirt strained across his muscled chest.

"Well, Miss Kim?" He slid into a chair behind his desk.

She wiped her sweaty palms on her coat, because for some reason she was nervous about being alone with him. He was, after all, an attractive man with impressively innate appeal. Nevertheless, her expectations had been high when she'd set out for Snowflake this morning.

Now she wasn't so sure. Now she was considering that their discussion might be unsuccessful at best and exasperating at worst.

She took a quick glimpse out the window. Tailor-suited men and women emerged from the entrances of multistory buildings, fastening their down coats and shoving fleece-gloved hands deep into their pockets. Even in this commercial part of town, dense pine wreaths trimmed with red bows decorated the businesses' steel doors. In Snowflake, the spirit of Christmas reached everywhere.

She glanced back at Tim. He stared at her intently, as if waiting for something.

"Well?" he repeated, folding his hands together.

Today he was all business. She sensed his standoffishness and couldn't understand why. Surely she'd done nothing to offend him since she'd entered his office.

She presented a level look. "Well what?"

"Miss Kim—"

"Holly."

"Holly, you're here at *my* workplace, so what can I do for you?" That velvety voice resembling a silky caress had changed to abrupt and businesslike.

In order for their meeting to go forward, she needed to speak, she told herself.

She swallowed. "The shelter needs our help."

"Ah, I see. The shelter needs *our* help." He glanced at his watch again. "Go on."

"There are countless ways to assist." She ignored his impatience with a good-natured smile. "I've brainstormed ideas with my aunt."

"And your aunt is—"

"My aunt Clementine," she flipped back. "She lives in North Carolina and we chat often. I try to visit her whenever I can."

"So your aunt is some sort of homeless shelter expert?"

"She's just my sweet, elderly aunt."

In the ensuing silence, his gaze slid to her mouth. Then he pushed out a deep sigh. "Therefore, you're not here to accept my offer for a date?"

Absolutely not was on the tip of her tongue, warring with an a*bsolutely yes.*

As her throat went dry, she reined in the enticing thought of actually going out with him.

A date ... with Timothy Stewart. At the same moment that the thought went through her mind, her heart thumped an erratic beat. She was in close quarters with him in his ten by twelve foot office, and the air was scented with leather and the outdoors—purely masculine scents.

She sensed there was an inordinate amount of life that he'd experienced beneath that handsome exterior, and for some reason, he'd sealed all of it behind a barrier of polite courteousness.

Besides, he was far beyond her reach. And she suspected he believed he was beyond God's reach as well.

She wanted to reassure him that God wasn't looking for perfection, and that Tim had made mistakes along with everyone else. God looked for people who were unsure of the next turn, not those who thought they knew it all and were full of their own knowledge.

Her fingers tightened.

So when it came to dating him?

Bad idea. The absolute worst idea.

Besides, she had a history of making poor choices with men, seeing the virtuous and never the unscrupulous. This had led her to marry a narcissistic man who cared only about what she could, or rather, *should,* do for him.

"I told you, Tim, I don't date." She managed a wavering smile. "As I mentioned, I'm here because of the shelter."

For a split second, disappointment flew across his rugged face.

He shrugged indifferently as his blasé mask slid back into place. "Did your visit with Jasmine and her mother go satisfactorily after I left the shelter?"

"As well as it could, considering the circumstances."

Along with a long-suffering look, he sighed. "Not my fault."

"I didn't say it was."

"Good, and Jasmine is an adorable child, by the way."

"She's quite out of the ordinary compared to other students," Holly replied. "For instance, she's mastered two-octave scales, both hands together. Her musicality is incredible for a child who practices only three times a week on an ancient upright piano in Snowflake's only music store."

"Encourage her to stick with it," Tim said. "Music can enhance verbal memory."

"How do you know that?"

"I've read articles, but my knowledge is all second-hand experience."

"Also important to remember is that when you play an instrument, you use both sides of your brain." Holly tried to sound human and not like a page out of a textbook. "I gather you don't play, Tim?

"I play the radio." He grinned and stretched out his long legs beneath the desk. "Other than that, I truly have no musical proficiency."

"You never had the opportunity?"

"That's one way to sum up my childhood. One sugary, polite way." The jaded drawl in his voice, his response immediate and conclusive, told her there was more, but she didn't pressure him.

Their brief cordiality floundered as Holly returned to the subject of the shelter and how to help the residents who were about to be turned out into the cold.

"They won't be 'turned out into the cold,'" Tim said curtly. "To begin with, the various lodgings in the area are willing to assist temporarily." He lifted the coffee to his lips and grimaced, muttering, "I forgot my three sugars." He set the cup to the side.

"Temporarily isn't the right answer," Holly said.

"*Temporarily* will have to do."

"It's a Band-Aid." She wasn't here to argue with him. "I'm assuming you can direct me to an electrician, the first rung in solving the problem. Do you have anyone in mind? I'm willing to help financially."

Understanding seemed to dawn, and Tim quirked a dark eyebrow. "Really? How?"

"A dear friend recently passed. Her name was Charity. She left money to me and several of our high school friends and tagged it for a good cause. This is certainly the case with the shelter needing all new electrical wiring." Holly struggled to stave off unanticipated hot tears. Wasn't grief supposed to subside with time? Would it never go away?

Tim's expression changed, the strain in his face replaced by compassion. He got to his feet and reached across the desk, touching her shoulders with both hands. "I'm sorry. Charity must have been young. My condolences for your loss."

"I take comfort from a sermon from Pastor Tom I heard a while back."

"Do you?"

"We must endure today's sadness. Remember, a blessed tomorrow is just around the bend." Holly wiped her eyes and repaid Tim's cool tone with a proud reply. "Charity wanted to strengthen her friends during her weakest hours by the gift of generosity."

Belatedly, Holly registered his unreadable expression. "What?"

He placed his hands on the desk. "You won't appreciate my answer."

"Try me."

"I've attended church, and it didn't work for me. I found the people there were judgmental and insincere."

"Then try again."

"No."

His flat reply reminded her of the teenage rebellions she'd dealt with when her adolescent students refused to take piano lessons, but were being forced to by their parents. "Why not?"

"Because I have an aversion to artificiality," he replied. "Which is one of the reasons I'm not in Hollywood anymore."

If Charity were alive, she would encourage Tim to embrace the season of Christ's birth with joy and church attendance. But Charity wasn't here anymore.

Holly drew a fortifying breath in a futile attempt to stave off more tears. She missed her friend considerably.

Tim came around his desk. "Holly—"

There was no distance between them now.

"You must think I'm a woman who cries all the time. I

don't usually break down like this. I guess I'm not as strong as I should be."

"I sense you're very strong." He cupped his hands on her shoulders. "Whatever your ideas, I'll make them work." The tender sincerity in his tone, coupled with the touch of his fingers, comforted her.

She gulped, and her blurry eyes searched his face. Tim had made an assurance without asking for repayment. She tied this with the realization that she simply believed him. His voice had been sincere, his response heartfelt.

"Thank you."

He gave a last encouraging squeeze, then swung back and settled in his seat.

She groped for a handkerchief in her handbag. This weeping must stop, she scolded herself. Charity would want her friends and family to move on with their lives.

"So you're not some rich model with millions of dollars to spare?" he asked teasingly. "Because you're extraordinarily beautiful."

"I'm certainly well past the age to start modeling." She focused on his coffee cup, the coffee he'd hardly touched. "Is that a compliment, by the way?"

He didn't miss a beat. "Actually, it was. Genuine and sincere."

Her cheeks grew hot. Had he also been genuinely sincere when he'd asked her out?

Frustrated by the direction of her musings, she chastised herself. How could she contemplate dating him when she was in the middle of mourning her friend's death and worrying about Jasmine and her mother's calamitous circumstances?

Tim observed her closely. "Holly?"

"To be clear, I assume fifteen hundred dollars isn't adequate for the shelter's rewiring." She tucked her lace handkerchief back into her handbag and placed the bag beneath her chair. "However, my aunt and I discussed a fund-raiser."

"Your lovable aunt Clementine." He smiled. "Let me guess, you're planning a bake sale?"

"No." Holly stifled a discomfited laugh. "Instead, my piano students and I will present a holiday recital and accept donations at the door."

"Are they any good?"

"Who?" she asked innocently. "My students?"

"Yes." He reached for his coffee.

"Well, they're not professionals, although they're extremely diligent."

He took a swallow of coffee, grimaced again, and slid the cup to the farthest spot of his desk. "Are you a hard taskmaster, Holly?" He kept his features straight for a moment before he chuckled.

"I'm not here to describe my teaching methods." She met his chuckle with one of her own. "What's more important is that my students' parents and friends will support the performance, and I expect the community will rally as well."

"And you'll also perform?"

"I usually don't, but I could."

"I'd pay to see you. You could end the program with a Christmas song."

"How about a sing-along?" she asked.

"Even better. I bet you're excellent."

Her pulse jumped at his enthusiasm. Nonetheless, she reminded herself that he'd acted for a living. "I'm okay. I studied music at a distinguished university in New York."

"I presume you have a shiny black grand piano in your home."

"On the contrary, I have a spinet piano in my apartment

that works just fine. Someday, I'd like to learn how to play the accordion. The instruments are similar."

"Miss Holly Kim, you grow more interesting by the second." He rolled up his shirt sleeves and fixed her with a direct look. "Where will you hold this recital?"

"How about Golden Birch Manor on Cedar Lane?"

"The senior residents will love it." He rummaged through the top drawer of his desk. Extracting a stack of business cards, he handed her one. "Here's Ralph's information. He's the electrician I recommend, so let's start with getting a cost estimate for the rewiring. By the way, Ralph recently erected a neon sign for the new ice skating rink in town."

"And that's why you recommend him?"

"He's fully qualified and the best in the area. We've been friends a long time."

"If he can erect a neon sign, then clearly he can rewire a homeless shelter," she said humorously.

A neon sign. That was exactly the sign she needed from God, pointing to the right guy before she fell in love again. Inwardly, she shook her head. As if that would ever happen.

What? The neon sign or the guy?

Both, she decided.

"Are you familiar with the rink?" Tim asked. The aloofness was gone, any former brusqueness in his tone subdued.

"I've driven past on many occasions, but I've never ice-skated before."

"You should try sometime. It's fun."

"Fun if you can stand upright on skates," she hedged. "I probably wouldn't even make it to the rink without falling."

He raised his eyebrows in a dare. "I'll hold you up."

She flushed, speechless. A vision of him and her ice-skating together, laughing, the sounds of smooth blades gliding across the ice, the enticing scents of nachos and popcorn from the concession stand, ignited an expectant warmth in her chest.

She gave herself a resolved mental shake. Talk about a fantasy. Most likely, her ankles would wobble, while he would make skating appear fluid and effortless.

"If you ever want to learn, let me know." It seemed like he wanted to prolong their conversation, and she sat back in her chair while he continued. "I played hockey on two high school teams."

"You attended more than one high school?"

"I attended five."

"Why so many?"

"My mother and I constantly moved around." His eyes darkened, and he looked away.

"I assume this was all before you became an actor?"

He raked a hand through his hair. "I've been on my own for most of my life, and spent several years in a variety of professions, yet that's the one everyone brings up. Thankfully, that stint is long past."

Abruptly, he stood, a firm conclusion. Their meeting was apparently over.

Holly scooped up her handbag. "Shall I call the electrician?"

"I'll text Ralph to arrange a discussion." Tim tugged his phone from his pocket. After quick back-and-forth texts, he read, "He can meet at the town center on Saturday, December seventh, the night of the tree-lighting ceremony. He's slated to be there in case anything goes wrong."

"Like if the tree doesn't light up?"

"Something like that."

"I haven't been to a tree lighting in ages, but I remember it was always held the first Saturday in December." She hadn't been since she'd gone with Charity and their friends when they were in high school.

"Neither have I." Tim studied her and smiled, and she had the most surprising thought. He seemed to definitely be admiring her. "So, we can all plan to meet there."

"*All?*"

"I'll come too," he said. "What's your phone number?"

Did she have a choice? It seemed as if he'd asked numerous times already. She offered her number, he put it into his phone, and then her phone pinged with a text. It was from Tim.

Five o' clock on December 7ᵗʰ? he'd texted. *I'll meet you in front of The Little Corner Bistro in Snowflake on Main Street. Ralph will be with me.*

I'll be there, she texted back.

This was absurd. He was standing right across from her and they were texting each other. She looked up at him, and their gazes locked.

And then, the strangest thing happened. They both laughed at the same time.

CHAPTER 6

a few days after meeting with Tim, Holly's thoughts continuously veered back to him—the strength of his fingers on her shoulders, his rich chuckle, his admiring smile. Everything about him melted her into an illogically thinking female. How could a man like him possibly be interested in a woman like her? She'd been told she was pretty, but she certainly didn't parallel a curvaceous starlet.

Surely she was the least stunning woman he'd ever bothered to flirt with. Did he assume he could lure her into a meaningless date with trite, empty flattery?

And then what, after he'd tired of her?

Why, he'd do what her ex had done.

She refused to dwell on the scenario, but had learned from experience.

Tim would abandon her.

At four o'clock on the day of Snowflake's tree-lighting ceremony, Holly gave herself a final once-over in the foyer mirror and smiled. She'd spent an hour getting ready, something she usually never did—opting for black mascara and a touch of blue eyeshadow to complement her dark eyes. Sparingly, she brushed on a light rose blush to her cheekbones, then applied lipstick in a sun-kissed mauve tone. Her reflection smiled back, and she attributed her shining eyes not to her makeup, but because she was seeing Tim.

She tucked her hair beneath a wool cap, and knotted a sumptuous blue cashmere scarf over her coat.

Snow had begun to fall when Holly stopped at the motel that was temporarily putting up Jasmine and Emily.

She insisted on bringing them to the tree-lighting.

At first Emily declined, her thin lips flattening, before finally complying for her daughter's sake.

They piled into Holly's car and arrived at the resplendently decorated town center where the unlit tree towered, and Holly snagged a parking space in a lot off Main Street. The town resembled an oil painting of a chocolate-box Christmas scene, enhanced by mouth-watering cocoa beans flavoring the air from Sheila's Gourmet Chocolates.

The dark green of the pines contrasted with their coating of pristine frosty snowflakes. Jasmine's breath left white puffs as she incessantly chattered, and the muted crunch of their boots on the hardened snow assured that the winter season had a firm hold on Snowflake.

As they approached the town center, they marveled at the winking silver lights in the shops' windows, and Holly ducked into the This and That Shop to probe their inventory of antiques before they closed. The observance of Christmas in a modest, Americana Colorado town was a sparkling and detailed affair. At one corner, a flashing red arrow pointed to Candy Cane Avenue, a side alley lined with candy canes.

"It even smells like peppermint!" Jasmine exclaimed, and the women smilingly echoed her enthusiasm.

At the end of the avenue the humane society had organized an 'adopt a dog' event. Multiple dogs wearing white-and-red velvet Santa hats chased an inflatable ball in a fenced-in area, while miniature piles of puppies, resting on each other, barked playfully and looked on.

Jasmine's cherubic face beamed, and she tugged at Emily's coat sleeve. "Can we adopt a puppy, Mommy? I always wanted a shih tzu."

"Maybe someday. And older dogs need companions too." Emily replied with cautious deliberation, which Holly attributed to an abundance of broken dreams. "Once we get back on our feet and have our own place, we'll see."

"That will happen," Holly encouraged.

"Will it?" Emily invariably had such a faraway stare. "It's difficult being a single parent, and I'm all alone."

"Not anymore. I'm here to help you." Holly offered an upbeat nod of confirmation. "In fact, the entire community is. Look at how the town rallied and found space for everyone."

As they proceeded, Emily declined Holly's offer of money so Jasmine could buy some hot chocolate or little trinkets. Respecting the woman's wishes, Holly placed her wallet back inside her handbag.

What made people too proud to accept a kindness, despite desperate circumstances? Didn't they realize it was a joy to give? Charity had often quoted a favorite Bible verse, 2 Corinthians 8:12: "For if the willingness is there, the gift is acceptable according to what one has, not according to what one does not have."

"Okay," Holly said. "But if you change your mind …"

Emily twisted the cheap wristwatch around her skinny wrist and didn't answer. Holly had the urge to place her hand over the woman's, calming the anxious gesture.

Farther down the street, they ducked in and out of local shops and grinned at holiday shoppers sipping mulled wassail. Jasmine inhabited her own little space, taking it all in

—the fruity scents of apples, lemons, and oranges mingling with cinnamon.

Seasonal markets clustered together selling residents' handicrafts. Spotting a unique stand, Jasmine tugged them over to a craft booth where an older woman was making handmade dolls. Traditional and beguiling, each doll was designed with a whimsical smile.

The woman used coffee-brown colored yarn to knot two eyes, then cut out a heart-shaped piece of red felt for the mouth.

"I loved dolls when I was young, but now I'm too old for them." Jasmine sighed and cupped a tiny doll lovingly. She handled the thick braids of yarn and dashed her fingers along the doll's gingham dress, circling the wide white buttons.

"You're never too old if it's something you love," Holly said. "The fact that you appreciate a beautifully handcrafted doll means you're imaginative and artistic. Which we already recognize, of course." Holly and Emily exchanged a smile. "Because you're a quick learner."

Beaming, Jasmine drummed her fingers on the counter as she leaned in to inspect the other dolls.

"Please let me buy this doll for you." Holly immediately noted Emily's frown and chided herself for not asking her permission first.

Jasmine jumped up and down. "Please, Mommy?"

Emily's face filled with regret. She surveyed the doll, then her daughter. Finally, her silver-gray eyes met Holly's. "Are you sure, Miss Kim?"

"It's my pleasure and we'll call it an early holiday gift," Holly said. "Agreed?"

"Yay, yay yay!" Jasmine snuggled the doll close to her chest. "Thank you, Miss Kim." The elation in the child's eyes was a reflection of the true spirit of Christmas.

"This gift gives *me* more happiness than you can ever imagine," Holly said.

A chill was in the air, and the scent of fire-roasted chestnuts permeated every inch of space. Food trucks sold homemade candy, and Holly was drawn to Nancy's Caramel Station, selling delectable, buttery caramels. She bought a half pound and shared the candies with her companions. The caramels were dense and chewy, a gooey delight.

The magical holiday atmosphere was furthered by evergreen wreaths twined with eucalyptus leaves and emerald satin ribbons placed uniformly on each shop door. The distinctive woodsy scent unmistakably proclaimed Christmas.

"I don't recall the tree lighting being anywhere near as wonderful when I was younger," Holly murmured.

"Life's defining stages." Emily's hands flew through her thin hair, and her severe features relaxed. "I read about it in my self-improvement book. Each stage you're in gives you a different perspective of the world."

"See, Mommy. I told you tonight would be fun." Jasmine supplied a tooth-filled grin and wiped a glob of caramel stuck to the edge of her mouth. "Let's go visit the dogs!"

"You two run along," Holly attempted to keep the jump of excitement from her tone. "It's almost time for me to meet the building inspector."

Emily removed her square-framed glasses and polished the lenses with the sleeve of her drawstring jacket. "You're meeting the bad guy here tonight, Miss Kim?"

Holly bristled, immediately coming to Tim's defense. "The shelter's defective wiring isn't his fault, and he's working with me and a host of others to get it fixed. I'll catch up with you two afterwards."

"Sounds good. C'mon, Mommy!" Jasmine quickly ended the women's verbal duel. "See you later, Miss Kim."

A chorus of brass instruments—several of Snowflake High School's band students playing the tuba, trombone, and trumpet—rang a medley of well-loved carols with "It Came Upon a Midnight Clear," succeeded by a jubilant "God Rest Ye, Merry Gentlemen."

Meanwhile, other members of the band played under the gazebo, and the melodies brought a grin to Jasmine's pale face as she raced off with her mother in tow.

Armed with an animated smile, Holly reached The Little Corner Bistro a few minutes later. She lingered, mesmerized by the tiny candles illuminating each window. Assorted restaurants were open, and patrons wearing sleek parkas with fur-trimmed hoods perused the outdoor menus. Scents of flame-grilled meats melded with basil and garlic, beckoning them inside.

Women idled as they passed the bistro, feasting their eyes on Tim.

Which was how Holly spotted him, as he reigned tall and straight and unbearably handsome outside the bistro. Because of the admiring women.

That, and because his athletic physique filled out his familiar quilted parka flawlessly. His attractive face showed the beginnings of a dark beard.

He was conversing with an older, gruff-looking man wearing round eyeglasses and a plaid wool coat. Tim tilted his head toward the man, suggesting that he was attending to the conversation, although he examined the crowd as if he was searching for someone.

He was searching for her, Holly thought with an inner tingle.

Seeming to detect her presence, he lifted his head abruptly, and their gazes locked.

Before she'd scanned the crowd a second time, he'd reached her.

"Holly?" He offered his usual charismatic smile, and her breath caught. "I haven't seen you in what … five days?"

She couldn't stand still and tried to relax her breathing. The magical atmosphere had transformed the night into one of enchantment, especially with a handsome, enigmatic guy at her side.

She stole a peek at him, appreciating the strength carved into his chiseled cheekbones and tanned face. Timothy Stewart was exactly what fairy tale princes were created from—broad-shouldered, hard-working, and compelling.

She bit back a grin. "But you text me all the time."

Since their initial meeting in his office, he'd texted each evening at eight o'clock when she'd finished teaching.

How was your day? he'd always begin.

Jasmine is the most precocious and talented student I've taught in several years, she'd texted back. *I only wish she had a decent piano to practice on, and a parent who was more invested in her progress. I've arranged to give her lessons at a music store in Snowflake.*

Slightly self-conscious by her chatty zeal for Jasmine, Holly described her other piano students and schedule.

Once, when silence lapsed, she'd informed him about how she'd subbed for the pianist at Snowflake Chapel. She'd been tempted to invite him to Sunday service, but didn't. He always brushed off every reference to church, changing the subject to inquire about her aunt or students or her cat.

What is Butterscotch doing? he'd ask, and she'd reply, *Nothing. Lazy, as usual. And your stray kitten?*

He'd confided that he'd revisited the shelter and adopted one of the kittens.

She is company for me, because my place is lonely.

Holly had studied the phone screen. Lonely? Him? What was he trying to tell her?

Hurriedly, she combed her thoughts for another topic but

fell short when she failed to think of anything. Finally, she texted, *Have you thought of a good name for your kitten?*

Taffy.

Sweet. For a man who was just as sweet.

As the days progressed, Holly clicked on her cellphone each evening with anticipation and delight.

The previous evening, she'd finished with, *Well, I'm calling it a night. I'll see you tomorrow.*

Can I tell you how much I'm looking forward to it? he'd asked.

Her pulse had given a leap of excitement.

Why?

Because I like talking with you, especially in person.

Calm down, she'd told herself after he'd sent that text.

And she was telling herself the same thing now. They'd arranged this get-together to figure out a solution to the shelter's dilemma. This wasn't about seeing Tim again.

The older man, who must be Ralph, approached, grinning broadly. "So this is the gorgeous lady you've been yakking about." Conspiratorially, he winked at Tim.

"Thanks for keeping my secret," Tim murmured.

"I didn't know it was a secret. Besides, you can't keep a beautiful woman under wraps forever." Ralph kept his unrepentant grin on Holly. "You don't live in Snowflake or I would have recognized you."

"I live in Pine Cone Valley," she answered. "I'm a piano teacher."

"So I heard."

"I teach a girl who lived at the homeless shelter with her mother."

"Jasmine, right?" Ralph quizzed. "She and her mother are staying at the motel in town at a heavily discounted rate until this electrical situation at the shelter is resolved."

"Yes. How did you learn about her?"

"Well, now, I wonder." Ralph sent a teasing look toward

Tim, then extended a hand to Holly. "Tim and I go way back. He was such a solemn little boy."

He really had been talking about her to his friends, she thought.

"You're a fountain of information tonight, Ralph," Tim said with an offhand laugh.

She smiled and shook Ralph's hand. "I'm Holly."

"Tim and I have texted the last few days." Ralph reached into his pocket, extracted a folded sheet of paper, and passed it to her. "I stopped by the shelter and the problem isn't as severe as everyone anticipated. But don't forget, the building hasn't been updated in twenty years, and chances are it will require upgrading."

Holly unfolded the paper and scrutinized it. "Three thousand dollars is your repair estimate?"

"Be warned. Rewiring is chaotic, disruptive work. Lou has a copy of my estimate too. It should be accurate, give or take any surprises."

"In this business, there are always surprises," Tim inserted. "So round out that number to thirty-five hundred dollars."

"I'll donate fifteen hundred toward the project," Holly said. "Somehow, we'll make up the difference."

"*We?*" Ralph's smile faded. "I'm working at a reduced rate already."

"I meant me and the business community, and anyone else who wants to contribute," Holly said. "I have various fund-raisers in mind."

"Like what?" Ralph countered. "A bake sale?"

Tim and Holly both laughed.

"Private joke," Tim explained.

Mayor Hardy, who prevailed at a podium by the tree, spotted Ralph and waved him over.

From where they stood, Ralph surveyed the tall, unlit

pine. "I'll catch up with you two in an hour," he called over his shoulder as he shuffled away.

"I brought Jasmine and Emily with me tonight," Holly said to Tim. "They're over on Candy Cane Avenue with the dogs. I'll meet them after the ceremony."

She regarded the steady stream of shoppers, the beginning of the retail rush. Why was the Christmas season so commercialized? Wasn't the holiday supposed to be a Christian holy day to mark the birth of the Son of God?

"How are they faring?" Tim's quiet tone jerked her from her reflections.

"Moderately well, considering the upheaval of moving into a motel." Holly placed Ralph's estimate into her handbag. "In addition, Emily is applying for a number of jobs this week."

"That's encouraging. I'm optimistic that she'll find a decent position soon." His hand on her elbow, Tim gently drew Holly away from the jam-packed sidewalk.

She glanced up at him. "Where are we going?"

He gestured to an outside seating area serving hot chocolate and tiny, fried cinnamon-glazed doughnuts. Portable heaters and a canvas canopy outfitted with Edison light bulbs created a snug, welcoming atmosphere.

"Do you want to grab something to eat?" he asked. "My treat."

This might be a date. She didn't want to date him. Or did she?

She hesitated.

"Do you prefer somewhere else?" He surveyed the various kiosks, looking like he could easily be hurt by her reply if she refused.

"No, this spot is ideal."

"Good." He guided her to a turquoise-colored bistro table and pulled out a chair for her. She liked that about him—

standing until she was seated, always courteous, calm, and considerate.

"It's not exactly quiet, and the menu is limited to beverages and doughnuts," he said. "It's more of a—"

"Everything is lovely. The vintage lights on the awning and the little place selling homespun sweets"—she gestured to the shop across the way—"smells wonderful."

He settled across from her. "So you're not teaching again for a couple days?"

His inquiry won him her astonished gape. "You remembered my text?"

He was so fine looking, and she loved the way he listened to her, honestly listened, as if every word she spoke—or texted—was important.

"I've learned a lot about you because I've been reading your texts over and over."

She tipped her head. "Why would you do something like that?"

His heated scrutiny of her sent her pulse into a double rhythm. "You really have to ask?"

On the tip of her tongue were the words, *Yes, I really do.*

But she really didn't, because that irresistible attraction tugged her ever closer to him.

In an attempt to avoid his searching gaze, she studied the menu as a freckle-faced teenage waitress started toward them.

"Hot chocolate and doughnuts?" Holly asked him.

"Sure."

After the waitress took their orders, Holly leaned back in her chair. "Hot chocolate reminds me of sledding, or simply sitting by a window and watching the snow fall." She smiled. "What about you?"

"Nope." He did the opposite of echoing her enthusiasm by

pressing his lips together and grimacing. "Hot chocolate isn't part of my childhood memories."

"Oh, I see."

Although she didn't see anything of the sort.

After they were served the piping hot cocoa laced with whipped cream and yeasty deep-fried doughnuts, Holly bent her head to say grace. Tim supported her lead. Granted, he didn't pray, but he bowed his head.

"Do you always say a blessing before every meal?" he asked when she whispered "amen."

"Absolutely. It's a way to show respect to God, and gratitude for our blessings."

Thoughtfully, he took a sip of hot chocolate. "So, tell me more about your fund-raiser."

"My students are all on board to play piano for the benefit recital." Holly savored a mouthwatering taste of whipped cream and hot chocolate, finishing with a bite of her warm doughnut. "Jasmine and I are working on a difficult duet arrangement of 'Silent Night.'"

Tim averted his head. "Duly noted."

"You don't like Silent Night'?"

"Everyone likes 'Silent Night.'"

"Is it because you don't like church?"

He shrugged. "Like I said, it's not for me."

"Did you ever attend church?"

"What do I look like, Holly? The Grinch again?"

"Sorry."

"We went, but certainly not often." He picked up a spoon and stirred the hot chocolate in his mug. "While we lived near Denver, we visited my grandparents. When we did, my mother often argued with my grandmother."

"What did you do? I mean, while they argued. You were a little kid."

"My grandfather was a contractor, and he'd bring me

along on his jobs. He taught me all about the building trade." Tim raised both his hands and grinned. "And thus, here I am. All that on the job training paid off, plus four years of taking college courses at night, multiple certifications, and passing licensing exams."

"You're a great guy."

"Me?"

She threw him a comic sigh. "You're not as cynical and hardhearted as I first suspected."

"Hmm. Gee, thanks."

"But we were talking about your grandfather."

"He was the best," Tim said quietly. "Unfortunately, there were days when he didn't take me with him and I'd be subjected to a firsthand blow-out between my grandmother and mother. My grandmother would go on and on about church, insisting religion was precisely what my mother needed—a clergyman to set her on a respectable path and enable her to overcome her many addictions."

"Which were?"

"Alcohol, pills, whatever she could get." He hesitated. He couldn't seem to find his words. "As usual, my mother expelled the idea as quickly as my grandmother fired it at her."

"She wasn't in favor of getting help?"

"She wasn't in favor of anything my grandmother suggested. They had a prickly relationship, which is stating it mildly. Grandmother disapproved of my mother's lifestyle, and looking back, I can understand why. My mother only visited when she was out of money."

A silence lapsed as Holly collected her thoughts. Nearby, the brass band launched into a jazzy rendition of "A Holly Jolly Christmas."

"Were you out of money often?" Holly asked.

"What do you think? Let's just say she would have fit in

seamlessly during the flower child era. She drove around in a Volkswagen bus with her friends like life was a never-ending party, while I hung out in the back seat."

"How old were you?"

"Eleven, twelve." He reinforced his recollection with an indifferent head shake. "My mother even changed her name from Sally to Astra. As you can imagine, my grandmother wasn't thrilled about that, either."

"Pretty name."

"Astra means star—derived from the star. My mother said it reminded her of Christmas. Ironic, in view of the fact that we didn't celebrate."

"Where is she now?" Holly surveyed his mug and half-eaten doughnut. He'd pushed both to the side.

"She passed away from pneumonia and a hard life." Tim's voice trailed off into silence. "Years ago."

"I'm sorry."

"Thanks." He swallowed hard. "The next day I headed west. I was nineteen when I arrived in Hollywood."

Hollywood at nineteen. A lively discussion about his adventures in that shiny town should have ensued. Instead, Holly felt an unexpected sadness for him.

"Forgive me, Tim." She concentrated on the festivities—youngsters carrying bags of buttery popcorn and skipping backward, their watchful parents close behind. "My questions were too intrusive."

CHAPTER 7

S he was right, Tim thought. Her questions, their confidences, brought up painful memories. They'd only known each other a few days, and he'd always kept his personal life off limits. Yet, as she watched him expectantly, he wanted to talk with her in spite of his inner hesitancy, in spite of his vow to never dwell on his childhood.

He inhaled, his memories peeling back fifteen years. "I remember sitting in the passenger seat of a rig after I'd hitch-hiked," he said softly.

"Where are you going?" the truck driver had asked.

"Wherever you are," Tim had replied.

"The trucker was driving to Hollywood to drop off some costumes for a movie set. He introduced me around, so I was able to get some work the next few years, doing various odd jobs at the studios and construction. I started auditioning for acting roles too, and even hired an acting coach." Tim shrugged. "Eventually I got a minor role on a TV show. That led to another, and finally I landed a spot on a popular television series."

"Congratulations," Holly said.

He smiled. Nodded.

Way before that, there were the do-gooders, the authorities who threatened to separate Tim from his mother. Sure, as an adult he understood that children should be safeguarded, but as a child, he only wanted to stay with his mother. And because of the fear that he might be taken from her, she often switched into protective mode and avoided appealing to the powers that be for help.

But this was Holly.

Sitting across from her, sharing the celebratory nature of the evening, compelled him to tell her more about himself.

And that was a first for him.

Besides, he wryly reflected, he didn't want to dampen her enthusiasm for their upcoming fund-raising conversation by answering her questions with curtness.

He steepled his hands and leaned forward. "Next, I suppose you'll ask me about my father."

"If you'd like to talk, I'm here to listen."

Clad in a crimson-red coat with a thick blue scarf wrapped around her, she was breathtaking—all fresh-faced complexion and enormous eyes framed by thick lashes and gracefully arched eyebrows. Her black hair was tucked beneath a wool cap and a stray wisp fell across her cheek. The glow of the vintage light bulbs highlighted her soft skin and softer, enticing lips.

"Tim?" Holly propped her small chin on her palms, suspending his delightful observation. "Your father?"

"I didn't know him well." His account was lacking, and Tim allowed a pause before continuing. "All my mother used to say is that he ruined her life."

Because she'd had a baby. And she'd named the baby Tim.

Holly slid her hand across the table. "Did your father desert you and your mother?"

"On the contrary, my mother left him." Tim closed his

hand over hers. Holly offered reassurance and comfort, and he decided to accept it. Another first. "My mother was a free spirit. Everything was done her way."

"Where is he now?"

"My father?" Tim tried to smile. "For many years he was absent from my life, and then he reappeared when I was cast in that television series. I suppose he was after money, assuming I was a rich and famous actor." He stared off, noting Ralph chatting with the mayor, the families gathering near the enormous tree.

Holly nodded toward his mug. "Your hot chocolate is getting cold."

He detected sympathy welling in her eyes, although she strove for a heartening smile. She'd clearly caught his distasteful tone at the mention of his father.

He picked up his mug. "I'm sure it's fine."

The last time he drank hot chocolate he'd been in grade school. These days, his likings ran toward a refreshing beer after work. Fearing she would disapprove because she was obviously a churchgoer and his mother had repeatedly lectured that God had strict rules you were supposed to follow, he amplified his sip with a smile. "This is excellent, especially during the Christmas season."

A season he hadn't celebrated in years.

Wait. There was that one Christmas when they'd arrived at his grandparents' house. Or rather, he'd arrived. He'd never been certain where his mother had disappeared to. He only knew that he'd bought her a gift with the money he'd earned working with his grandfather.

He shook his head. Those memories, that gift, were too difficult to deal with, and he shoved them aside, preferring happier reminiscences. His mother had loved him, but if she was pushed, she loved the drink more. Surely by now, he'd accepted that.

And then there were the pleasant emotions, the giddiness of waking up Christmas morning in his grandparents' secure home, despite he and his mother always being despairingly broke.

That remembrance of a happy Christmas gave birth to a heartening possibility; and a chunk of his resistance, the barricade he'd firmly erected from one end of his broken dreams to another, began to split.

Was a real Christmas in the future for him—that elusive spirit of goodwill? Was Christmas about receiving, like the child he'd been as he'd contentedly unwrapped his grandparents' gifts? Or was Christmas truly the season of giving, per Holly's intent?

And was it about God's love and forgiveness, as Christians proclaimed?

He kept his hand around Holly's, studying her lips, rosy from the invigorating air.

"What people don't understand," he said, "is that just because an actor gains a modicum of success doesn't mean he's amassed a fortune. Especially if you give most of it away."

"You gave the money you earned away?"

"Just about." He gentled his reply with a smile. "I didn't make millions, as most assumed. I wasn't the lead in the series. Actually, I got the role of a secondary character when the actor who originally had the part opted to work on a different show."

"So who did you give your money to?"

She didn't seem interested in the amount of money, which surprised him. That was initially the first thing everyone wanted to know.

He focused on the brass band performing a rousing rendition of "The Twelve Days of Christmas" while the crowd chimed in with, "'And a partridge in a pear tree'" at the end of each verse.

Holly toyed with her doughnut, apparently waiting for his reply.

"Who do you guess I gave the money to?" he asked.

"Your father?

"He claimed he was in a jam." Tim gave a derisive snort. "But my grandmother had stated countless times that he was constantly in a jam, which she blamed on compulsive gambling." Tim scrubbed a hand over his face, as if he could rub away the memories of his father's betrayal. "He was supposed to use the money to check into a treatment program. By the time I reached out to see how he was doing, he'd disappeared. I haven't heard from him since."

Tim caught Holly's expression of understanding, the slight slump of her posture, and tugged his hand from hers. He didn't need her sympathy, he cautioned himself. He didn't need anything from anybody. He'd made his own way and had done just fine.

She blinked.

"Holly?"

"Hmm?" Her eyes welled with tears.

"You're crying?" he asked skeptically.

She flapped a dismissive hand. "Don't mind me. I cry when the commercials appear on television about sponsoring an abandoned puppy in a shelter."

"Please don't feel sorry for me." He tipped up her chin. "My mother cared about me and my grandparents were wonderful. I don't have any emotional wounds. I promise."

"You must. Your parents were neglectful, and—"

"No more talk about me or my past." With an indifference he didn't feel, he blew out a breath.

"You're important too Tim."

He dropped his hand. "Let's discuss your fund-raiser, all right?"

"All right." She faltered, then plucked a sheet of notepaper from her handbag. "I consulted the internet and discovered that it's best to start with a name."

"And what name did you come up with?"

"I hadn't decided on any until now, but what about Astra?" She perked up. "Because we're reaching for the stars to create a better and safer shelter."

"No, no." He crossed his arms. "You initially blamed me for the electrical problem, and now you're thinking about naming your fund-raiser after my mother?"

"It's a lovely name and ideal for the season. The star of Bethlehem guided the three wise men, and a star is the glowing symbol of hope."

"Astra. My mother. A star of hope." Tim sucked in a quick breath. "And then what?"

"Then we formulate a plan. But wait. Are you okay with the name?"

He saluted.

"Good."

Her infectious smile, her eagerness, made it challenging to concentrate on their conversation, or take a nibble of his doughnut or a gulp of tepid chocolate. Holly was unabashedly enthusiastic, and her energetic voice captivated him.

He uncrossed his arms, taken aback at how his heart spun in his chest, precisely the same as when he'd first laid eyes on her at the shelter.

"There are state regulations and building permits," he murmured, half to himself. "I'll look into them."

"And I'll solicit the parishioners in my church for donations. They're always generous. Plus, I'm going with the idea of a Christmas sing-a-long at the conclusion."

"Okay." He raised his mug for a toast, feeling slightly foolish for his youthful excitement. "What about a tree decorating? Ask the attendees to contribute money, plus bring an ornament to hang on a Christmas tree."

"I like that." Deliberately, she nodded. "But where is this tree? There was a pine at the shelter, and Jasmine and the other children trimmed it before they left."

A Christmas tree. He'd never hung ornaments on a tree before, not even at his grandparents' house.

"We'll set up a tree at the nursing home. I'll donate it." He took her hand, drawing the shape of a pine tree on her palm with his thumb.

He feasted his gaze on her glistening eyes, her ready smile. Could she truly be genuine and so different from the do-gooders he'd dealt with when he and his mother were homeless? Individuals who claimed they would help, but did so only for publicity?

"I phoned the Golden Birch Manor, and the director said she is thrilled to support us." Holly lifted her face, shimmering with delight. "The residents will enjoy hearing the students play holiday carols, and the facility will place the donation box at the entrance."

He squeezed her hand in encouragement. "Thank you for sharing your vision with me. You're an inspiration."

"Because this is my vision and my mission," she declared, with a satisfied wag of her head. "I've scheduled the recital date for December twenty-third at three o'clock, which gives me a little over two weeks to raise the funds. Will Ralph allow the shelter any leeway if he doesn't receive the full payment when the work is completed?"

"He's a hard man to get to know, but once you do, you'll discover he's good-hearted," Tim replied. "Though I can't predict what he'll say because he must pay his employees too."

"I'll donate my fifteen hundred dollars immediately, and that should move things quicker." He was aware she looked to him for a smile to soothe her unspoken concerns. He obliged, then stated he was ready to render assistance to Ralph and the shelter, and that he was well-connected to the community because of his job. Moreover, her fund-raiser seemed feasible.

"I'd like all the residents to move back by New Year's Eve," she said.

"That will make for a happy New Year?"

"A very happy New Year."

"Attention." The mayor's microphoned voice boomed, accompanied by a drum roll from the band's percussionist. "Our very own Snowflake High School chorus is singing Christmas carols by candlelight, and the tree-lighting cere-mony begins in fifteen minutes."

"Ready?" Tim checked the time on the town clock. At Holly's affirmation, he signaled for the check and paid the bill. As they rose, he took her hand as if it was the most natural thing in the world.

She stalled when they passed a candy stand. "I'd like to buy Jasmine a bagful of caramels. She loves them."

"Whenever you mention her, your face lights up," Tim said. "And being well-acquainted with Mayor Hardy's fond-ness for speech-making, I guarantee there's plenty of time."

"I feel a love for Jasmine that's difficult to explain."

He chuckled at her sincere smile, then gestured toward the candy stand. "Will you buy candy for me too?"

"I suppose I can spare you some." She purchased two separate pounds and provided him with his own bag.

"You're a generous woman, Holly." He popped a caramel into his mouth, offered her one, then shepherded her to a quiet area behind the crowd. "This spot is just right."

"We can't see the tree lighting from back here."

"We will once the tree is lit."

"Shouldn't we move closer?"

"I can't imagine why, when here is perfectly fine." He leaned against a tree trunk and nestled her in his arms.

"Jasmine and her mother are here." Holly squirmed and went up on her tiptoes. "I told them I would meet them afterwards to bring them back to their motel. I pray that her mother—"

"If she's struggling with an addiction, she'll need support. The shelter offers excellent resources, and seeking a job is admirable."

She prompted him to look toward a booth selling beverages—bottled water and warm cider and soft drinks.

"They don't serve alcohol at these events, Holly."

"It's just that … I would do anything for that little girl."

"So you mentioned." Tim scanned the crowd. "I don't see them and the ceremony hasn't started yet, so they're probably playing with the dogs on Candy Cane Avenue and it's all good."

"Maybe we should—"

"Holly." He inclined his head and brushed a kiss on her temple, his lips gliding down her cheek and settling on her mouth for a kiss. "Thank you."

She drew back. "Why?"

"Because you are kind and determined and thoroughly gorgeous." He smoothed his hands across her cheeks to lighten the moment before he recognized that the look in her glistening gaze wasn't confusion. She felt the same tug of emotion that he did.

"I should get another bagful of candy for Jasmine before the stand closes, and—"

He grinned, not intending to change his plans in the least.

"Tim? Did you hear what—"

"Holly." Again, he touched her lips with his, exquisitely gentle. "Let's stop talking."

CHAPTER 8

She must have dined at the Cozy Coffee Shop a dozen times, Holly thought as she snagged one of the few empty tables, tucked by the entrance. Invariably, she appreciated the comfortable interior—sunny and lively with light-colored walls and a splash of brilliant-red poinsettias decorating each table—and detected the aroma of freshly ground coffee beans and the daily baked baguettes. A rolling jazzy arrangement of Christmas music played softly in the background.

Tim strode to the table and set down their tray. "Eggnog latte and a peppermint brownie for lunch?" He raised his eyebrows.

"Technically, eleven thirty is still morning." She smoothed down her red V-neck velour sweater that matched her red slacks as she defended her choices, which were startlingly lacking in nutrition. Unapologetically, she inspected his plate. "Should I have ordered your selections? Double smoked-bacon on a croissant and a cup of black coffee?"

"What's wrong with it?"

"Black coffee cancels out the calories of a buttery croissant and bacon?"

Amusement flicked over his features. "If you recall, I take my coffee with three sugars, so there goes your calorie-counting theory."

She took a swallow of latte—steamed eggnog, dark-brewed espresso, and a dash of cinnamon. "You should try to look a little embarrassed by your choice of food groups."

"I will if you will," he teased in response. When he smiled, his eyes crinkled up at the corners, flashing with wit and keen intellect.

The same overheating of her senses she'd experienced the night of the tree-lighting ceremony flooded through her. She avoided his gaze and focused on his navy-blue parka as he hung it on a rack beside her coat.

"I'm paying for lunch," she reminded him, "because you treated last time."

"That's why I ordered the early luncheon special, to save you money," he teased. "In fact, I might order the daily dessert too. Muffins are half price on Saturdays."

"Be my guest," she said graciously. "But first, let's say grace." She bent her head. Tim didn't participate, but he kept his head bowed until she completed the prayer.

The shop's glass door swung open heralding a burst of wind, casually teasing his coarse, dark hair. Thick and rich and the color of root beer, she decided. His hair was styled to lay flat on the sides, fairly long at the nape, the waves sweeping against his shirt collar. Over his shirt, he wore a fisherman knit sweater.

She sampled her brownie and briefly closed her eyes to savor the sweetness of mint chocolate laced with peppermint buttercream icing. "It's delightful. Do you want a bite?"

"Only if you let me pay for lunch." He slid onto the seat across from her so that their knees touched.

"I told you—"

"It's the least I can do to thank you for your commitment to the homeless shelter."

"You mean the Astra project," she corrected.

"My mother wasn't exactly the poster child for Christmas." Wryly, he smiled. "And may I point out that we were talking about lunch and concluded with my refusal to allow you to pay?"

"Tim, you agreed to let me treat today."

"I don't recall ever actually agreeing." His dark eyes glinted with mischief. "In any case, I changed my mind."

"Are you the persistent type who won't quit badgering me until I agree?"

"I'm known for being extremely tenacious, especially if I want something." The serious tone of his voice robbed her of any retort, and she avoided his roguish expression by staring at the poinsettia.

She'd been thrilled when he'd suggested meeting at the coffee shop, hoping all week that he'd ask her out. And with that hope, she'd questioned herself.

What was she doing? These feelings, these rose-colored glasses, were completely out of character. She'd sworn off men after her unpleasant experience with her ex.

"A bite of your brownie?" he repeated. "Or do you intend to eat it all by yourself?"

Obligingly, she offered him a nibble.

"Just like I imagined." He laced his fingers through hers. "Delicious."

A hazardous warmth invaded Holly's bloodstream. Warily, she lifted her hand from his.

In the days since the tree lighting, she'd taught a full schedule of daily piano lessons, and Tim had put in a seventy-hour workweek. Still, he'd texted or called nightly, and they'd compared notes on the progress of the fund-raiser, whom they'd spoken to that could help raise funds, and the arrangements with the nursing home that was hosting the performance.

And in those texts and calls, an easygoing companionship had developed between them which was established by spur-of-the-moment remarks and mutual laughter, peppered by recurring, relaxed silences.

She arranged a napkin on her lap. "So what was your urgent need to see me on this sunshiny morning?"

"Well, the first urgent need was that I was hungry. Starved, actually, but not only for food."

Pointedly, she ignored his innuendo, as well as the flush of heat creeping up her cheeks. Self-consciously, she tucked a strand of hair behind her ear.

Earlier that morning, she'd taken particular care with her appearance, applying rosy lip gloss. Then she'd brushed her black hair until it gleamed and refrained from wearing her usual woolen beanie.

"Well, I'm starved for conversation," she joked.

"I told you about myself." He dove into his croissant. "Now I'd like to learn more about you."

"We've corresponded nearly every day since we met."

"And from the little I gathered from your brief responses, you were adopted from South Korea when you were six months old." He reached for his coffee cup. "Is Holly the name you were born with?"

"I didn't have a name. I was dropped off on a church's stairs."

He stopped in the middle of drinking his coffee. "Truthfully?"

"Many children in Korea are abandoned. Many more are abandoned all over the world."

His stunned expression prompted Holly to explain, "Nonetheless, I believe I was loved by my birth mother. She chose to give me the advantages of adoption—a healthy home and solid education—opportunities she couldn't have provided as a single parent. Most likely she had limited choices, and she 'abandoned' me in a way that permitted me to be found."

He sent her a blank look. "So, who named you? Your adoptive parents?"

"Yes. I required hospitalization in South Korea, which was why I wasn't adopted immediately. Because I was born near Christmas, my parents called me Holly. They were Asian as well."

He put his cup down. "They must have been thrilled with an adorable baby girl to cherish."

"Perhaps in the beginning." She nibbled at her brownie. "But as I grew older, I acted out. I assumed I was the only Asian adoptee in town and felt out of place."

He set down his croissant and regarded her. "Were you?"

"No. There is an extensive Asian community in this area. Still, as a child I was bullied for being homely and awkward."

"Surely not?" He leaned forward and gently cupped her chin. "Looking at you, that's hard to believe."

Airily, she waved him off. "The teenage years are difficult for a girl who hasn't figured out where she belongs. Maybe my insecurity showed."

"You were special. You were chosen by your adoptive parents." His brown eyes reminded her of the finest chocolate, and involuntarily, she memorized them. Oftentimes, the scorching heat of his gaze melted her. Now that gaze was slightly hard, as if he was ready to protect her from the insensitive actualities of the real world.

She repaid his protectiveness with a sincere smile.

"You must have fought off the boys in droves once you hit high school." He threw a quick, grim laugh, and the thought crossed her mind that he might be jealous.

"I was short and skinny, and no guy even looked cross-eyed at me." She reflected on those distressing, uncomfortable years, knowing she'd been thankful for Charity's friendship. Later on, when they'd reached adulthood, Charity often reminded Holly that God was in everyone's heart, even the classmates who had cruelly tormented her. Often, she spoke about sadness and happiness growing together.

"Praise God when things go perfectly," she'd advised. *"And praise God when they don't."*

"Fast forward, and you could be a model on a runway," Tim was saying.

Though she glowed at the flattery, Holly reverted to their earlier conversation. "Certainly, Snowflake and the surrounding areas are welcoming and diverse. The residents are down-to-earth and genuine."

Tim responded by folding his arms and leaning back. "Tell me about your parents. I spoke honestly about mine over hot chocolate and doughnuts."

She caught the aloofness that threaded his tone whenever he mentioned his mother or father, and perceived the hidden frustration and sadness and, yes, bitterness.

"They were loving and bighearted. Both were missionaries and adopted me later in life." Holly fiddled with the charm bracelet on her wrist, hearkening back to her father's chuckle, her mother's arms enfolding her. The delicate scent of violets and shared giggles and bedtime stories enveloped her.

"You mentioned in one of our phone conversations that they passed away?" he asked.

She took a deep breath. It was a question that was challenging to answer, despite the five years that had gone by. She'd learned a hard lesson the day they died—that the people she loved could be taken away from her in an instant.

Precariously close to tears, she fingered the silver charms.

"Their small plane went down on a missions trip in Asia. I was supposed to go, but my work schedule interfered at the last minute."

Soon afterward, she'd met Jim and plunged headfirst into a hasty marriage. With hindsight, she'd figured out that she'd coped with the void in her life, seeking to fill it with love and companionship, and had married a man incapable of either.

Tim's steady fingers covered hers. "I expressed my sympathy the other day, but I'm truly sorry for your loss."

"Thank you. This bracelet was a gift from my mother. She bought all the charms too."

He lifted her wrist and inspected each charm individually as she described the momentous occasions in her life.

"By the way, did I mention that you look as beautiful as your charm bracelet?" His intimate grin, the way he adeptly piloted the conversation in a different direction, prompted her heart to do a little flip in her chest. He lifted her hand and kissed it.

"I remind you of a charm bracelet?" she challenged with a jaunty smile.

"A beautiful one."

She busied herself with stirring her latte and beamed. "Thank you. Again."

Many folks had complimented her beauty once she reached college, a respective number of men poetically expressive. She'd extended a gracious acknowledgement while harboring the belief that they weren't speaking the truth. With clear precision she would flashback to the tongue-tied girl she'd been, the girl who'd worn glasses and been nicknamed a studious geek. And sometimes, even if she didn't entirely admit it to herself, the baby who had been abandoned in South Korea.

While she'd attempted to tuck away those long-ago

memories of youth, as an adult she placed little significance on something as fickle as external prettiness.

"I've learned from God that I'm sufficient just the way I am. I'm sufficiently attractive and sufficiently tall."

Tim grinned. "You're five feet."

"That's tall." She recited a favorite pastor's message that had been her mantra through those difficult adolescent years. "God made me, and He is perfect."

"I'm not following."

"I'm enough because God is in me. My talent and intelligence are sufficient."

Without taking his gaze from her face, Tim replied, "I agree."

"It took me a long time to come to peace with that. And Tim, you're enough too."

"With all my baggage?" Despite his outward unconcern, his voice caught ever so slightly.

She clutched her hands together. "I'm subbing at Snowflake Chapel for Sunday's service. I'll be playing Christmas carols, and you're welcome to attend. You mentioned you like 'Silent Night.'" She kept her tone neutral, but inwardly entertained the wish that he would accept her offer.

"Nope. Not my thing, Holly." Idly, he traced his forefinger along the table's wooden surface. His fingers were rough and callused. He was a man who worked with his hands. This charismatic man sitting across from her wasn't a television star anymore. "Thanks for accepting my invitation to see me today," he added.

Accepting? No decision there.

Anytime, she wanted to blurt. Instead, she viewed his guarded expression, his unswerving approach to navigating their discussion away from church.

They ate in quiet camaraderie, interspersed with Tim's queries regarding Jasmine and her mother.

When they finished, a college-aged woman with spiked blond hair wended past the other tables to them, ready to whisk off their plates. "Dessert?" she suggested, and Holly debated. The excellent service in the shop made her wish they had dined somewhere else. Her time with Tim had gone by much too fast. They'd been in the coffee shop less than an hour.

"No dessert for me," Tim told the waitress, grinning at Holly's quirked eyebrow.

"I thought you said—"

"Seeing you is a heap full of sweetness for a Saturday morning, and enough for any man."

Holly rolled her eyes. "Uh-huh. Me and your three packets of sugar."

With a smirk, the waitress placed the check between them.

Neatly, Tim covered the bill with his hand before Holly tugged it toward her.

"My treat, remember?" He reached into his pocket and laid several bills on the table. "No change," he instructed the waitress.

"Thanks, Tim. Annie is cooking in the kitchen but saw you come in. She said hello." Friendly and breezy, the waitress swept up the bills and carried their plates away.

"Who is Annie?" Holly asked. Through the large glass window, she watched pedestrians with ruddy cheeks hurrying along the sidewalk.

"The owner of the place."

"And the waitress knows your first name?"

"I've lived in Colorado ever since I was born, except for my stint in California." He gave an unabashed smile. "When I was a child, I came here with my grandfather."

"Where was your mother? Was she with your grandmother?"

"Sometimes. Other times, she'd take off for a spell and leave me with my grandparents. We never quite knew when she'd come back."

Or if.

She expected him to say more.

How long did his mother leave him? Days? Weeks? Months? Unnerved, Holly waited while a hush took up the space between them.

"Tim?" she eventually said.

"Did you want to ask anything else?" He looked at her as if he'd practically forgotten she sat across from him.

"Not unless you want to tell me more about yourself and—"

"Let's move on to your fund-raising business, all right?" It wasn't a question. The discussion concerning his mother was clearly over.

Holly didn't think she could ever learn enough about him to be satisfied, but she understood that his feelings about his past needed to be respected.

"Yes, of course." She picked up her latte and gazed at him over the cup, attempting to banish the downhearted mood that had settled. "Is Ralph making progress on the shelter?"

"He began the initial-stage fix, which is installing cables and wiring." Tim slid his coffee cup to the side of the table. "His crew removed furniture and carpeting and are running wires under the floorboards, through the walls and in the ceiling. New back boxes have been fitted, and sockets and switches are being rewired."

"The shelter needs all that?"

"Present-day demands are different from the past. High-tech is a part of everyday life, so might as well do it now when they're rewiring."

"So that's just the first stage?" She shook her head. "There's a considerable amount of work involved."

"Ralph and Lou are using a graph, so they're literally on the same page."

"What's the second stage?"

"The floor, ceiling, and walls are replastered, modern light fittings, switch plates, you name it."

"How is the timeline?"

"So far, Ralph and his crew are on track." When she reached for her cup, Tim lightly touched her arm. "Holly, your contribution is an immense help. You came at exactly the right time."

"God's timing is perfect, and every moment matters." She quoted another beloved saying from her pastor.

"Every moment matters," Tim repeated with a wide smile. "I like that. So let's make the most of it by spending the afternoon together."

"Don't you have to work?"

"Not on Saturday." Boyishly, he grinned. "And you aren't teaching any lessons, so you're free."

She swallowed a last gulp of latte. "Are you certain you know my schedule?"

"I memorized your texts, remember?"

She couldn't help her smile. He seemed to regard their texts as a higher form of communication, to be studied, analyzed, and gauged. "Tim, I may not be teaching, but I arranged to stop by the nursing home to prepare the final recital arrangements. Consequently, I'm not free."

"You're an educator, correct?"

"Yes."

"Educators are fond of learning new skills, right?"

She eyed him warily. "What did you have in mind?"

"The nursing home is right down the street from the ice-skating rink."

"So?"

"So, Miss Kim, we can visit the nursing home first and spend time with the residents." He grinned, extending his hand and bringing her to her feet. "Afterward, I'll teach you how to ice skate. And I'm looking forward to your reaction when you see the neon sign that Ralph installed."

CHAPTER 9

*F*our days later, Tim was still grinning when he parked his truck near town and walked the short distance to Musical Notes, the local music store.

Flurries were blanketing Snowflake in a fresh covering as evening neared. It was as if he'd phased into a scene from Norman Rockwell's colorful oil painting, *Main Street At Christmas*, complete with the faded brick town hall and country store. All Snowflake lacked were the vintage automobiles.

Sprigs of mistletoe and holly intermingled with whiffs of pine, and candlelight spilled across the pathways.

Taking Holly ice-skating had been a splendid idea, he decided as he neared the store. The rink had been a cacophony of giggling children and adults, and the bustle of hockey and figure skaters competing for ice time reminded him of his limited seasons as a high school hockey player.

Despite having never ice-skated before, she'd been a good sport.

She was infinitely appealing—her dark almond-shaped eyes and black hair flying with abandon over her shoulders—

and she possessed an elegant poise when she'd eventually skated around the rink twice without falling.

Her movements had been graceful, the gentle sway of her hips alluring.

"I did it!" she exclaimed as she skated back to him, her pert nose held high, her fine, sculpted cheekbones flushed with excitement.

Wholeheartedly, he'd applauded.

Because, why not? She was stunning.

He'd been attracted to her since the first night they'd met at the shelter. He recalled her stunned stare when he'd asked if she was homeless and needed a room.

In the ensuing days, she'd occupied all his attention. Brilliant and gifted, righteous and honorable, all wrapped up into one mesmerizing package.

He'd missed seeing her, understanding that she was entrenched in organizing the final fund-raising details and juggling a demanding full-time teaching schedule. Still, he had texted her numerous times each day and phoned her in the evening.

And now he wanted to buy her a gift. Nothing elaborate, just a thank you for all she'd accomplished, and the happiness she'd given him.

In jovial spirits, he brushed a fluffy snowflake off his face and couldn't contain the expanded emotions in his chest. He was behaving like an infatuated adolescent boy.

His mind went back to their day together. After they'd ice-skated, Holly had requested that he build a snowman with her. With her hair tucked beneath a forest-green beanie and her clear complexion devoid of makeup, she was magnificent, and thoughts about anything other than her vanished.

"Sure," he replied, although he never remembered ever actually building a snowman before.

Because again, why not?

And then she did the most childish thing as they strolled toward Cedar Lane Park. She stuck out her foot and tripped him, and he fell into a pile of snow like a piece of sawed timber.

As he lay sprawled on the ground, he'd gaped up at her cherubic grin. "What was that for?"

"Let's call it payback for teaching me how to ice-skate while the entire town of Snowflake watched me fall a half-dozen times."

"But what about when you got up? Do those times count?" He brushed snow from his jacket and advanced on her as if he were a silent leopard ready to pounce.

"Don't you dare, Tim." Stifling a giggle, she backed away.

He made a grab for her, she twisted, and he tumbled forward into another high snowdrift.

Hands primly on her hips, she hovered over him. As ever, her eyes held him spellbound, an intense dark brown, fringed by long lashes. Eyes that were pure and tender.

However, as he was quickly understanding, the true glimpse of the woman was her determined chin and alert gaze.

"Are you lounging there all afternoon?" She rocked on her heels and tossed her hair back, and all he craved was to gather her in his arms and kiss her full lips.

Instead, he fixated on the trees standing starkly above him and the dove-gray sky covered in clouds. "It depends on whether you'll try to push me down again."

"I didn't push you. I tripped you, and it was bad of me." Her gaze sparkled with mischief. "Are you hurt?"

"Only my pride." He gave a guileless smile and held out his hand. "Will you help me up?"

Exactly as he figured she would, she extended her hand, and he pulled her down beside him. With a shriek of merriment, she paused to catch her breath as he curved her onto her back.

"That's the thanks I get for teaching you how to ice-skate?" he challenged.

She giggled and squirmed. "Yes."

"Say thank you."

His answer was a face full of snow while she giggled louder.

"Now I deserve a thank you *and* an apology." He mopped the snow from his face, but when she started to scramble to her feet, he linked his arms around her waist.

"I didn't hear you," he whispered in her ear.

"I'm sorry." Out of breath with laughter, she gasped, "And thank you."

"A vast improvement." He nuzzled her nape. "Kiss me and we'll make up." His lips slanted over hers, and he tightened his hold. With a quiet sigh, she molded herself to him. "Holly, you are so beautiful," he murmured.

And the thought came. If only they could stay like this.

She was with him, he could see her, feel her enticing lips on his.

But then snowflakes began to fall, swirling in all directions, and he feared he would lose her in the thickening flurries. Just as he'd feared losing everyone he loved—his mother, his father, his grandparents. And he had, for they were gone.

He cautioned himself that this was present day and here was Holly. She was honest and vital and kissing him back in delightful surrender. Their future was unexplored, their pasts filled with obstacles, but with her he felt entirely at peace and in agreement with a world that hadn't lived up to his expectations.

That is, not until now.

A few minutes later, the snow stopped, and the clouds

cleared. He helped her to her feet and reached for her hand—two people falling in love, strolling outdoors beneath the dazzling vastness of a winter sky, holding hands. They were surrounded by a Jack Frost wonderland.

He squeezed her gloved fingers. Her hand fit into his as if she were made for him.

And there was no mistaking his feelings, because he was in love with her.

She was free of the pretensions he'd witnessed in Hollywood. She was funny and enthralling and generous. And she was bursting with affection for her students, most notably Jasmine.

Her love for God was forever present, and she clearly accepted God's gift of salvation. "Faith and love begins on the inside," she'd declared, and he was humbled by her attributes, particularly kindness.

Once they arrived at the park, they located a flat, shady area near the gazebo. Nearby on Snow Hill, a popular hilltop ideal for sledding and inner tubing, children zipped down and landed at the bottom. Their parents watched, cheered and hastened down the hill.

"Tim?" Holly said as she shaped and flattened the top of a medium sized snowball.

Whenever she spoke his name, the melodic sound of her voice had a hypnotizing effect on him.

"Hmm?" He evened out the edges of a gigantic snowball and fixed it on the ground. To his astonished pleasure, she made a great show of liking his creation, though he'd only just started. But then, as he'd discovered, she had an ability for making even the ordinary seem extraordinary.

"We've been acquainted only a short while, yet it seems like we've been friends forever," she said. "We shared a great deal about ourselves."

"I've revealed more to you than anyone. We're certainly

never at a loss for words." He paused, observing her. "I like to think we're more than friends."

She polished the angles of the snowball she'd placed on top of his, then gazed up at him. "I would too," she said quietly.

He heard the uncertainty in her voice and his breath halted. Unreservedly and effectively, she was beginning to thaw his heart.

Briefly, he closed his eyes, pondering why she had this magical effect on him. A few seconds later, he managed to speak. "How does the phrase, *a couple,* sound?"

He was surprised at how effortlessly the words came. He'd avoided serious relationships with women and any endearments he'd used were surface only.

"I like it," Holly was saying. "We're a couple, then."

"Let's shake on it." He extended his hand. "Deal?"

She laughed and shook. "Deal."

He lifted her into his arms, twirled her around, and thoroughly kissed her.

As he held her, he reflected on her biggest surprise, which had occurred when they'd parked in front of the ice-skating rink.

Tim had hurried around his truck to open the door for her, looking forward to her reaction when she saw the neon sign Ralph had fixed to the entrance of the rink.

Lips parted, she stared, while he suppressed a chuckle.

"Every moment matters." She enunciated the words she read in a shaky tone, then veered to him. "The owners of this rink must attend my church. They obviously chose phrase after they heard the pastor's sermon."

"Could be," he said with mild cynicism. "I'd wondered where they got that slogan, and then when you said the same thing in the coffee shop …"

"*Every moment matters* is more than a slogan, Tim." Their

gazes held. "It's a way of life whether you attend church or not."

Their silence was charged with a growing, mounting awareness for each other. He felt it, because there was no denying its existence; and by the softening of her expression, Holly felt it too.

Now, Tim rehearsed exactly what he'd say to her when next he saw her. He wanted them to spend Christmas together. He didn't usually celebrate the holiday, save for serving meals in a Denver soup kitchen in the morning. He didn't cook, so he'd usually bring leftovers back to his apartment, or order a takeout pizza and spend Christmas afternoon reading by himself.

Of course Felicia, his ex-girlfriend, would observe the holiday in high style. Fortunately, that high style didn't include him, and there was no wandering through that mine field anymore of struggling to satisfy her with lavish dinners at overpriced restaurants.

He'd broken things off with her shortly after he'd met Holly. It had been insanity to get involved with Felicia in the first place, but he knew she cared for him.

The breakup had been quick and honest. He saw her in person and tried to do everything right.

She'd been angry. She'd screamed at him. And then it was over.

At the intersection of Main Street, Tim crossed at the stoplight. Outside the entrance to Musical Notes, he paused and rubbed the back of his neck. He hadn't purchased a gift in years, and then only once, when he was twelve and waiting for his mother's recent disappearance to end. Had she been in a treatment program, or run off hot-rodding with her latest boyfriend? He couldn't remember.

It had been mid-December, and the weatherman forecasted a massive storm producing significant snowfall. He'd tried not to upset his grandparents by asking where his mother had gone and spent the empty hours staring out their front bay window at the whirling snowstorm.

He'd watched. He'd waited.

"She'll come back," he'd determinedly told his grandmother. Why wouldn't she? He was an exemplary son, a son to be proud of, so of course his mother wouldn't leave him.

Two days later, Ralph, who worked with his grandfather on construction jobs, had taken Tim shopping. He'd earned a few dollars by running errands for his grandfather at the construction sites.

That day, he'd bought his mother a Christmas gift.

Tim shook his head, chiding himself for overthinking.

This wasn't the same. He wasn't buying a Christmas gift for Holly. He was buying a thank-you gift because of her generous contribution to the community.

And because they were … a couple.

Besides, his mother and Holly were entirely different people.

He pushed the door to the shop wide open and banished the old memories.

The timbered space was crammed with musically themed gifts, from pencil pouches to statues of composers, to frames embellished with string instruments and posters of Beethoven and Bach.

"Do you sell charms for a bracelet?" he asked the middle-aged salesclerk behind the counter, rushing his words. Thoroughly engrossed in scrolling through her cell phone, she gave a start and swiveled around.

"Yes." She beamed. "And anything musical you can imagine."

Tim took a step forward. "I'd like to purchase a charm."

"Brilliant." She ushered him to a display stand. "Any particular instrument?"

"She plays piano, but she already has a piano charm." He picked through the charms, examining each one.

"Gold or silver?"

"Silver. But she wants to learn how to play the accordion." He perused the display and selected a sterling silver accordion charm polished to a shiny finish.

"This charm is accordion accurate," the sales clerk said.

"Music isn't my forte." He chuckled a little too loudly at his pun. His insecurity about purchasing a gift for someone was showing.

Suppose Holly didn't like it? Or worse, suppose she discarded his gift in search of something more appealing, as his mother had done?

"See?" The clerk rode her thumb across the accordion's tiny keyboard. "Complete with white and black keys similar to a piano."

He nodded. "I'll take it."

"Our store offers gift wrapping at no extra charge."

"Sure." He'd only wrapped one gift in his life, a young boy's clumsy attempts using the Sunday newspaper comics and string.

"Hello, Mr. Inspector! I mean, Mr. Stewart."

A chirpy young voice prompted Tim to spin around. "Jasmine, what are you doing here? And please, call me Mr. Tim."

Jasmine, carrying an armful of music, sprinted to him. "Okay."

"What are you doing here?" he repeated.

"I just finished practicing in the back room. Miss Kim and I are playing 'Silent Night.' It's a duet arrangement."

He grinned. "So I heard."

"And I counted the beats out loud for each measure so I don't go faster than Miss Kim." Perky-pink flags of color enhanced Jasmine's pale cheeks. "I'm preparing a solo too. 'We Three Kings of Orient Are.' Have you ever heard it?"

"Yes. Many times." He paid for the package, carefully wrapped in ivory paper embellished with lime-green musical notes, and he placed it in a purple bag embossed with the store's logo.

His gaze strayed. "Where's your mother?"

"Working." Jasmine scooped up a heavy quilted coat from a peg rack and traded her shoes for a pair of glittery shearling boots. "Mr. Tim, guess what else?"

"What else?"

The slight girl fairly beamed with excitement. "I won't need to practice at the music store anymore because I'm going to live with Miss Kim. She's been alone since her divorce, so I'll keep her company."

He froze, nearly gasping while his brain recorded disbelief. *Holly had been married?* Never once had she mentioned it.

And what was this about Jasmine living with her?

"Is that what she said?" he casually asked.

"Yep. It's all arranged."

"How?" He struggled to assimilate everything. "Miss Kim lives in Pine Cone Valley."

"I know. I went to her house every week for piano lessons."

"When?" He heard his voice. He'd raised it. "When are you moving in with her?"

"This afternoon."

"With your ... mother?"

"No." Jasmine filed her music into a canvas bag and hoisted it over her shoulder. The strap slipped off, and she slid it back up her arm. "My mother isn't coming."

Then how ...

Unable to extend any more than a head bob, he kept his features bland.

Once he exited the store, the questions exploded in his mind.

Had Jasmine's mother relapsed? Was that why Jasmine was staying with Holly? Or was Holly planning to take over the little girl's life?

His muscles quivered and his body tensed.

Memories of the incidents when the "men in suits," as his mother had called them, threatened to remove Tim from her home, or rather, lack of home, whenever she lost the battle to her addictions, climbed to the surface.

No. It couldn't be. That wasn't Holly. She'd never take Jasmine away from her mother. She loved the girl and wanted what was best for her. And a child belonged with a loving, caring parent. Holly knew that. Everyone knew that.

His heart hollered the denial. But his mind mulled over Holly's words, the smidgens of conversations regarding Jasmine, and his pulse raced.

"I would do anything for that little girl."

CHAPTER 10

Seated on the tufted couch in her living room, a pen in hand and a mountain of paper beside her, Holly studied her list of things left to do. The baby grand piano in the nursing home had been tuned, a donation box set up, and her students were prepared. The media had publicized the fund-raiser on television, radio and newspaper at no charge, and colorful brochures noting the date and time were posted in shop windows everywhere.

Plus, an extensive three-part email marketing event had begun, with an announcement sent to area businesses. The first was a Save the Date; the second, an Event Reminder; and the third, a Last Chance email.

The Astra Project Fund-raiser to benefit the Snowflake Home-less Shelter
Holiday Piano Recital at Golden Birch Manor
5 Cedar Lane, Snowflake, Colorado
December 23rd at three o'clock
Bring an ornament for the residents' tree!
Donations accepted at the door

Tim had mentioned that he'd provide the tree, and Holly counted on him staying true to his word.

Luckily, she'd started her annual winter recess, which meant lessons were scheduled only for students who opted to participate in the fund-raiser.

But she hadn't finished decorating her apartment, nor hoisted her "Charlie Brown" tree from the attic.

And she hadn't heard from Tim.

Her hands fluttered, and she set the pen aside. She sagged against the couch, trying to ignore the prick of anguish that came with a stark realization. Tim was avoiding her. He hadn't reached out in days, and her texts had been greeted with replies so short and clipped that she'd actually flinched.

Why had he suddenly lost interest in her?

All the jubilant expectation of spending the holidays with him had drained out of her. And that awareness left her shocked and rejected.

Unfocused, she stared vacantly at the paper.

She'd done it again. She'd placed her trust in a man. A man who obviously considered her nothing more than a diversion that had run its course.

Her chin quivered as she succumbed to a rush of tears. These days, she did that a lot. When at last her tears subsided, she dried her eyes and went in search of a soft cloth to press over them.

That morning, her views had swung the opposite way, and her battered pride had prompted her to push her shoulders back and silently banish him.

Of all the nerve. Of all the insensitive nerve.

She'd thwarted her heartache by telling herself that there was no reason for her sadness. He'd go on to solid-gold charm another woman and … And so what?

So what if that thought caused her to feel hollow inside?

She rubbed her temples and swung her legs to the side of

the couch, weary of the mental conflict harboring her disbelief and bewilderment.

Finally, she'd decided not to contact him anymore. No longer did she leave him cheery voice mails, or any voice mails at all.

"*How does the phrase* a couple *sound?*" he'd asked.

She'd detected the revealing huskiness in his voice and believed his admission sincere. Apparently the actor could carry off a deliberate deception without a second thought.

Determined that the recital would be a success, she'd resolved that nothing, not even a shattered heart, would preclude her from achieving her goal. Her aunt had pegged Holly's quest as a personal penchant, a private pursuit to raise all the money the shelter needed. And that was exactly what she intended to do.

Nevertheless, she also had an eleven-year-old girl living in her apartment. A girl who left scuff marks on the tiled floor in the foyer and often seemed despondent. A precocious child who chatted only when she was in the mood, Jasmine spent hours after school practicing the piano in Holly's living room, or straggling her legs out in front of her as she flopped on the couch. Hands jammed into jean pockets, she resembled a tiny pixie with round, impish eyes as she declared how bored she was.

Holly suggested she read a book or play with the cat. That occupied the girl for about ten minutes.

The previous afternoon, the principal of the elementary school had phoned because of a discipline issue. Jasmine, it seemed, had a tendency to associate with the wrong crowd, claiming that she should stick with "kids who understood her best."

Considering her age and how she'd been displaced and lived in multiple homes, the principal assured Holly that Jasmine's behavior was normal, and her scores on intelligence tests rated higher than average. Still, Holly spent numerous hours on the phone with Jasmine's mother discussing the situation.

The last morning before winter break, Holly phoned her aunt while Jasmine was in school.

"Try to relate to the depth of Jasmine's plight," Aunt Clementine advised. "Understandably, she misses her mother. Focus on the good news. She secured an excellent job with a generous salary and benefits, and they'll be reunited soon. But I'll continue to pray for them, of course."

Silence surged for a beat.

Holly tapped her foot on the floor. To split the stillness, she inquired, "Are you still seeing Justin, Aunt Clementine?"

"His arm is looped around my shoulders as we speak."

"You both fit in the recliner?" Holly teased with a delicate chuckle.

"We're a perfect match."

Holly smiled at the mental image of two seniors ultimately finding love. "Are you housing any new rescue dogs?" she asked.

As if on cue, a dog bayed.

"One adorable long-eared beagle, and a Yorkshire terrier who insists on yapping at everything."

Holly giggled and then immediately sobered when her aunt inquired, "What's new with Tim?"

She tightened her grip on the cell phone. "I … I wouldn't know."

"I understood that you texted or saw each other every day." Holly heard a smooch and assumed Justin had kissed her aunt.

"Tim isn't talking to me," Holly replied.

"Why not? What's the problem?"

It was useless to hide the facts. Her aunt was extremely discerning.

"The problem is he's avoided me ever since …" Frowning, Holly sat up straight as a notion struck her. "Ever since Jasmine moved in. I assumed he liked children. Apparently not."

"So he's aware of the situation with Jasmine?"

"Yes. She met him in the music store in Snowflake and told him before I had the chance." Holly gulped to steady her emotions. "It all happened so quickly when her mother was hired for her dream job in Denver."

"And now along with caring for a youngster, your fundraiser is in a couple days," Aunt Clementine said.

"Tim is supposed to donate the tree. I hope he will."

"If he said he will, then I have no doubt he will. He seems a man of his word, so I wouldn't worry. Have faith."

"I do."

"Then the odds are in your favor. Tim will come through."

Holly collapsed against the back of the couch. "Will he?"

"Your expectations flow from God. In the end, it is God who provides."

Holly gained strength from her aunt's belief, as well as her conviction regarding Tim's solid character.

"I invited him to the recital so often that I lost count, but his replies were always noncommittal."

"What did he say exactly?" her aunt asked.

"Just something about working that day." Holly bit her lower lip. "But the town offices are closed for the holiday break, so he wouldn't work unless he was on call."

"From the sounds of your romance, I presumed you were falling in love."

"You were wrong." Unconsciously, Holly pressed a hand to her heart. "We only met a short while ago."

"But still, it sounded wonderful."

But still, it WAS wonderful.

311

So wonderful, in fact, that when Holly clicked off, she curled her arms across her chest and wept.

FORTY-EIGHT HOURS LATER, Holly entered the lobby of the Golden Birch nursing home, carefully balancing a pile of music with a container of Chinese Christmas cookies stacked on top. Garland outlined the door, spelling out the words *Noel* and *Joy*.

She'd chosen to wear cashmere slacks in a rosebud-pink, and a notch-collared faux wrap blouse in a vibrant silk print. She'd arranged her hair into an elegant chignon at her nape, secured with a faux diamond clip, and a pair of tiny diamond earrings. Her gingerbread-colored tote bag doubled as a handbag.

Jasmine, endearing in a red ruffled lace dress and black patent leather shoes, her blond hair styled in ringlets, skipped beside Holly. Clutching her music to her thin chest, she glowed with optimism when her mother hugged her.

As arranged, Emily had met them at the recital and would take Jasmine home with her to Denver when it was over.

"Thank you, Holly, for allowing Jasmine to finish the semester in Snowflake while I started my new job," Emily said. "It was helpful that you drove her to and from school every day."

"No worries," Holly said. "Jasmine even helped me set the table for dinner two nights in a row. That is, when she didn't practice or play with my cat."

Holly realized that Jasmine's mother deserved whole-hearted accolades. She was a single parent who'd resolved to make a better life for her and her daughter and raising a child certainly wasn't easy. "I'm happy this is all working out for you."

The previous afternoon after church service at Snowflake

Chapel, Holly and Jasmine had baked Christmas cookies. They'd snacked on leftover butterscotch chips and velvety chocolate that melted on their tongues, and Holly had explained that the Chinese Christmas cookie recipe was from Tina, her college friend.

And they'd discussed Pastor Tom's sermon based on John 3:16, concerning God's unconditional love. "The outlook in your heart replicates the judgments in your mind," he'd preached. "God sees how your narrative begins and ends. He loves us, even though we oftentimes feel inadequate and make mistakes."

Holly had taken the message to heart and prayed for forgiveness. She'd recognized that she'd lost patience with Jasmine on occasion.

She was brought back to the present when she shifted to allow a professional caregiver to pass. He wheeled a white-haired fellow in a wheelchair and both extended a smile. Inspired, she smiled back. The home was evidently devoted to its seniors.

To celebrate the holiday, multicolored lights in the shape of an angel were affixed with tape to a blank wall, and individual stockings were tacked on each resident's door. Down the hall, an engaging game of bingo sounded over a loudspeaker, and an outdoor area beyond the dining room enabled residents to enjoy the gardens when the weather was warm.

While parents made space for the residents, Holly's students guided the elderly men and women, some with canes, others with walkers, to the enormous parlor where the recital would take place. The glossy ebony-black piano commanded center stage.

In the meantime, Holly conferred with the director about organizing the refreshments and donation box, and reminded the attendees to hang their ornament on the eight-foot-tall tree.

"The crowd is larger than we expected and donations started pouring in yesterday," the director informed Holly. Her ash-blond hair was coiled in an upsweep, a bouffant hairstyle that Holly hadn't seen in years. She headed toward the hallway and began setting up extra chairs.

"Yes, I'm thrilled." Holly tailed her. "Thank you for allowing us to perform."

"Our pleasure. And the tree." The director regarded the tall pine. "The tree was donated by Mr. Timothy Stewart. A local Christmas tree farm delivered it this morning."

"Is he here?" Holly couldn't help herself, her anxious gaze pinned to the front door. Then she foolishly regarded the tree, as if Tim might materialize from behind it. "The man who arranged the delivery?"

"He was here earlier, but disappeared shortly before you arrived."

Holly stopped herself from asking any more questions about him. "Right. Thanks." She reverted to her professional teacher tone and stepped into the parlor.

A half hour before the recital, Holly knelt by each of her thirty students, who ranged in age from six to eighteen years old. She offered encouragement and reminded them to sing along with the Christmas hymns for the finale. However, she was no match for their eagerness, their love of music, which, she ascertained with a tinge of pride, she'd helped to instill in them.

At five minutes before the hour, Holly's heart rate doubled in nervous anticipation. She seated herself in the front row and creased the page turn of the first piece, "Silent Night." She'd decided to commence with a strong opening, foreseeing a seamless performance because she and Jasmine had practiced the duet for hours.

"You don't like Silent Night?" she'd asked Tim.

"Everyone likes Silent Night," he'd replied.

Her eyes burned with tears. A lump settled in her throat, and she swallowed determinedly. She certainly couldn't break down here. She was a woman with mettle and resolve.

Something caused her to swivel, and her stomach fluttered. Privately, she wished that a broad-shouldered handsome man had shown up at the last minute to support her and her cause. Instead, she locked gazes with a recognizable fellow sporting a plaid coat and wearing round eyeglasses. He'd planted himself at the far end of the parlor and passed her a sociable nod.

"Ralph?" She chewed on her trembling lip and prayed her disappointment didn't show. She came to her feet and hastened to him. "What are you doing here?"

"I finished work early, and I'm always up for supporting a good cause." He gave a half-laugh. "After the recital, let's meet in town at The Little Corner Bistro. Say, seven o'clock? They close at eight."

It was a subtle order, not a request.

"All right."

"Will you be bringing Jasmine?" he asked.

Startled, she shuffled back. "No. She'll be with her mother."

"Excellent. That's where a child belongs." He stepped away. "Be prompt. I have some news you'll want to hear."

CHAPTER 11

They'd done it. The recital was over. By the ringing applause from the residents, friends, and family, the students' performances and sing-along were an emphatic success. Even better, they'd raised an additional five hundred dollars, and the director assured Holly that donations would continue throughout the holiday season.

Holly kissed Jasmine and her mother good-bye, and congratulated the girl on a flawless recital. She promised to send recommendations for piano teachers in the Denver area. On their way out, Holly overheard Emily reveal to Jasmine that they were heading to the humane society. A seven-year-old shih tzu named Leo had been given up for adoption because the owner's landlord didn't allow pets.

"But our new landlord does?" Jasmine asked tentatively.

"Yes. He gave the okay. Merry Christmas, Jasmine!"

The girl flung her arms around her mother's neck. "Merry Christmas, Mommy!"

After lemonade was served and the remaining students and parents departed, Holly lingered to converse with the residents and joined in a high-spirited game of bingo.

At six o'clock, she yanked on her coat and headed for the exit. An hour was enough time to drive the short distance to The Little Corner Bistro in town.

"Holly?"

She swiveled at the recognizable male voice, deep and achingly familiar.

Tim perched on the edge of a folding chair, arms crossed, the color rising in his handsome, tanned face. She struggled to still the traitorous responses unfurling within her, struggled to keep her expression blank in the same way he had mastered.

"Excellent recital." He stood and came forward. "You were magnificent."

Guardedly, Holly contemplated him. "How would you know?"

He brushed his hand along her cheek. "I was here."

"I didn't see you." She'd scanned the parlor countless times.

"Do you think I'm lying?"

"I'm not certain what to think anymore when it comes to you."

He reached out to take her hands.

She jerked aside and spun for the door. The director at the front desk peeked up, and Holly ignored her soft bark of laughter.

"She's watching us," Tim murmured. He'd beaten Holly to the door. He propped his hand on the frame, successfully delaying her departure.

Holly sent a commendable imitation of a smile toward the director, committing to revisit on Christmas Eve at three o'clock, which would allow ample time to attend the church service at six. She'd made arrangements to play carols for the residents.

She placed her fingers on the door's brass handle. "Even

more of a reason to let me pass, then," she sputtered.

His jaw hardened. "Where's Jasmine?"

"She left already."

"I'll walk you to your car." His tone was as unmoving as his stance. "I ... I bought you a gift."

Her breath caught as she stared up at his earnest, attractive face, and once again she cautioned herself that he'd been a successful actor. "I'm not interested in your gifts. Please excuse me." She wrenched the door open and held a stiff posture as she marched past him.

The nursing home's parking lot was silent and nearly empty. A nipping, icy sleet had begun to fall, fierce and relentless.

Across the street, the neon sign of the ice-skating rink flashed *Every Moment Matters.*

She thrust her freezing hands into her coat pockets and observed the nursing home. Frost clung to the windows and night had fallen. In December, the days grew short so rapidly.

She hurried to her Jeep.

Tim quickened to keep up with her. "Why are you ignoring me?"

Holly grabbed her beanie from her tote bag and drew it over her raw ears. "Now there's a million-dollar question."

"What's that supposed to mean?"

"You're the person who disappeared."

His forehead creased into a scowl. "I've been around the nursing home all day."

"Where? Invisibly?"

"I stayed in the hallway for the entire recital, and rushed out the minute it was finished because I was called to a job in town. I assumed you'd chat a while with your students. I intended to return within a couple hours, and I did." He grasped her forearms. "So, can we talk?"

Meticulously, she wrenched free from his grasp, first one arm, then the other. "No. Not anymore."

"Can I give you … this?" Undeterred, he smiled, but the smile wavered. "I thought you might like a little something."

She drew a trembling inhale at the sight of the miniature box wrapped in ivory paper, embellished with lime-green musical notes. "Why?" Rubbing a hand over her heart, she readied to end the conversation. Being near him hurt too much.

His smile faded, his eyes bottomless pools of anguish. "Don't you like gifts?" His voice sounded very odd, very unsure.

"Not your gifts, Tim. Please keep it."

With a proud tilt of her head, she whirled, striding away on legs that felt too weak to support her body.

CHAPTER 12

A hollow numbness settled over Holly as she drove the few blocks to The Little Corner Bistro. Instead of being emboldened by refusing Tim, she was despondent, and heavy with remorse for her inexcusably bad behavior.

Negotiating the busy traffic into the center of town took longer than she anticipated, compounded by waiting at an intersection until there was a break. Nonetheless, she reached the bistro before seven o'clock and parked at the curb. The street was dark save for the bistro's muted pendant lighting stretching from the rustic interior.

As she got out of the car, she hardly noticed the sting of icy pellets on her heated cheeks. Unblinking, she shivered and clutched her coat closer, half hoping that Tim had pursued her. He hadn't, and she shook her head in mock derision, feeling foolish for thinking otherwise.

She shuffled to the front entrance. An illuminated reindeer in the lobby greeted her, along with background instrumental music, a classical rendition of "Silver Bells." White pine roping adorned the mantel of a crackling fireplace, and each tabletop sported a mason jar chock-full of red and green ornaments.

Ralph sat at a table near the back. He sprang to his feet, took her coat and hung it on a coat rack.

"Where's Tim?" He asked so casually that Holly was immediately put on her guard.

"I have no idea." She tugged off her wool beanie and flattened back the wet hair plastered to her cheeks. They both slid into chairs across from each other at the table. "Why?"

"I expected he was coming with you." Ralph's gray eyebrows rose at what he evidently assumed was an oversight. "Didn't you see him after the recital?"

"Only for a short while." Somehow, she kept her tone nonchalant.

A waitress scurried over, gripping a pad to take their orders.

"Peppermint tea for me," Holly said.

Ralph nodded agreement. "The same."

After tea was served, Ralph silently observed Holly while he stirred in cream and sugar.

"Do you want to discuss what happened at the nursing home and why he's not with you?" he asked.

"And spoil a perfect chat? Let's just say we had a disagreement." Ruefully, she shook her head and fixated on the mason jar between them. "Truthfully, I've thought about him so much, I've run out of words."

Ralph's forehead furrowed. "In my opinion, you two care a great deal about each other. However, I'm not certain who is more stubborn, you or Tim."

His reproof made Holly straighten. "It's Tim. He's impossible. I assumed I understood him, but he's an enigma."

Ralph hunched forward. "He was angry when he found out you had taken Jasmine in."

"First, that was none of his business," Holly said. "Second,

Jasmine's mother secured a job in Denver and asked me to keep Jasmine at my apartment so that Jasmine could finish out the school semester. Of course I was happy to help."

A gleam sparked in Ralph's eyes, partially hidden behind his round glasses. "Ah, so that explains it."

"I don't understand."

"Tim's mother wasn't the best, but she was fiercely protective." Ralph bent his head and surveyed Holly. "She instilled in him a deep fear of being taken by the authorities, an 'us versus them' philosophy. Because of Tim's previous experience, he probably assumed you intended to pull Jasmine away from her mother for good. He's got deep feelings about subjects of that nature."

"So in his mind he charged me with a crime, and the verdict was guilty?" Holly drew in a small breath. "All without actually speaking to me?"

"And yet he still came around today and forgave you."

She studied her hands. "For a crime I didn't commit."

"Why didn't you explain Jasmine's situation to him?"

"Well, to begin with, he's completely ignored me these past few days. He didn't respond to my texts or phone calls." Holly broke off, unable to put her heartache into a coherent sentence.

"And that hurt you, because you're in love with him," Ralph replied.

"Yes." Her face heated. She'd blurted her admittance too quickly.

She couldn't bear to face Ralph's perceptive smile and averted her gaze, peering out the double-hung windows facing the street. Sleet had frosted the overhang, and the hand-painted stone fountains flanking the entrance were glazed with ice.

"Good news." Ralph didn't hide the delight in his gravelly voice. "He's in love with you too."

Suppressing the flare of optimism in her chest, Holly kept her gaze on the outside fountains. There was nothing else to say, but in all honesty, there was everything.

"Does Tim ignore every woman he loves?" she finally asked.

"To my knowledge, he's never loved another woman. Sure, he dates women and treats them with respect, but he never reveals anything about himself. But you—you touched a nerve. You brought out a part of his past he's tried to suppress." Ralph shook his head. "Instead of confronting you, he closed up. That's what he does."

"Why?" Holly's mouth went dry. "We've spent hours talking about our lives."

"But not talking about everything." Ralph fairly swooped down on her reply. "Tim is a complex man, Holly. I first met him when he was a little boy. He was lovable, appealing, and into mischief at every opportunity despite his attempts to appear angelic."

Holly smiled and leaned forward. "Please tell me more."

"He was smart, sharp as a razor." Ralph grinned. "And solid and sunny. Any mother would be bursting with pride to have him as her son."

"Any mother except … his?"

"Oh, she was proud, all right. Sometimes. Sometimes not. It all depended on if her addictions got the better of her. Tim never knew where he was going to wake up from one week to the next—under a bridge or at his grandparent's house. His mother was an original and even called herself Astra for a spell. When I saw the name on your advertisements, I knew Tim had told you about her."

"A star of hope," Holly said. "I must have explained the significance of that name a hundred times this week."

"Or a falling star."

"I refuse to believe that." She frowned. "Where did you and Tim meet?"

"His grandfather and I were friends since we were both in the building trade." Ralph lifted his cup to his lips, and Holly noticed a subtle tremor in his hand. "We all called him Timmy back then, that is until he forbade it."

"How old was he at the time?"

"Probably nine."

"And his mother?" This close, Holly counted the numerous lines on Ralph's wide forehead, the gray whisker stubbles on his chin. "From what I gather, she was everything to him, although he shuts down whenever it comes to actually discussing her."

"Despite her lifestyle, she was the center of his life." Ralph folded his hands. "Can I tell you a story?"

"Of course." There was the tiniest catch in her voice. She wondered if Ralph noticed.

"His mother was drop-dead gorgeous until her addictions wore her looks away. One Christmas soon after I met them, she left him with his grandparents, and, after a few days, he begged me to take him shopping. He'd saved some money by working for his grandfather, doing odd jobs at the construction site, and he wanted to buy her some jewelry. He found an adorable charm on clearance that was engraved with the words *Mama Bear*."

"Precious."

"To you. To me." Ralph fell silent for a heartbeat. Firelight cast dim shadows on his creased cheeks. "Tim didn't have the money for the store gift-wrapping, so he wrapped it himself with old newspaper and string."

"His mother must have been thrilled when he gave her the gift."

"I was at his grandparents' when she finally showed up on Christmas Eve. Tim was so excited he could hardly keep still.

He grabbed the gift from beneath the tree and pressed it into her hands. 'Mommy, I got you a gift,' he said. He looked so small standing there." Ralph's tone rang with sadness. "I assumed she would welcome him into her arms and apologize for being gone so long. And that she'd make a big show of opening it."

"Didn't she?"

"No. A car horn, her latest boyfriend, and off she went out the door."

Holly's entire body tensed. She was unable to hide her sadness and righteous anger for the little boy Tim had once been, for the man she loved.

For she had, indeed, fallen in love with him.

"What happened next?" She dabbed tears from the corner of her eyes.

"He called out to her, he still held the gift. She dismissed it. Dismissed him." Ralph's eyes were damp. "Sure, he probably spent exorbitant amounts of money on women when he was in Hollywood, but he never actually bought them a present. He's been blessed in his professional life because of his exceptional looks and hard work ethic. In his personal life, not so blessed."

A painful silence emerged, despite the bustle as the bistro began shutting down for the night. Holly was perilously close to weeping, recalling her heated discussion with Tim only an hour before, and the contemptuous way she'd informed him to keep his gift.

She covered her face with her hands. "Did he ever forgive his mother for her callousness?"

"In one sense, yes, but forgiveness is difficult. Tim's heart is kind, but he's careful. Understandably so. It takes a big person to forgive."

"'As far as the east is from the west, so far has he removed our transgressions from us.'"

"Psalm 103:12," Ralph responded. "I'm a church-going man, and listened closely to Pastor Tom's recent sermon. Does that surprise you?"

Holly smiled at the reference to church. "Not at all. You strike me as a compassionate man, who has obviously formed deep friendships."

"I never married. I wanted to."

Holly chuckled. "Until a few weeks ago, I might have matched you up with my aunt. But now, in her sixties, she is dating a wonderful man."

"I never found the right woman." Ralph held up his left hand, devoid of a wedding band. "Fortunately for Tim, he has."

"I appreciate what you're trying to do, Ralph." With a ragged laugh, Holly reached for her tea. It was cold. "However, your efforts are wasted."

"I read a study once. Within three days, you'll be able to identify whether or not you're attracted to another person."

"Hardly a lifetime. I didn't go to the homeless shelter looking for love."

"Let's call it a fortunate accident then."

"A fortunate accident." She sought to match his upbeat tone. "What's the good news, by the way?"

The waitress pointedly placed a check on the table and peered at her watch, then posted the closed sign on the entrance door.

Ralph paid the bill and got to his feet. "An anonymous businessman in the community has offered to pay the entire rewiring project, and the work should be completed by the end of December. Lou will deposit the money you've given toward services, food, and clothes for the residents."

"Ralph, that's wonderful." He helped Holly on with her coat, and she swung her arms in excitement as they exited. "Who's the businessman?"

He winked. "Anonymous, remember?"

"Is it Tim?"

"I'm not at liberty to tell. But since you mentioned Tim again … I watched the way he looked at you the night of the tree lighting, and in truth, I was surprised. When he acted in that popular television series, women swarmed all over him. They still do. He's always been immune, which hardly shocks me, given his history. Still, despite the fleeting fame, he's a street kid at heart. Nonetheless, that man is deeply in love with you."

And Holly, in turn, was in love with him.

But would he ever forgive her for being so insensitive— rejecting not only his gift but the man himself?

CHAPTER 13

*E*arly on Christmas Eve day, Holly hoisted her spindly tree from her apartment building's attic and arranged it by the living room window. Outside, luminous rays of sun highlighted wintry trees, and a light snowfall resembled crystal lace.

She hadn't heard from Tim, and although the possibility existed, she certainly didn't expect to.

Consequently, she pondered how best to approach him.

Phone? Maybe. Maybe not. Suppose he ignored her calls?

Text? Probably the same.

There was so much she wished to say, so much to explain. But where to begin?

Completely immersed in her musings, she balanced on the garden stool to hang tinsel on the higher branches. From the corner of her eye, she glimpsed the box of ornaments on the floor—the glittering baby-blue icicles, the winter angel, and the lighted manger.

"How does the phrase a couple *sound?"*

Tim's rugged face seared in her mind, and she recalled each detail of their afternoon building a snowman. The scene jerked her from her task, and the restraint she'd relied upon crumpled.

She sank onto her tufted sofa. The tears she'd vowed not to shed streamed down her cheeks.

"I'm sorry, Tim." She wept hot, broken sobs. "How do I ask for your forgiveness? How do I know you won't reject me?"

With a semblance of control, she grabbed her cell phone. Butterscotch skirted across her ankles, purring and flicking his cream-colored tail. She reached down to scratch his head. "I'll stop at the This and That Shop before the nursing home, then I'll return here after the church service," she informed him.

Already wearing a red crushed-velvet dress that skimmed her curves, Holly styled her hair long and loose. Her silver bracelet decorated her wrist, the charms gaily jingling.

The only thing left was to contact him. Easy. She'd invite him over for Christmas Day. She paused, swallowed and cradled the phone to her chest.

And how would she begin that invitation, exactly? Her courage dissolved as she anticipated his curt reply. Or worse, if he didn't reply at all.

SEATED IN HER FOUR-WHEEL-DRIVE JEEP, Holly focused on the road to the nursing home and arrived at three o'clock. Streetlamps misted beneath a fine snowfall, and the sun struggled to appear through gray clouds.

Earlier, she'd ducked into the This and That Shop to purchase a tree topper. On the spur of the moment, she'd requested the topper be gift wrapped because she planned to give it to a special someone.

Voices were muted as she entered the nursing home. When she walked into the parlor, she noticed quite a few of the residents visited with family members. Holly sat at the piano and introduced herself before launching into the first Christmas carol.

After the sing-along ended, she reminded each man and woman individually how remarkable they were and wished them all a joyous holiday.

After embracing the last resident, she stepped out of the home. Pausing, she hesitated in the parking lot and stared at the unpretentious yet expressive words flashing from the ice-skating rink's neon sign.

Every moment matters.

But it was the person standing beneath the sign who captivated her.

There it was. And there he was.

From his dark furrowed eyebrows to the sturdy jut of his jaw, he was her beloved. The mark of his strong physique, the same potent appeal that had chased her nightly dreams, caused tears to slide down her cheeks.

His hands were at his sides, the familiar cranberry-colored scarf around the neckline of his navy-blue parka.

Silently, he acknowledged her.

The director stepped out from the home, calling to Holly that she had forgotten her music, flapping it in the air. Holly hardly heard her. She rushed through the snow, the parking lot, quicker now, then raced across the street into Tim's outstretched arms.

"What are you doing here?" Her shoulders quaked. Her face nestled against his chest as he embraced her.

"I came for you. I waited." His deep, gripping voice. She'd ached to hear it again. "I wanted to wish you a Merry Christmas. And to tell you I'm sorry. I'm so very sorry."

"I planned to call you, to text." She swallowed the lump of remorse in her throat and curved her arms around him. "I was afraid you'd reject me. There were things I wanted to say, beginning with my apology for the way I treated you yesterday."

"You're forgiven. Now please forgive me." His tone was a raw whisper, hoarse and sincere.

"I forgive you." Her eyes moistened as she gazed intently into his. "You're a good man. You inspire me to become a better person."

"You inspire *me*." He pressed his forefinger to her lips to prevent her from speaking. "To care. Really care, even if I get hurt."

"You won't. I promise." She placed a hand on his chest. Beneath his jacket, his heart beat vital and solid.

He brushed a strand of hair off her cheek. "If I could undo—"

"There's nothing to undo." Her heart constricted with a love so deep that she held him ever closer. "An hour earlier, I felt alone and sad. Now I feel like dancing."

"And singing?" he teased.

"Yes." She sniffed, and a tear trickled down her cheek.

"Then why the tears?"

"Because you're here," she whispered. "And I'm happy."

"Has anyone ever mentioned," he kissed her, leaving her breathless, "that your smile lights up the entire town?"

Her merriment muffled against his chest, before she glanced around at the empty sidewalk. "It's probably wise if we go to my car. I have something for you."

The director still stood on the nursing home's steps, apparently impervious to the cold.

"She isn't going to go inside until she sees us kiss again," Tim murmured.

"Again?" Holly offered a winsome grin. "All this kissing in front of the entire town?"

"Yep." He tightened his hold and lowered his head, and she encouraged his stirring kiss with one of her own.

He was here, Holly thought. On Christmas Eve, Tim was really here.

A HALF-HOUR LATER, evening had fully descended.

Tim and Holly were seated in her Jeep, in the parking lot of the nursing home. She sat in the driver's seat, he settled beside her in the passenger seat.

A dozen questions raced through his brain and he drew in a breath.

"I've missed you very, very much," he began.

"I've missed you too."

He responded with a kiss, trailing his fingers through her silky black hair and holding her near. She reacted with the same yearning that had awakened him from sleep and kept him up at night.

"Tim, we need to talk," she said.

"For a while," he granted. But not for long, he grinned.

"When I told you to keep your gift ..." Her features swelled with anguish, her tone subdued. "I was hurt and baffled and lashed out at you."

His grin sobered. "I assumed you were seeking to take Jasmine away from her mother. My judgments were uncalled for."

"Don't ever shut me out like that again. You didn't even allow me a chance to explain."

"I'm sorry." He enfolded her in his arms and kissed the top of her head. "And you were married. You never told me."

She shuddered. "I assumed I would never get over it."

"Did you?"

"Thoroughly. Charity was correct. A joyous tomorrow is straight ahead."

He smiled at her infectious tone. "Because?"

"Because I found you."

"And I found you." He fished in his pocket for the small wrapped gift and presented it to her.

"For Christmas?" she inquired.

"Guess again."

"My birthday?"

"January first is a week away and I'm buying you something special." He would ask her to marry him, to embark on their future together as *a couple*. "This gift is for you for being … you."

Silently, she unwrapped the package, broke into a wide grin, and leaned forward for a closer look.

"Do you like the charm?" he asked.

"I love it. But how did you remember I wanted to learn how to play the accordion?"

He fastened the charm onto her bracelet and kissed her wrist. "Because, if you recall, I memorized all your texts and our conversations."

"I have something for you too." She reached behind her, then handed him a bag imprinted with the words This and That Shop.

He gazed at the star he unwrapped, a simple five-point design with gold glitter, and smoothed his forefinger along the sleek edges. At one of the most touching moments of his life, he could only smile.

"Thank you." His voice was husky and he cleared his throat.

"It's a tree-topper. At first I bought it for myself—for my Christmas tree. But in my heart I knew it was for you."

"Astra," he murmured.

"A shining beacon of hope."

This was Holly's gift. An act of generosity, the true spirit of the holiday, an acceptance of Christian grace and love.

"Will you spend Christmas with me?" she asked. "Will you help me decorate my tree? More often than not, I'm alone."

"So am I."

"I usually order a pizza."

"Me too. Takeout."

Her beautiful face brightened with color, her almond-shaped eyes glistened with love. Tenderly, she touched the tiny accordion charm.

"And I accept," he added. "In fact, I thought you'd never ask." He smiled and peered through the foggy windshield. Arms crossed and a cardigan sweater thrown over her shoulders, the director remained on the nursing home's steps and glared at them. Or was she grinning? He couldn't tell.

"I'm guessing she aims to throw us out of the parking lot," he said.

"Should I tell her I'll pick up my music some other time?"

"You can text her. Tomorrow."

The peal of Snowflake Chapel's church bells made him pause. The first star appeared in the sky, radiant and twinkling.

"Church service begins at six o'clock," Holly said softly.

"I'd like to attend."

He couldn't judge her reaction at first. That is, until she gazed up at him with a radiant smile. "Really?"

"Really."

"God is calling. He must've found you."

"I'm easy to find because I'm with you. If He will take me with all my shortcomings—" Tim wavered. "He's bound to be disappointed."

"You can't disappoint God." She started the car, letting it idle as she hummed "Silent Night." He chuckled. She glanced at him. "You don't like 'Silent Night'?"

"Everyone likes 'Silent Night.'" Laughing quietly, he nuzzled her neck. "And Holly Kim, I love you."

She skimmed her hand against his cheek.

In the midst of a wondrous Christmas Eve, he reflected

on the unexpected circumstances that had brought this exquisite woman into his world.

At the age of thirty-four, when he was toughened by what he'd seen as a child, by what he'd done in Hollywood, he bowed to a consideration he'd never allowed himself.

He was good enough for God. And he was good enough for the woman he cherished.

THE END

A NOTE FROM JOSIE

Thank you for reading *Holly's Gift*, set in the charming fictional town of Snowflake, Colorado.

If you loved this sweet inspirational holiday romance as much as I loved writing it, please help other people find *Holly's Gift* by posting your review here.

This book is available in ebook, paperback, Large Print paperback, Hardcover, and audiobook.

I've always looked forward to the holiday season, and wanted to give the title, Holly's Gift, personal meaning when Holly offers the hero, Tim, her most precious gift.

A gift of faith.

Like Holly, I am also a pianist, and I happily brought music into the season. Holly's students, notably Jasmine, were an inspiration.

Many of my readers will chuckle about the shih tzu who is adopted in the story, as my shih tzu, Henry, occupies a special corner beside me while I write. He is a sweet dog!

I'd love to meet you in person someday, but in the meantime, all I can offer is a sincere and grateful thank you. Without your support, my books would not be possible.

As I write my next sweet or inspirational romance, remember this: Have you ever tried something you were afraid to try because it mattered so much to you? I did, when I started writing. Take the chance, and just do something you love.

My Spotify Play List for Holly's Gift is here.

With sincere appreciation,

Josie Riviera

Love sweet romance Holiday stories? Be sure to check out my book bundles:

Holiday Hearts Book Bundle Volume One
Holiday Hearts Book Bundle Volume Two
Holiday Hearts Book Bundle Volume Three
Holiday Hearts Book Bundle Volume Four

RECIPE FOR TINA'S CHINESE CHRISTMAS COOKIES

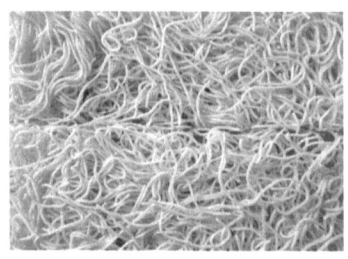

Ingredients:
- 1 cup semisweet chocolate chips
- 1 cup Butterscotch chips
- 1 cup chow mein noodles
- 1 cup dry-roasted peanuts

Preparation Steps:
1. Melt chocolate and butterscotch chips until smooth.
2. Put chow mein noodles and peanuts in a large bowl.
3. Pour chocolate mixture over the noodles and peanuts and stir until well coated.

4. Drop rounded tablespoonfuls of mixture onto wax paper. Refrigerate until set.

Enjoy!

RECIPE FOR NANCY'S CARAMELS

Ingredients:
    6 cups sugar
    3 cups light corn syrup
    6 cups cream
    1 cup butter
    1 ½ Tsp. Salt
    1 Tbsp. vanilla

Directions:
Combine sugar, syrup and 3 cups cream in a large heavy saucepan. Cook over medium heat: boil about 10 minutes.

Add remaining cream slowly, keeping at a boil, stirring constantly. Boil 5 minutes longer.

Add butter, 1 teaspoon at a time; stir in.

Lower heat so mixture remains at a slow boil and cook to a firm ball stage (248 degrees) (45 minutes to an hour).

Remove from heat; add salt and vanilla. Let stand 10 minutes, then pour into greased (about 12" x 17" pan). Let sit for several hours to cool before cutting and wrapping in waxed paper.

You can make 1/3 of this recipe and pour into 2 greased bread pans.

Enjoy!

ACKNOWLEDGMENTS

An appreciative thank you to my patient husband, Dave, and our three wonderful children.

ABOUT THE AUTHOR

Josie Riviera is a USA TODAY bestselling author of contemporary, inspirational, and historical sweet romances that read like Hallmark movies. She lives in the Charlotte, NC, area with her wonderfully supportive husband. They share their home with an adorable shih tzu, who constantly needs grooming, and live in an old house forever needing renovations.

Become a member of my Read and Review VIP Facebook group for exclusive giveaways and free ARCs.

To connect with Josie, visit her webpage and subscribe to her newsletter. As a thank-you, she'll send you a free romance novella directly to your inbox.

josieriviera.com/

josieriviera@aol.com

ALSO BY JOSIE RIVIERA

Seeking Patience

Seeking Catherine (always Free!)

Seeking Fortune

Seeking Charity

Seeking Rachel

The Seeking Series

Oh Danny Boy

I Love You More

A Snowy White Christmas

A Portuguese Christmas

Holiday Hearts Book Bundle Volume One

Holiday Hearts Book Bundle Volume Two

Holiday Hearts Book Bundle Volume Three

Holiday Hearts Book Bundle Volume Four

Candleglow and Mistletoe

Maeve (Perfect Match)

A Love Song To Cherish

A Christmas To Cherish

A Valentine To Cherish

A Christmas Puppy To Cherish

A Homecoming To Cherish

A Summer To Cherish

Romance Stories To Cherish

Romance Stories To Cherish Volume Two

Most books are available in ebook, audiobook, paperback, Large Print paperback and Hardcover.

Many are FREE on Kindle Unlimited!

I HOPE THESE SWEET
CHRISTIAN ROMANCES
WARMED YOUR HEART.

www.ingramcontent.com/pod-product-compliance
Lightning Source LLC
Chambersburg PA
CBHW022003050726
47499CB00002BA/278

9 7 8 1 9 5 1 9 5 1 8 0 1